Books by Rita Mae Brown & Sneaky Pie Brown

WISH YOU WERE HERE • REST IN PIECES • MURDER AT MONTICELLO • PAY DIRT
MURDER, SHE MEOWED • MURDER ON THE PROWL • CAT ON THE SCENT
SNEAKY PIE'S COOKBOOK FOR MYSTERY LOVERS • PAWING THROUGH THE PAST
CLAWS AND EFFECT • CATCH AS CAT CAN • THE TAIL OF THE TIP-OFF
WHISKER OF EVIL • CAT'S EYEWITNESS • SOUR PUSS • PUSS 'N CAHOOTS
THE PURRFECT MURDER • SANTA CLAWED • CAT OF THE CENTURY
HISS OF DEATH • THE BIG CAT NAP • SNEAKY PIE FOR PRESIDENT
THE LITTER OF THE LAW • NINE LIVES TO DIE • TAIL GAIT • TALL TAIL
A HISS BEFORE DYING • PROBABLE CLAWS • WHISKERS IN THE DARK
FURMIDABLE FOES • CLAWS FOR ALARM • HISS & TELL • FELINE FATALE

Books by Rita Mae Brown featuring "Sister" Jane Arnold

OUTFOXED • HOTSPUR • FULL CRY • THE HUNT BALL
THE HOUNDS AND THE FURY • THE TELL-TALE HORSE • HOUNDED TO DEATH
FOX TRACKS • LET SLEEPING DOGS LIE • CRAZY LIKE A FOX
HOMEWARD HOUND • SCARLET FEVER • OUT OF HOUNDS
THRILL OF THE HUNT • LOST AND HOUND

The Mags Rogers Books

MURDER UNLEASHED • A NOSE FOR JUSTICE

Books by Rita Mae Brown

ANIMAL MAGNETISM: MY LIFE WITH CREATURES GREAT AND SMALL
THE HAND THAT CRADLES THE ROCK • SONGS TO A HANDSOME WOMAN
A PLAIN BROWN RAPPER • RUBYFRUIT JUNGLE • IN HER DAY • SIX OF ONE
SOUTHERN DISCOMFORT • SUDDEN DEATH • HIGH HEARTS
STARTED FROM SCRATCH: A DIFFERENT KIND OF WRITER'S MANUAL • BINGO
VENUS ENVY • DOLLEY: A NOVEL OF DOLLEY MADISON IN LOVE AND WAR
RIDING SHOTGUN • RITA WILL: MEMOIR OF A LITERARY RABBLE-ROUSER

Feline Fatale

A MRS. MURPHY MYSTERY

Feline Fatale

RITA MAE BROWN

Illustrated by Michael Gellatly

BANTAM BOOKS

NEW YORK

Copyright © 2024 by American Artists, Inc.
Illustrations copyright © 2024 by Michael Gellatly

Published in the United States by Bantam Books, an imprint of Random House, a division of Penguin Random House LLC, New York.

BANTAM & B colophon is a registered trademark of Penguin Random House LLC.

ISBN978- 0-593-35763-7

Printed in the United States of America

Book design by Diane Hobbing

Dedicated with love to Jahnae Barnett,
President Emeritus of William Woods University,
and her husband, Eddie.
They will never know how many thousands of lives
they have touched.

CAST OF CHARACTERS

THE PEOPLE

Mary Minor Haristeen, "Harry," was the postmistress of Crozet right out of Smith College. As times changed and a big new post office was built, new rules came, too, such as she couldn't bring her animals to work, so she retreated to the farm she inherited from her parents. Born and raised in Crozet, she knows everyone and vice versa. She is now forty-five, although one could argue whether maturity has caught up with her.

Pharamond Haristeen, DVM, "Fair," is an equine vet specializing in reproduction. He and Harry have known each other all their lives. They married shortly after she graduated from Smith and he was in vet school at Auburn. He generally understands his wife better than she understands herself.

Susan Tucker is Harry's best friend from cradle days. They might as well be sisters and can sometimes pluck each other's last nerve, as only a sister can. Susan bred Harry's adored corgi. Her husband, Ned, is the district's delegate to the General Assembly's House of Delegates, the lower house.

Deputy Cynthia Cooper is Harry's neighbor, as she rents the adjoining farm. Law enforcement is a career she is made for, being meticulous, shrewd, and highly observant. She works closely with the sheriff, Rick Shaw; adores Harry; and all too often has to extricate her neighbor out of scrapes. Harry returns the favor by helping Coop with her garden. It probably isn't an equal exchange but they are fine with it.

Tazio Chappers is an architect in her late thirties, born and raised in St. Louis. Having been educated at Washington University, she received an excellent education, winding up in Crozet on a fluke. Just one of those things, as Cole Porter's song lets us know. Warned off a job at an architectural firm by many people back in Missouri, due to her being half black and half Italian, she came to Virginia anyway. No one can accuse her of being a chicken. Now owner of her own firm, getting big jobs, she is happy, married for two years, and part of the community. She is also terrifically good looking, which never hurts.

Amanda Fields is a first-term Republican delegate to the Virginia statehouse, the House of Delegates. She is a smashing-looking former TV reporter in middle age. Bright, self-possessed, she usually knows how our political system really works.

Aidan Harkness—Facile, in his late thirties, a rising star among the Democrats. Reasonably intelligent, good at avoiding the tough issues, he goes head-to-head with Amanda. He struggles to contain his emotions.

Lucas Dennison is Amanda's right-hand man, a dear friend from William and Mary days. He wears many hats: secretary, campaign planner, willing ear. He loves her deeply but is not in love with her.

Ellis Barfield shoots Assembly meetings, which are streamed in real time. He makes a good living creating alluring videos for small businesses and individuals. The state job is steady money. He pays attention to what goes on on the floor and is good at capturing events and personalities.

Reid Ryder is a fourteen-year-old page; like all of them, he is enraptured by state politics. He has been handpicked to be a page, which means he is an outstanding student.

Miranda Hogendobber worked with Harry for years at the old post office. In her early eighties, she knows everyone and she herself is well known for her beautiful singing voice.

Aunt Tally, who is now 103, has become frail. Her mind is very good, but her body is slowing down. Given the harsh winter, she is lonely and snowbound. Harry drops in on her. There is not one person in Crozet who knows life without Aunt Tally.

THE ANIMALS

Mrs. Murphy is Harry's tiger cat. She is bright, does her chores, keeps the mice at bay when need be. Harry talks to her but not baby talk. Mrs. Murphy just won't have it.

Pewter is fat, gray, and oh so vain. She irritates Tucker, the corgi. She takes credit for everyone else's work. However, in a pinch the naughty girl does come through. She's also quite bright.

Tucker, the corgi bred by Susan Tucker, runs around everyone. She's fast, loves to greet every person once she has checked them out, and particularly likes to herd the horses. The horses are good sports about it, which is a good thing. Tucker is brave and she loves Harry totally.

Pirate is a not-yet-fully-grown Irish Wolfhound who landed in Harry's lap as a puppy when his owner died. Huge, able to cover so much ground, he can be dominated by Pewter sometimes. Tucker has to give him pep talks. Like Tucker, Pirate has great courage, loves being part of the family. He is trying to understand people. The others help. A sweet, sweet animal.

The horses, the big owl in the barn, and the possum aren't in the forefront in this book but they are around and will be their usual selves in the future. This also applies to the barn mice, who have a really good deal at the farm.

Feline Fatale

1

A snowdrop peeked out, a little white bloom sur-rounded by glistening snow. Two inches fell last night. The six-petaled flower was protected by the farmhouse overhang.

Mary Minor "Harry" Haristeen knelt down to examine its pristine beauty.

"Spring." She smiled. Snow or not.

Eventually a palette of color . . . peach, yellow, pink shimmer-ing purple, and subtle lavender . . . would fill the yard, pastures would begin to turn electric green.

"*Those bulbs she planted will all come up once it's really spring,*" Tucker, the corgi, informed the Irish Wolfhound, now mostly grown but still a puppy at a year and a few months.

"*She spent a lot of time digging last fall,*" the handsome fellow replied. "*But she can't eat flowers. So much effort.*"

"*Pirate, everything doesn't need to be food. She likes color. Fragrance. Humans are like that.*"

"Oh." The big fellow sniffed the tiny bloom while Harry watched.

The summer screened-in porch was closed in winter with wooden siding, and windows to allow light in. The animal door remained in the wooden door to the kitchen. The screen door was removed, replaced by a solid door to the outside. This, too, had an animal door.

A gray cat head pushed out the flap, but nothing else. Pewter, the large gray cat, hated the cold. *"I am not getting my paws wet."*

"Who asked you to?" Tucker sniffed.

"Everything is more fun when I'm involved," came the saucy reply.

"You are mental." Tucker sounded authoritative, then under her breath whispered to Pirate, *"Nuts."*

"Oh," the big youngster again said.

Mrs. Murphy, the pretty tiger cat seated on the old wooden bench alongside one wall, advised Pewter, *"Don't get her started. She's been in a mood since you snitched her dog biscuit. You don't even like dog biscuits."*

"Was fun to hear her whine."

"Are you talking about me?" Tucker asked.

Pewter pulled her head back in, relieved to be away from even a brief time in the cold. *"Dogs aren't worth talking about."*

Deciding she'd go into the kitchen in case Pewter decided to whap Tucker when the corgi's face pushed through the door flap, Mrs. Murphy flicked her tail up and jumped on the kitchen table. The kitchen, warm, seemed to her the happiest room in the old white clapboard farmhouse.

Tucker, wisely fearing a slap, hung back, waiting for Harry to open the door. As she did, the corgi pressed next to her leg, Pirate behind the two of them. When the slender woman opened the kitchen door, Tucker shot inside, Pewter right behind her, a paw swinging at the tailless butt.

"Pewter, leave her alone," Harry quietly commanded.

Leaping onto the kitchen table, the gray cat blinked, then washed her paw. *"Dogs are a lower life-form. I don't know why you bother."*

"What are you two doing on the table anyway?"

"*All the better to see your pretty face,*" Pewter mocked her, although Harry was pretty.

Opening a big porcelain jar on the counter under the window, Harry plucked out two kitty treats. Then she opened a cabinet door for two greenies for the dogs.

"Beggars."

With everyone happily chewing, she flicked on her new electric teapot. In minutes she poured boiling water over a tea ball filled with loose orange pekoe tea. The aroma lifted her spirits.

Sitting down, she got up again to grab a paper napkin. Linen was so much better, but then you had to wash them.

"Off." She slid the paper out from under Pewter's considerable butt.

"*I was going to read it,*" the cat protested.

"*You were going to shred it.*" Mrs. Murphy wiped her mouth.

"*What's the difference?*" the cat protested.

"*I like the pictures.*" Mrs. Murphy observed a full-page ad on the back of the paper for Jaeger-LeCoutre, a watch designed in the 1930s for horsemen so they could flip the watch face over, protecting the crystal while they rode or played polo.

"*Watches are a waste of money,*" Pewter announced. "*Look at the sun.*"

"*What if it's cloudy?*" Pirate sensibly said.

"*People pay too much attention to time. It's not,*" the cat thought for a moment, "*natural.*"

Mrs. Murphy picked at a few crumbs that had fallen while she ate her treat. "*Pewter, there isn't much about human life that is natural. Our mom and dad live closer to real things than most humans. She'll finish the paper, look at the wall clock, worry about the time, and go get ready to leave.*"

Tucker, half a greenie still in her mouth, dropped it but put her paw on it. You never know. "*No fur. That had to be the start of it.*"

"*Some of them have lots of fur.*" Mrs. Murphy giggled. "*Remember the badminton party they had last summer? Got hot. Some of the men took their shirts off. But I don't see how that bit of fur can keep them warm. Maybe Tucker is right.*"

"*I am,*" came the forthright answer. "*Furthermore, they can't smell but*" so much. Their hearing isn't sharp. They miss a lot. I love our humans no matter what but they are easy prey. They can't climb a tree like you cats. No claws. Okay, I can't either, but I have a terrific sense of smell, a golden nose, and I run fast. They are really slow."

"Their eyes are good." Mrs. Murphy tried to find advantages.

"Can't see in the dark." Pewter really wanted another treat so she patted the newspaper page.

Harry shook the page. "I'm reading."

"You can't see in the dark. Big deal, reading," Pewter huffed. "I'm hungry."

"We had breakfast. I don't think she's going to get up and hand out more goodies," the small dog predicted.

"Right," the tiger cat agreed.

Sipping her perfect cup of tea, Harry wondered at the write-up of the county commissioner's meeting. A contentious issue was whether to sell county-owned land to developers. No details were provided, so it seemed like a rhetorical issue. Then again, the county was growing, facing more demands than before. She then flipped to reading about what was going on in Richmond, seat of the state government. She slapped the paper down.

"Can't anyone agree on anything?" Looking at the clock she gulped the last of her tea, repairing to the bathroom to smack on a bit of makeup.

"She's fooling with her face." Pewter thought it funny when Harry drew the mascara brush over her upper eyelids. Once Pewter had jumped on the sink to bump Harry's arm. Harry had a big black dot of mascara on the side of her eye. Curses followed.

"Maybe Tucker is right. No fur. They have to buy fur or something." Mrs. Murphy pondered this from the bed where she now reposed.

The dogs, in the kitchen, were already asleep. Nothing like a morning nap after breakfast to start the day.

As the cats talked, Harry emerged from the bathroom, flipped through her closet, and picked out a long tartan skirt. Then she opened drawers, finally settling on a dark green turtleneck sweater.

"Have no idea how warm or cold the statehouse is."

"A shawl will take care of that." The tiger cat had studied clothing.

As if understanding her much-loved cat, Harry walked back to the closet, snatching the shawl off a sturdy hanger.

After putting her clothes on she checked herself in the mirror. "Well, I've looked better, but I've also looked worse."

"You look fine," Pewter reassured her. *"Now can I have a treat?"*

"Ha." Murphy laughed.

"Worth a try. Maybe I'll rub on her leg."

Pewter didn't get the chance, because Harry pulled on her hunting boots. Given the cold, she would wear two pair of socks. Anything to help keep her feet warm. The long skirt reached the top of the boots. It was a good look, particularly in cold weather.

Back in the kitchen, she opened a drawer, pulling out a thin notebook plus a ballpoint pen. Slipping these in her winter coat, she again checked the clock. Almost eight-thirty. Just in case she and Susan, her best friend, had to walk far to get into the statehouse in Richmond, she would take her winter coat. Filled with man-made insulating stuff, it wasn't fat like goose down, but the five-year-old Eddie Bauer kept her warm, plus she had the shawl and her sweater. She hoped she wouldn't need to bring the coat into the statehouse.

"Susan." Tucker woke up hearing the tire tread about a quarter of a mile away.

The cats, back in the kitchen, and Pirate, looked at the door.

"She doesn't hear it yet," Pewter remarked. *"Plus she won't know it's Susan's tires."*

"She'll know it's Susan because she's expecting her," Pirate chimed in.

"But she can't identify tire treads. If it weren't Susan, but say Cooper from the farm next door, she wouldn't know. Humans can't hear tire treads. They can hear tires but not the treads."

"Really?" Pirate was fascinated by such things.

"Doesn't matter. We can hear. They can't hear details. If it's a stranger we can bark, plus we can check out whoever that person might be. Our job is to protect Harry."

"I can protect all of you." Pirate surprised them.

"Cheeky for a big puppy, but you are big." Mrs. Murphy liked Pirate.

"Okay, gang. Behave." Harry swung the shawl over her shoulders, grabbed the coat, opened the door, and hurried outside. Opening the door to Susan's Audi station wagon, she flung the coat in the backseat. The car was comfortably warm.

"We're off." Susan smiled.

So they were. The trip was the beginning of an adventure. If the two women had the keen senses of the animals, it might be more of an adventure; nonetheless, adventure sharpens all your senses. Even the weak ones.

2

Passing the turnoff for Goochland, Susan slowed a bit. "Traffic."

Harry noted the line up ahead, which was thankfully moving. "Gets worse every year. We at least aren't in Northern Virginia. Can you imagine battling that every day to get to D.C.?"

"No. This is bad enough. And now look at that."

A few snowflakes twirled down, promising more from darkening skies.

Harry looked up at the sky through the large windshield. "The weather report called for light snow showers."

"I don't think this will be light. The weather changes so fast."

"Does, but maybe this will help Ned."

"True."

Susan's husband, Ned Tucker, was going to introduce a bill in the House of Delegates for improved road clearing during bad weather. The terrible snow and ice storm of January 3, 2022, had people trapped in their cars on I-95 for thirty hours, one of whom was Virginia's senator to D.C., Tim Kaine. He finally made it to his D.C. office after twenty-seven hours.

"Do you think our DMV is bad?" Harry wondered.

"No. But we don't have a very good response to a weather crisis. Granted, Virginia is not Vermont, where they are more accustomed to this, but given the crazy weather these last few years, we need to be ready for anything, and that includes the state police and fire departments. We need clear mandates, as my husband would say."

Harry smiled. "He's going to get his chance to say it."

Susan smiled back. "The buzzword now is *situational awareness*. I told my husband if he blabbers it, no fried chicken for two weeks."

"Ha. I can think of more effective punishments than that."

A sly smile crossed Susan's lips. "Harry, you save that for big problems. This is verbal detritus."

"Our late high school English teacher would love to hear you say that. So, what do you think will happen?"

"He'll present his idea with Aidan Harkness. Won't take long. The other side will fuss a bit, but given that the bill's so sensible, I think this will go quickly. At least I hope so. For one thing, I can't sit that long and neither can you."

"That was always the problem in school. Sitting. I'd stare out the window. How many times can you get up to go to the bathroom?"

"Mrs. Lordes might allow it once." Susan flashed back to their strict English teacher.

The two had known each other since before kindergarten after which they were in every grade together. There were things one need not explain when you've known someone that long. Mrs. Lordes was one of them.

"Do you think our schools were too strict?"

"Harry, how would I know? I mean, it appears to me that there is no discipline these days; even when my two kids were in school

I thought things were getting lax. Now I guess parents would be happy even for that time. Children can't learn in chaos."

"Not sure anyone can. Before I forget, when is the next time the kids will be home?"

"Easter, I hope. Izzy has to come from Dallas. Danny, Boston. You know, I am glad my children have made their own lives but I so wished they lived closer. Neither of them is married yet. Worries me. Ned says he isn't worried."

"Don't start, Susan. They'll find the right person."

"I know, I know. But Danny is twenty-four and Izzy is twenty-one. I know it takes young men longer, at least that's what Mother says."

"Listen to your mother." Harry laughed, as both of them did listen to Susan's mother as well as her grandmother, who was pushing ninety. "Remember when Izzy decided that's what she wanted to be called, by her middle name. She said Isabelle, Izzy, would stand out?"

"She has a point, but Emily was Ned's mother's name, so it was a bit hurtful when she dropped her first name."

"I know, but the older I get . . . not that I think we are getting old, but still . . . the more I think people have to find their own way and we burden them with expectations."

"Spoken like a woman who does not have children. Harry, how are young people going to come up to the mark if there aren't expectations, rules of conduct? It was simple in our house. Be calm. Be productive. Be helpful. You aren't the only person on the planet."

A silence followed this. "Okay. But Danny and Izzy had good parents and no constant social media. Mucks up the works. To shift gears, someone out there looking to make a name for himself will attack Ned's plan and accuse him of visiting prostitutes, speaking of social media."

"I'll put a red light by the door." Susan raised one eyebrow.

"Damn fool."

A car shot past her, skidded in the gathering snow, still very light but slick; the car nearly went off the road.

"You know, it's four-wheel drive not four-wheel stop." Harry flipped the vents more toward her.

"I can turn up the heat."

"No. This is fine. Back to prostitutes. Do you think we can get out of this mess? Democrats vilifying Republicans and vice versa."

"If we want to, we will. Maybe we have to crash and burn first. Obviously I can't say that out loud. My husband is an elected delegate for the great salary of $17,640 per year. Fortunately we can afford an apartment in Richmond so he doesn't have to go back and forth every day, but it's still a drain on the budget."

"I know it is. You don't complain. I would." Harry took a breath. "Maybe the low salaries aren't a bad thing, because they keep delegates and state senators working, which keeps them closer to the people."

"I think about that, but for someone who doesn't have much of a career . . . I mean, Ned can and does practice law, but you can't be in politics without money, so the House and Senate chambers are skewered, you know?" She slyly grinned. "Back to prostitution, right?"

Harry laughed. "I don't have an answer, plus I really hate politics. I didn't even like our high school elections."

"Maybe so, but you worked for me." Susan slowed again. "You were good at rounding up people."

"Maybe. It was fun talking to everyone, plus your opponent was such a snob . . . and by the way, she still is. Ginger Stein, you know one of the first things she still tells new people is that she isn't Jewish in case they think *Stein* is a Jewish name?"

"Where did you hear that?"

"From Big Mim." Harry cited the older woman who essentially ran Crozet through her husband, the mayor.

"What an ass."

"She married well. Makes it worse." Harry laughed. "The old prejudices die hard."

"Yes, they do. All right. I'm going to shift over to the right-hand lane; traffic gets even worse here. We've got about ten miles to go."

"You're okay."

"Thanks."

"Who is Aidan Harkness? I don't think I've met him."

"First term as a delegate. Seems to have ambition. He's attractive, well-spoken, quite a bit to the left of my husband, who is the quintessential middle-of-the-roader. But they work okay together on most things. Aidan is maybe late thirties. Northern Virginia district. Maybe early forties at the most. I should know. He rarely veers away from the party line . . . then again, few do."

"Another reason I hate politics. However," she quickly added, "I love Ned."

"I do, too. I married a good man and so did you. You and I have seen enough divorces to be glad about that. As I recall, Harry, you got divorced. Then you married him back pretty quickly."

"We were both stupid. But I'd been dating him since I was a junior in high school. He was in the class ahead, an older man. Captain of the football team. You know."

"I know. Sometimes we learn the hard way. I've asked Ned who does he think is having affairs among his compatriots, and he says he doesn't really know and he doesn't want to know. So I put it to him, 'Do you think the personal is political?' And he said 'Yes.' Then he said what I guess so many of us think, 'If you lie about one thing, you will probably lie about another.' "

"Pretty much, but some people can compartmentalize better than others. I think it's all too much work. Then again, the thrill of getting away with something must be very seductive."

"Ha. What's seductive are women's bodies," Susan replied.

Harry laughed. "Women cheat, too."

"I know, but I swear the percentage has to be less than men. But those who are caught often say they have good reasons."

"Maybe politics provokes this. You're beat up. You're tired. Your wife and kids are home and you aren't. You're in some condo or apartment too much of the time. Sex lifts one's spirits. I don't know. I'm not condoning it, but I do try to understand."

Susan then came back with, "Do you think the gay guys cheat as much as the straight ones?"

"Do we have any gay men in our Assembly?"

"Good question. I don't know about any gay women either. I never paid attention, but if one is a Republican I doubt there's an ounce of support. As to the Democrats, they will at least say it's okay. I find it all a ploy to get us away from the real problems. If no one can solve the problem, they divert your attention. And I will really give Ned credit, he doesn't do that."

"Talking earlier about expectations, I think people live up or down to expectations. We've revealed our expectations about the different behaviors based on gender or at least what we are identifying as gender. Maybe we're part of the problem."

Susan took the last right turnoff of what was now I-95 so she kept her eyes firmly on the road. She knew Harry, and Harry was capable of deep thought when she applied herself. But her heart's sister rarely shared it.

"Maybe we are, Harry, maybe we are."

They were about to see something they would never have expected, nor would anyone else.

3

Sitting in the gallery, her shawl draped over her shoulders, Harry noticed what natural light there was in the room was darkening.

Susan also noticed. "We're really going to get it."

"Yep. I've only been in here once, during grade school. I never realized how much natural light there is. You don't think about that in old buildings."

"Built from 1785 to 1788." Susan knew the state buildings well. "It's a Palladian temple, really. Our General Assembly is the oldest lawmaking continuous body in the Western Hemisphere."

"I should know that. But I don't."

"July 30, 1619, we had our first elected delegates. I take comfort in it when Ned is home on weekends. No matter how tired he is or frustrated, I always tell him to think about who came before him. All men, of course."

"Well, that has changed." Harry smiled.

"Not enough."

"Susan, if this deliberative body were all women, do you think it would be better?"

"I do, in the sense that I think most women are more pragmatic than most men."

"You'll get an argument there." Harry hastily added, "But not from me."

Susan waved as her husband walked into the large room. He looked up at her then winked, took his desk seat. Aidan came over to stand at his desk and after a few words with Ned he, too, looked up at Susan. He smiled broadly. She smiled back.

The room filled up. Only a few seats remained empty. Standing along the side walls were the pages. These young people were selected by the Speaker of the House from applicants across the state. They were thirteen, fourteen years old, in good academic standing. Their school principal and teachers agreed they would receive lessons and study from seven PM to nine PM at the study hall at the hotel where they live when the Assembly was in session. Their days were spent in the Assembly.

Each of these young people dreamed of politics. Being here was a thrill. They carried bills, notes, and amendments between delegates. They performed errands for the delegates, including running back to their offices if necessary. People under stress can be forgetful.

They were expected to support one another and they were allowed to go home on weekends. Friday's session let them out at noon.

Harry scanned the group. Eagerness shone from their young faces. They were so young.

She could only imagine how this experience could set their paths in the future.

"Doesn't he look good in that deep navy suit I bought him?

The tie sets it off. Magenta. He complained. You know how Ned doesn't want to shine or show off, but I told him that now that there's live streaming, he needs to look as good as possible."

"He does look good."

"Having everything tailored to him, bespoke, makes all the difference. And the fact that he is fit. Everything looks good on him."

"You're the one with the eye."

"Thanks. Live streaming makes all the difference. As you can see, some of the delegates get the message, but others don't. Poor old Mike there; my God, how many terms has he served?"

"Probably since 1619."

They both laughed.

"He looks like he's wearing a colored potato sack."

"His wife passed away four years ago and he is hopeless, poor thing. The older delegates give us stability, even if Ned gets frustrated with them, as he feels they are behind. I tell him 'Behind on some things but rock solid on others.' Not that I am trying to influence my husband. The district elected him, not me."

"Susan." Harry's voice hit the low register.

"Well."

"Susan."

They both burst out laughing as Susan and Ned discussed everything from politics to her desire for miniature crepe myrtles.

The room was almost filled.

Click. Click. Click.

All heads turned toward the sound emanating from the highly polished hall floor leading to the chamber. Within a minute, a terrific-looking woman strode into the chamber, the carpet silencing her red-soled high heels.

Harry gasped. "Christian Louboutins. Cost a fortune."

Amanda Fields also wore a luxurious cashmere turtleneck in deference to the weather. Her upper assets, amply displayed, could create conversation, as did her shoes. Her skirt, a longer length, again a nod to the weather, flowed with her. Amanda,

elected from a district just south of Henrico County, had been a newscaster on a Richmond TV station.

"I'm tired of reporting the news, I want to make it" was her battle cry during a hard-fought campaign. Over time her Democratic opponent was worn down. Were he a woman, people would have called him dowdy. Since he wasn't a woman they didn't call him anything. Those stinging terms were usually applied to females. The best that could be said for Newton Miner was "unexciting." As for Amanda during the campaign, she got called everything from "a bombshell" to "a woman not ready for the rough and tumble of politics." Boy, did they get that wrong. Not only was she ready, she could manipulate the media like a pro, which she was.

Knowing where the cameras were, she smiled a big wide white smile as she took her seat, sitting down in a becoming feminine manner, practiced . . . but then, those things are.

The Speaker of the House, a Republican, elected from the delegates, took his seat and lightly tapped the gavel on the round wooden disk. The session began.

The gallery was half-full. As nothing volatile was up for discussion, plus the uncertain weather, things were on the quiet side. Took one hour to get through routine business, with pages quietly handing notes to delegates from other delegates. Nothing much at stake. Harry tried not to fidget.

Finally Ned was recognized. As he stood up, Aidan, at a nearby desk, organized his papers, preparing to be recognized when needed to provide more facts. He motioned for a page, giving him two pieces of paper to deliver to a lady delegate at the back row.

After properly addressing the Speaker and members of the Assembly, Ned got right to the point. "The weather is changing. Granted, it can never be accurately predicted, but in the last ten years our Virginia weather has included terrific blizzards, howling rainstorms, blistering heat, and floods. My colleague Aidan Harkness and I are presenting a bill to address the difficulty of transportation. VDOT is pressured to the maximum. Can the state afford a fleet of expensive large snow-removal machines? There is another way to handle this problem." He turned to address his colleagues, then returned to the Speaker. "We would like to hire more independent contractors. Yes, the state will need to find money for that, but it costs far less than buying equipment plus paying people to operate that equipment. Also this will be welcome income in those districts comprising the Blue Ridge Mountains and the Alleghenies as they and the Shenandoah Valley receive more snow than counties and districts to the east. Our counties in the southwest especially need a boost." He then quickly read off the counties most affected.

Before he could launch into numbers, Amanda raised her hand, asking for an interruption. Ned, being a gentleman, stepped back.

"This is a misuse of state funds. Given that the number of counties are mostly in the west of the state, if we do allocate funds then the eastern counties should receive equal funding for roads and improvements. Otherwise this is preferential and unequal treatment."

Aidan leapt to his feet. "That's not preferential. It's a fact of nature. You come from a county that gets light snow infrequently."

She shot back, "Equal treatment. My district has great need of road repairs, and we need roundabouts."

The Speaker banged the gavel. "Mr. Tucker has the floor." Amanda smiled sweetly at the Speaker and sat down. Aidan also sat down, reluctantly.

Ned continued. "The cost of a tractor powerful enough to handle an interstate road or, say, Route 250, a state road, would be roughly a hundred and sixty thousand dollars and that would be for one with smaller horsepower. Say 80, which sounds big to many of you, but really a tractor big enough to handle the steep grades in the mountains and the Valley is a 150 HP, minimum. And then you add the cost of the attachments. A wing blade is well over twenty thousand dollars. Just one simple front blade, not all that wide, runs about ten thousand dollars depending on the tractor. Big snowblower attachments would run you twelve thousand for a lesser horsepower tractor . . . say an 80 HP which, while versatile, will not hold up under the weight of wet snow or the steep grades. And if the state is buying snow removal equipment we have to factor in repairs. A man, or I should say person, driving his own equipment is going to take very good care of it. If this body will consider this proposal, a committee should be set up to review all possible costs. I think if that is done, the cost of renting or paying people who own their own equipment will be seen to give us substantial savings. We must do something. We can't afford another January 3, 2022."

Amanda was recognized. "That blizzard was so unique. Using it as an example makes little sense. Yes, there is more snow in the west, but not so much that it is a VDOT issue. Our VDOT people do very well. Furthermore, snow removal is very profitable. Often a fifty percent profit. This isn't a money-saving proposition."

Aidan furiously scribbled while Amanda spoke. He handed the note to a page, Reid Ryder, who hurried over to give it to Ned.

Opening it, Ned read. "Who prepped her? How did she know about our proposal? She's done research."

Ned scribbled back. "I have no idea. She was a reporter. Maybe she found out what we were researching. We need to push for a committee."

As Aidan read, Amanda, making a few more statements about budgetary waste, sat down.

Aidan was recognized. "Does our esteemed delegate have no concern for a Virginia citizen out of her own county? After all, Delegate Fields, they can't vote for you. Those counties are some of our poorest. This would be a great help to them as well as keep us from spending millions on equipment plus servicing same."

"Delegate Harkness, not only am I thinking of my constituency, I am thinking of yours since obviously you aren't. This is an enormous expense for a spotty issue. Our state does not regularly encounter paralyzing snows. Once in a great while. To squander money in this fashion deprives people in your district of vital services, such as a diminution of state police members or no extra funds for those in your district needing housing. Oh, but I forgot, your district is rich. So what do you focus on, Mr. Harkness? I care about all of our residents, even the poor ones, as they are not well served." Down she plopped.

"I resent that," he shouted.

The Speaker banged the gavel. "Order."

Aidan raised his hand. The Speaker ignored him.

Ned was again recognized. "We are all concerned with money. Our state is one of the best run in the country; the reason for that is our wise use of our resources to meet the needs of our citizens. No one can predict the weather or the cycles. But if a person cannot get to work, that is a problem for everybody. If a child cannot get to school, that is also a problem. Look at the learning losses now identifiable from COVID closing schools or people simply refusing to send their children to school during the pandemic. Anything that interrupts commerce or learning is a detriment to us all. Mr. Speaker, may I propose we form a committee to study hiring individuals to clear our roads, be it a terrific monsoon or a blizzard?"

Amanda called out, "That's a dodge. We don't need a committee. We need numbers and a sense of weather cycles. That isn't that difficult to find, despite what you and Delegate Harkness say. You Democrats, all you want to do is throw around money. We Republicans are far stronger than you are in rural counties. You're just trying to buy them off."

"That's bullshit." Aidan forgot himself.

The Speaker banged the gavel as poor Ned wiped his brow. Susan leaned to Harry. "Ned will hold it together, but look how red his cheeks are. This isn't going to plan."

"How dare you swear in this chamber, which has seen far better public servants than you, you lowlife," Amanda said.

"Bitch." He totally lost it.

So did she. She flew out of her seat, ran over to him, and slapped his face. Then she slipped off one of her frightfully expensive shoes and beat him around the head with it. The page, Ryder, tried to stop the enraged woman, but couldn't. Finally two capitol guards came in and pulled her off. She stopped immediately, flashing a radiant TV smile, then walked to her seat.

"This chamber is in recess." The Speaker banged the gavel, stood up, and left the podium. He was seething and needed to get to his small room in the back behind the podium to get under control.

Meanwhile, the streaming service people were beside themselves with joy. Ellis Barfield, head videographer, slapped hands with two assistants. This would be watched by jillions.

Amanda took a deep breath, stood up, and looked composed as she turned toward the cameras. She could easily handle millions, even jillions.

Ned, on the other hand, put his arm through Aidan's and forcefully led him up the aisle.

"I'll kill that bitch." Aidan spoke too loudly.

"If you give her enough time, she'll dig her grave with her teeth. Now calm down. You know you are both going to be censured. That won't help us and it isn't going to help the party."

As Amanda walked out, the Majority Leader, who was from her party, fell in with her. "Amanda, that is going to cost us."

"I make you a promise, it will work for us. Trust me, Mr. Kilgore, I know the media."

He did not want to argue with her in front of people, but the Majority Leader was a strong believer in decorum, tradition.

"I'll see you after everyone calms down."

"Mr. Kilgore, I know how proper you are. You are such a good majority leader but do remember that John Randolph tore into Congress in Washington urging his pack of foxhounds into the chamber while he ran on ahead to beat with his crop those he felt deserved it. I promise you, Sir, I was out of order but still not that bad." She smiled that melting smile.

He nodded, knowing he really had his hands full.

Susan sat there, stunned, as did most of the people in the gallery. "Harry, we need to go to Ned but I don't know what we will find."

"I give him credit for not losing his temper."

"I do, too." Susan breathed a stream of air out of her nostrils, then stood up as Harry joined her.

They had to get to the Pocahontas Building, where Ned's office and everyone else's were. The snow was really falling now. Harry pulled on her coat, which wasn't easy given her shawl but she was glad to have both. They zipped and slipped into the building, snow sticking to their shoes.

"Oh dear." Susan saw the crowd outside her husband's office.

"Why don't we wait here until they disperse?"

"Actually, this may be one of those times when my husband could use my presence. And yours, too. Okay, sugar. Time to remember cotillion."

Harry moaned. "Oh God."

"We are about to be the quintessential Virginia ladies." Susan took a deep breath.

They reached the crowd.

Susan beamed. "Bill, haven't seen you in far too long. Harry, this is Bill Donovan. I think of him as king of the Shenandoah Valley."

This made him laugh and those who heard it. Delegate Donovan took Harry's hand when she extended it, and a few pleasantries were exchanged.

Susan walked in. People parted. Harry stuck with Bill. "I am so proud of you." She kissed Ned on the cheek.

As most of the people in there were Democratic delegates, with only one or two Republicans, smiles greeted her. Aidan, still fuming, also smiled at Susan, although it was more like a twitch.

Susan took his arm. "Aidan, you said what the rest of us think."

Everyone laughed, including Ned. The mood shifted. Aidan breathed less heavily. The delegates started talking about issues in front of them, plus the possibility of a committee.

Harry realized although she had known Susan all her life, she often forgot how smart, emotionally smart, her beloved friend truly was.

As the group chatted, Amanda strode into her office, closing the door.

"Well?"

Lucas Dennison, her chief of staff, raised his eyebrows. "No one will forget it."

"Good. What I need are numbers. Will you call John Deere, Kubota . . . and, yes, VDOT? Numbers. How much equipment does the state own? What condition is it in? What would be the ideal tractors and implements for clearing snow? The cost? Would they give the state a price break? I know you may have to couch that in different language. You'll think of more stuff. By the way, how did I really do?"

"Brilliant, baby doll. Brilliant." He beamed at her.

She then sat at her desk and picked up the phone to call her old TV station. "Jenny, hi, it's Amanda. Can you get me Frederico?" A pause. "You saw it. I'm so glad. That's what passes for leadership today, and yes, I lost my temper." Pause. "Thanks, honey." Another pause. "Frederico, darling, I am ready to give you an exclusive interview on tomorrow's morning news. I promise it will be a zinger." Longer pause. "All right. I'll be there at seven. Don't worry about makeup. I'll come in full war paint." Pause. "Be good to see you."

She hung up her landline phone, better reception, and leaned back in her chair. It was too easy, really. Just too easy.

Looking at the bottom of her shoe, she rose, opened the door to her closet. Lucas walked in.

"That was fast," Amanda said.

"Sent emails. Once I have tractor numbers I'll make calls. What's with the shoe?"

"Took a chip out of the heel. This will be hard to fix. Fortunately, I have a lot of pairs, but still."

"High heels are a form of torture."

"No one's leg looks as good as it can unless you're in high heels." She then grinned mischievously. "I'll be thrilled when the red bottom of this Louboutin is red from that jerk's blood."

Leaving the gathering at Ned's office, Aidan hurried all the way to the Assembly chamber.

Going behind the front, where the Speaker sat, he sprinted to a small door at the back of this space. Most auditoriums have side doors or back doors so speakers and special guests can come out. Not only is it theatrical, it gives the guest, say a prime minister from another nation, the opportunity for a moment of quiet to collect their thoughts.

"Ellis," Aidan called.

"Right."

Aidan opened the door to the video room where Ellis Barfield collected his gear.

Looking up, the videographer, maybe in his early thirties, grinned. "That was a hell of a show."

"I'm sure you recorded every syllable, videoed every twitch."

"Aidan, you and Amanda are front and center. Anyone who thinks state politics are boring will change their mind."

"Well." Aidan paused. "I guess they will. I'm hoping this doesn't impact my reelection campaign fund."

"Maybe for a short time, but I'm willing to bet over time a lot of those liberal males, your people," he emphasized *people*, "will toss coins your way. They may deny it, but how many men have wanted to call a woman a bitch?"

Aidan's humor returned. "I take your point."

Footsteps reverberated. Reid Ryder stuck his head in. "Mr. Barfield, any errands for me? Hello, Delegate Harkness. Do you have errands for me?"

"Not right now, Reid."

Ellis handed the young man a small carton of empty Ball jars.

"Here you go. I owe a constituent Ball jars."

He also handed him his car keys.

"Thanks."

"Reid, my RAV4 is good in bad weather, but be careful."

"Yes, Sir."

"Reid. Here." Aidan handed him a fifty-dollar bill. "For gas and a sandwich."

"Thank you, Sir." Balancing the carton, the young man . . . underage driving, no less . . . was on his way.

"If he gets stopped, you'll both be cooked," Aidan warned Ellis.

"He's fourteen. Just. But he looks so much older. It's his height. He doesn't have far. This way I can do some editing. And no, I won't edit you out."

"You'll make me a star." Aidan laughed. "Still shooting locations, old buildings for Thanatos and other developers?"

"You bet. The pay is good. And being here, I have a good idea of what is possible, can be bought without hassle."

"All best done quietly."

"Your tips are golden." Ellis smiled.

"You'd be surprised by what I hear. People are so indiscreet."

"Aidan, given that some of these old guys, regardless of party, have run this state for decades, they have no fear."

"Well, I do. My generation is beginning to fill the pews, if you will. And a lot of my younger colleagues believe in transparency. I think it sounds great but impossible."

Ellis shrugged. "I don't much care. Give me more political drama."

"Next time I hope it won't be me."

"Aidan, getting footage is golden. Amanda is already a star. She'll make you one."

"You really think so?"

"Right now anger, rudeness, and hate sells. Look at what's on your TV, your phone. Washington is a cesspool. People are hooked. There's room for name calling, shouting, throwing things at other delegates. Go for it." Ellis beamed. "You're also getting me more work. I can't charge the state any more, but small businesses and corporations will hear I'm the videographer. Anger sells. Anger correctly filmed, edited, sells bundles."

"I'll remember that." Aidan took a breath.

"Does Reid know what goes in the Ball jars?"

"I don't think so. He traded in the empty jars. He doesn't deliver anything. Once the jars are filled, my associates deliver them."

"I see."

"Nothing as good as country waters." Ellis threw on his knapsack.

"I agree totally. And I have a blind eye. Income from illegal liquor or cigarettes is good for Virginia, as long as you don't get caught."

"I hear you."

Both men walked down the stairs.

Ellis headed in the direction opposite Aidan. "One of my associates is picking me up briefly."

"How many associates do you have?"

"A handful." He stopped, turning to Aidan. "I mean it. Don't hold back. You give me more footage like today and you'll get a national name."

"As a jerk," Aidan replied.

"Doesn't matter. People will know who you are."

4

The ride back took an extra hour, given the roads. Lots of small accidents on I-64, people sliding off. Harry and Susan talked the whole way home. They never ran out of things to discuss, but today was a bonanza.

Getting out of the wagon, Harry blew a kiss to Susan then opened the kitchen door to a rapturous greeting.

"I missed you." Tucker danced on her short hind legs.

"Me too." Pirate put his head under her hand, while the two cats rubbed on her.

Harry hung her coat on a hook, put her shawl there temporarily while she fetched treats.

"I need a cup of tea. Boy, it's dark outside."

Sitting down at the table she gratefully sipped the warm tea, a special dark tea with a light lavender infusion. Harry liked to try different kinds of teas. Restored, she walked into the living room, immediately noticing the bookshelf was missing some books.

"Pewter, I know it was you."

"*Not me*," the gray cat lied.

When disgruntled, Pewter would leap onto a shelf, wedge behind books, and push them to the floor. She dislodged half a shelf about shoulder high, since she had jumped from the back of the old, comfortable couch.

Harry, kneeling down, picked up the books, some old, beautifully printed, the letters cut into the page unlike today's thermographic books. Cheaper, yes, but ugly.

"Pewter, you are bad." She carefully wiped off the John Donne, sliding it next to another volume of poetry. She loved Donne, was relieved the old book wasn't damaged.

The books back in order, she picked a framed photograph off the floor, very happy the glass hadn't broken. The picture was of her grandfather sitting in front of his communication equipment in a destroyer. Grandpa Beaufoy, who had been a well-muscled man, had headphones on and was wearing a T-shirt. Seeing him so young reminded her of all the questions she'd never asked him. The radio operator, the fellow who sends signals, is often one of the last men off a sinking ship.

It was his job to continually send distress signals.

Putting the frame back on the shelf, in front of Churchill's many volumes, she looked at Pewter, now sitting on the sofa.

"I know it was you."

"*Was Pirate. He's so big he can get his face on the shelf.*"

Mrs. Murphy, now on the back of the sofa, said, "*Pewter, Pirate wouldn't dump books on the floor. You were tired of waiting for more treats.*"

"*She was late,*" the gray cat huffed as Harry studied her grandfather.

"How many of our men and women went to war? At least a million, right? Would we do it today?" She spoke to the cats and the two dogs. "If our country were in danger, I'd like to think we would defend it. They called G-Pop Sparks. Think that's what they called the men who did this job on land or on sea. Can you imag-

ine keeping your nerve under fire?" She stared into four pairs of eyes giving her their full attention. "We make war. You don't. Ah, here comes Fair."

Her husband drove up, parking his big truck in front of the barn. He didn't sprint to the back door, the snow getting too deep and slick.

"Hi, honey," she greeted him.

"How was it?"

"Oh, I have a lot to tell you, but first, are you hungry?"

"I can always eat."

"There's shepherd's pie in the fridge. If you warm it up I'll go bring in the older horses. The younger ones have their run-in sheds and blankets, but I worry about our senior citizens."

"I'll do it with you. We can knock this out in twenty minutes. A handful of grain works wonders." He smiled.

They bundled up and, accompanied by Tucker and Pirate, who were impervious to the cold, went outside to bring in the old geldings and mares, then went back into the house and filled the house animals' food bowls.

Once the shepherd's pie was ready, the two sat down and Harry told her husband about the wild Assembly meeting.

"What's the big deal about the shoes?"

"They have red soles and cost over a thousand dollars."

"What?" He nearly choked.

"A thousand dollars. Aren't you glad I spend most of my time in boots?"

"You look good in anything, but yes I'm glad. Why would any-one pay one thousand dollars for shoes?"

"Same as with expensive cars, honey. Because they can. The rest of us are supposed to be impressed."

His eyebrows knitted together for a moment. "Okay. I think I'm missing the impress gene. I mean about money. You can't take it with you."

"True. I sort of get it. If you aren't sure of yourself or if you want to look as though you belong, you know, you're on the cutting edge, you throw your money around."

"I can understand that." He sliced himself another piece of pie. No one made shepherd's pie like his wife.

"Your dually truck, if you bought it new, would be over one hundred thousand dollars today."

"It's awful. Then again, I will be babying that truck for another ten years, but it's my business. Look at all the stuff I have to carry. And no one is impressed by a dually unless it's another country person."

"What would you rather have? More time or more money?"

"More time," he replied without hesitation.

"Me too. You know what Queen Elizabeth I's last words were? 'All my possessions for one moment of time.'"

"I would have liked to have known her," Fair thoughtfully said. "Moment of time. What an incredible realization. Obviously, she didn't want to die."

"More food," Pewter demanded.

Harry, knowing well her naughty cat, looked down. "I know what your answer would be. Not money. Not time. Food."

"Indeed."

5

Studio lights, bright, could wash one out if one's makeup wasn't suitable for the hot lights. Amanda looked perfect. After all, this had been her business. She sat in a comfortable chair, a coffee table to her left, her interviewer on the other side of the table. The cameras could easily focus on each woman.

"Aidan discounted me. I marshaled my facts, which certainly diminished the approach he and Ned Tucker were taking to yet another appeal to blow our citizen's money. And I confess, I lost my temper. I can't promise I won't do it again. I can't endure mansplaining. I am sick of it."

"Amanda, it would be hard to dismiss you," Grace Dudley urged her on with a knowing smile.

"Is there a woman out there looking at us who has not had this experience? I've reached my limit. I have been elected to represent our district. I thought I would be able to introduce a minimum of financial responsibility, but I don't know if the Democratic

Party will ever do anything but raise taxes and blow money on its favorites."

"Possibly, since whoever is in power generally rewards those who put them there."

"Grace, that's why I am trying to do this." Amanda grabbed the setup. "We are facing rising inflation. Prices are through the roof. And if we are not careful, the interest hikes will really throttle the economy."

"Are you saying it's a no-win situation?"

"Well, it didn't have to be, but the Federal Reserve waited far too long then dropped the hammer. And people here are paying for it. What is this project for snow removal? Is it snowing now? Yes. We've got a foot. But that doesn't mean this will be a common condition. We are usually facing rain. This is unusual. That doesn't mean we spend a lot of money renting people and their equipment, I'm not sure I phrased that right, but you know what I mean. If anything, the state has to trim the budget, not fatten it."

Grace slyly asked, "How long did it take you to get to the studio today?"

"An extra forty-five minutes. I left early. You adjust. Is it too much to assume people are intelligent enough to factor in the weather? And if it's really horrible, stay home. Now, if one of my male colleagues said that, would Aidan have exploded as he did? No."

A pause followed this. Then Grace said, "As you said, we women are accustomed to such belittlement or dismissals, but on the floor of the House of Delegates it is surprising, especially since the sessions are streamed."

"Exactly. So the people in his district ought to be asking, why did they elect someone so ignorant of the media? Or so sexist? If a committee is formed to study maintaining our roads, which I am sure will happen, then half of that number better be Republicans. Someone has to keep an eye on the dollar."

"Madam Delegate, speaking of the dollar, don't you think everything is commercialized?" Grace, who had worked with Amanda, set up straw men, easy for Amanda to attack.

Looking very thoughtful, Amanda slowly agreed. "Actually Grace, I think that is the major problem in our society. Yes, I keep my eye on the money. I don't want my people taxed more and more, but what I fear more than anything is everything being monetized. Our campaigns are a disgrace. Where are the ethics? Then again, who goes to church anymore? We are sailing into a full-blown crisis. All I am doing in my own small way is hoping to trim our sails."

Lucas, watching her in the green room, smiled. Amanda was good. She just rattled her woman viewers, including the most liberal, by presenting Aidan as an unrepentant sexist, then she slid into her hopes for her constituency and then for all women. With time, he believed his boss could become the first woman governor of Virginia. She was not a Christian Nationalist but she appealed to them. Lucas had known Amanda since their days at William and Mary, when both were pledges to Delta Delta Delta. She shone brightly then. Her career in media gave her every tool for this media-obsessed age. For the next few years she had to walk the line. As to their being Delta Delta Delta sisters, that, too, would boost her appeal. And when necessary, he would make sure to deliver emotional testimony on their friendship through thick and thin.

Grace glanced at the red light on top of the left camera, swiveled to it, then turned back to the middle camera, red light on top now lit. "One last question, as we are running out of time. What do you suggest for our General Assembly, given its sexism, so much of it unconscious?"

"For those of us in the General Assembly, I think it's time we worked together regardless of party. Do I expect one of my female Democratic colleagues to agree with me regarding trimming the budget? No. But we can all work together to ensure that we are treated with respect and taken seriously. And I hasten to add, I was wrong. Wrong to go after him, but I do think he will bite his tongue before he calls another woman a you-know-what."

Grace looked at the camera, ending the conversation. A commercial came on for the big Ford dealership.

Amanda rose, hugged Grace. "Thanks. I have no idea what will happen next. I will approach the Democratic women. This is only going to be addressed if we address it together."

Grace hugged her back. "I hope you can. This issue is bigger than party. Be careful driving." She pointed to the weather lady, ready to come on after the commercial break, putting up all manner of snow symbols.

"I will."

Harry, having come in from turning out the oldsters, wearing their heavy blankets, to play in the snow with the younger horses, stood in front of the fireplace to warm her hands. Her phone rang, so she trotted into the kitchen, the next room.

"I know it's you."

"Is," Susan replied. "I just watched Amanda Fields on the morning show. She made Ned's proposal that much harder. She put everything under the heading of Aidan dismissing her. Talk about an appeal across the aisle."

"She has a point. He should have never called her a bitch."

"It was pretty stupid," Susan agreed. "How many years have I known Aidan? Four? Long enough. Do I think he's sexist? Well, no more than any other man. It slips out, you know."

"I try to ignore it."

"Sometimes you can't. I care about my husband and his proposal, which I think is helpful to the state. It will cost a lot less money than buying the equipment. But yes, it will still cost money. I don't know about you, but I'm looking at a foot and a half of snow. I expect Richmond is getting less, but even the eastern counties are getting hit. Our weather is changing."

"About a foot and a half here. You know Ned is the best in my book. I hope they can push this idea before a committee drags it out for a year. Because of course there will be a committee. But I actually worry more about droughts than snow. The snow helps with the water table, kills a lot of bugs, and ultimately it melts. A drought is hopeless."

"Is," Susan agreed. "If you want to see the interview, I'll send it to you on your computer. It's worth a look."

"Okay. Do you need anything? No? All set. The snow should stop soon and I have enough pasta for weeks. Eggs. By the weekend, all will be well and your Ned will be home, which means ribeye steak. He lives for red meat."

"Do you believe in this fake meat?"

"I hate killing cattle, but no, I don't believe in laboratory meat. Seems odd. Weird, really."

Back in Richmond, Ned had made it to his office, as had Amanda. The snow kept those away who had to travel to get to the Capitol.

A pile of papers sat on Amanda's desk. Carefully scrutinizing each one, she made notes on a pad. "Lucas."

"Yes," came the response from the adjoining room.

"Do you have the latest figures, for my reelection campaign?"

"Give me a minute. I'll run them off." He knew Amanda didn't want this on her computer, as she liked to spread papers out side by side.

Delegate terms are so short, two years, so one starts planning for reelection while taking the oath of office.

He walked in, placing three pages on her desk. "Doing well. I think today's interview might bring in more funds, even though you didn't mention the next election. Pretty much most people know it."

She quickly read the three pages then looked up. "It's growing. I need to find better ways to reach out."

"Your speeches help."

"I know, but it's more difficult to make speeches when we're in session. Doesn't mean I won't do it, but there are some votes that come up at odd moments. I like time to prepare."

"I think everyone does, but that's what Majority and Minority leaders are for, as well as the whips, to give you information, schedules, and to push you on your committee meetings."

"Actually ours does a good job. Can you believe Aidan and I are on the budget committee together? When I first got elected I, of course, took what was assigned to me. Budget is important, so I was pretty excited. Then I started going to the meetings, and what a wake-up call. Party politics to the max. You know I support fiscal restraint. If either side even tries to find common ground, we hear once the meeting is over why that will hurt the party. Aidan never veers from his party's position. Never. Every now and then a man ought to think for himself. This woman does." She looked up at him.

"You always have." He paused. "Well, after watching you this morning, I was reminded of how good you are in front of the camera. Can we afford a, what do they call it, vlogcast? There are a few good studios here, you could easily create a fifteen-minute or half-hour show. Or instead of sitting in a studio, and this would be more work, but what if you shot a half-hour weekly show wherever you wished? Hollywood Cemetery; Cary Street; a child-care center; a landlord losing his building, his mortgage closed on because his tenants didn't pay their rents. It's endless. You'll get a big following."

She quietly digested this. "If I'm on location I'd have to pay for the videographer. That and the editing."

"There's no reason that can't come from your reelection funds.

By being back on the air you will increase the non-profit gifts. I promise that. For one thing, you look relaxed. For another, you'll ask good questions if interviewing another person, plus your research will be solid. Doesn't matter if it's 1627 or today. And you have an audience remembering you from your newscaster days."

"Let's start talking to people. We have to find the right outlet. That will cost us, too."

"I'll get on it."

"Apart from the snow removal issue, what's next?"

"Fires in salvage yards."

She wrinkled her nose. "It surprises me that there aren't more of them. We can pass all the laws we want, Lucas, but it takes only one idiot to throw a match, especially if it's tires or shredded rubber."

"Couldn't agree more." A knock on the door diverted Lucas's attention.

He opened the door. The delegate from Northern Virginia, Nola Feinstein, smiled.

Amanda, seeing her, motioned for her to come in. "Sit down. Lucas, perhaps Nola would like coffee?"

"Nothing, thank you. I'll get to the point. A group of us met. All elected Democratic women. We are appalled at Aidan's behavior. I can't apologize for him, nor can I apologize for my party. If you and other Republican women are willing, we would like to meet." She shifted her weight. "Sometimes it's like butting your head against a wall."

"Yes, it is."

Nola, voice low, said, "A few of us saw your interview today. We really do need to get together. I can't promise that all the Democratic delegates and state senators will meet with the Republican women, but I can promise that a number of us will. For some, obviously there are other considerations. There are those who worry if they cross the aisle it will hurt their reelection chances. I am hoping we can offer women support. All this does is pit people against one another, and like you, Amanda, I'm sick of it. Yes, I support my party's position on many issues, but I'm tired of being taken for granted. Who is worse? The Republican men or Democratic men?"

"I am so grateful that you chose to meet me face-to-face. I'll start calling, shall I say, my sisters?" Her smile was wry.

Nola, smile also wry, replied, "This will be interesting."

After she left, Lucas pulled up a chair. "You hit a nerve."

"What do you think? You were once treated like a woman."

"It's real. Being accepted as a man, I see it even more clearly, and some of what I hear offends me. Not all men, of course, but so many are unwittingly dense. They do not identify with women on any level, including a lot of gay men."

"No surprise. I expect the brotherhood to stick together." A dark note crept into her voice. "No one gives up power. You have to wrest it from them. So I must have done a good job this morning. Grace asked me excellent questions, plus she kept her distance, which helped. Okay."

"Okay what?" He grinned.

"Keeping Fields as my last name," she joked about the family habit. "That was the first big discussion Ron and I had before getting engaged, back in the dark ages. I said I wouldn't take his last name. Seems small but you'd think someone like Aidan would figure out I won't be put in my place. I have my own identity."

"I remember."

"Ron was fine about it. You know, Lucas, he is a good guy. He works hard. He has his career and I have mine. When we are home, the rule is, 'I won't talk about my day if you don't talk about yours.'"

"If I ever marry, I'll remember that."

"I'll be there." They laughed over this. Old friends.

6

The small propane fireplace sitting on a slate and fire pad warmed the tack room up quickly. Electric heat along the wall was left on low during the night. Harry worried about the cost. Fair had installed, as a Christmas present, a small fireplace with a glass door so she could see the flames.

She had saddle pads for the cats and dogs. The cats lately wanted special houses so they could step in, curl up on a saddle pad inside. Other times, they would climb up to sleep on the saddles covered with pads. These were in a vertical row. More work to get up, especially for Pewter. The dogs were happy in front of the fireplace.

Tapping on her computer, feet in heavy woolen socks, her boots outside the door since the soles were wet, Harry frowned.

"This is awful."

"*What?*" Tucker felt upset when Harry was upset.

Looking over at her best friends, who had mumbled at her, Harry replied, "Fertilizer has gone up two hundred percent. Seed costs aren't far behind. I can't pay this."

"*Maybe it will come down.*" Pewter loved being in her house even though she sometimes shared it with Mrs. Murphy, who had her own. They took turns.

Harry dialed on the old phone. "Honey, I can't find any store or company with lower fertilizer costs. All are the same."

Fair, in his own office at the clinic, commiserated. "It's everything. My medical supplies are jacked up. The delivery costs are added to everything. I guess the truckers have no choice. The only thing I can suggest is we don't fertilize this year. You have your big compost pile. That will help."

"It will. That's why I fill up that manure pile year after year. But that is better for my garden than the pastures. Think of the weeds. I can pull them out of the garden but not the pastures. You know, honey, in my whole life I have always fertilized and overseeded. That's why we have such good hay, plus my sunflowers are pretty good, too. I don't know what to do."

"I don't think anybody does. When I filled up the dually with gas this morning, it was over one hundred dollars. It's eight weeks to the spring equinox. Maybe fertilizer will come down."

She sighed. "It's a gamble. Some of this is the war, Ukraine. You know, seeing the news then looking at my grandfather's photo in the destroyer, taken during a world war, a war that slaughtered millions, brought a question to mind. Do you think it could happen again?"

"I would hope not, but I don't think we learn from history. If the war ends or some kind of truce is called, I think fertilizer prices will go down."

"What about inflation?"

"I don't think inflation is tied to Ukraine. Sweetie, I am a veterinarian, not an economist, but I've lived long enough to see cycles. Inflation will eventually come down or we'll all be eating ramen every night. As to a truce, a peace, I don't know. Take a deep breath. We aren't going to starve. Even one year without fertilizer or overseeding won't hurt the nutrition for the horses. More than that, we'll face it when we must."

"You're right. What were you doing before I interrupted you?"

"Looking at X-rays. Cannon bone X-rays. There's a tiny splint. And a nervous new owner. I'll tell her to turn the horse out for two months and don't ride him. I'll check each month. The splint should reattach. Of course, I am sure she will want a second opinion. Will be interesting what happens next. Most every vet I know will tell her the same thing but a few will prescribe drugs. People love to get prescriptions." He laughed.

Harry laughed with him. "Mother said the best medicine is tincture of time. Don't think that would get much of a hearing these days, for people or animals."

"Your mother had good sense. I am thrilled with the advances in my profession, but so much of what I try to get people to do is just let a horse be a horse."

"How do we get people to just be people?"

"I don't know if that's possible. We are a lot more different from one another than horses are different from one another."

"Well, this is an interesting way to start the morning," she teased him. "Okay, I am going back to trying to find anyone with a price drop in fertilizer. Another half hour. Will make me feel I've done my duty."

"You are persevering. Perseverance furthers. Who said that?"

"Fair, that's from Chairman Mao."

"Ah. Okay, sugar. Back to work. Love."

"Love you back." She stared at the screen. "I hate this."

"Don't do it," Pewter advised.

"She won't be happy until her eyes water," Tucker answered.

"It's her eyes not mine." The gray cat curled her lip.

"You know she worries about money. She worries about her hay. She wants everything just so." Mrs. Murphy was sympathetic to Harry.

Pirate, on his back, turned his head to observe Harry tapping away at computer keys. He closed his eyes.

The phone rang.

"Susan. What are you doing?"

"Listening to my husband curse. I figured if I called you I'd get more imaginative curses."

"Is that a compliment?"

"Yes."

"What's the buzz?"

"Aidan won't apologize to Amanda. Apart from what I think of it, she is rallying women, and having watched her interview, I get it."

"Called you after I saw what you sent me. She clearly says she lost her temper. But her reasons will win a lot of fans even if they aren't with her politics. Did I say that right? Every day Aidan sits on his high horse, she wins, know what I mean?"

"I do."

"Okay. Now can I bitch and moan?"

"Of course." Susan laughed as Harry launched into her fertilizer tirade.

7

Light snow fell after a cold night. Low clouds slowly moved west to east, finally opening at nine-thirty. This snow, unprecedented, surprised few living by the Blue Ridge Mountains. The area had its own weather system.

Harry plowed the main farm road again. A lumberjack hat kept her head warm. Wearing an old, serviceable, thin goose-on-top down coat, she was also covered in layers of sweaters, plus an undershirt. A cashmere scarf warded off the biting air. That, lined gloves, and two pairs of socks in her work boots did the job. The snowflakes hitting her face felt invigorating. The rest of her remained warm.

Fair drove out early this morning before the snowfall. They each took turns plowing the driveway.

As she pushed snow to the side of the farm road, she reflected on Ned and Aidan's idea. She thought it sensible. Her tractor wasn't big enough for heavy roadwork, but if she kept at it each time it snowed, she could ensure her road would be serviceable in all but a blizzard or heavy snow.

This snow would add maybe five inches to the previous snow, now pouring down and unfortunately covered in thin ice. A new snow falling on ice creates more accidents.

She drove slowly. The tractor, having deep-treaded huge tires, usually wouldn't slide. A car or truck could.

She shut the animal doors to keep the dogs in. Tucker was too short. Pirate could handle it even though the snow would reach his stomach. Better they be together.

Reaching the end of her one-and-a-half-mile driveway, she noted the two-lane state highway, not heavily traveled, had been plowed yesterday.

Turning right, she headed to Aunt Tally's farm. The westernmost border touched the old Jones Homeplace, her neighboring farm, rented by Cynthia Cooper, who was now in the process of buying it.

The dirt roads that could take Harry to Aunt Tally's would be dicey. The snow was too deep. Best to go on the state road; that would make the drive two miles minus a yard or two.

Dark though the sky was, she could see the farm sign sway in the wind.

Aunt Tally's great-niece, Little Mim, and her husband, Blair, were in Ocala. Their daughter attended Westover in Connecticut. This was her first year. A caretaker lived with Aunt Tally, 103 years old. The caretaker, a nurse, would not be clearing the farm road.

Harry wanted to make sure an emergency vehicle could reach the farm. Tough as Aunt Tally was, she was increasingly frail. Her niece, Big Mim, in her early seventies, might try to check on the beloved centenarian.

Harry began pushing now; she thought Blair and Little Mim had picked the perfect time to leave. They rented a house in Ocala for January and February. As they, like Big Mim, were in the horse business, Ocala was ideal.

The snow fell more heavily. Harry thought if it continued maybe they'd get another half foot. She kept plowing, coming up to the outbuildings, all Federalist architecture; she was reminded of the farm's starting year, 1831.

She passed a small house. Now empty but could be used for a farm worker. A quarter mile ahead she could just make out the main home, two stories, clean lines. Through the snow, the dark green door, protected by an overlay, looked inviting.

She kept going until she reached the stable, pushing a circle in front to the side. She had to remember where the road was, as snow now covered everything. The big red barn had one hand-dug walk to the main doors. She decided to let that be.

After ten more minutes of pushing, she returned to the main home, on the side where a garage with architecture and paint matching the home stood, doors closed.

Climbing down from her high seat, she lifted one door; no electric doors here. Two spaces were empty, a third was filled by Aunt Tally's old used car.

Back up in the tractor, Harry drove in, happy the seat wouldn't be covered in snow. She just wanted to check on the woman she had known all her life, as had everyone else in Crozet.

Stomping her feet, she opened the door to an enclosed side porch, then brushed on the side house door.

Teresa Becker, the live-in assistant nurse, smiled as she saw Harry. "Come on in. You're almost white."

"Coming down harder. Let me take off this coat. Shake it out."

"Hang it inside. It will be warm when you leave. Keep your boots on. Can I get you a warm drink? Coffee? Tea? Hot chocolate?"

"No thank you. I just wanted to check on you and Aunt Tally."

A voice called from down the hall. "Harry, I'm in the living room."

Teresa led Harry to the living room.

"I'd know your voice anywhere." Aunt Tally held out her hand for Harry to immediately hold.

"Your ears are good."

"That's about all that's left. Sit down." She looked at Teresa. "Hot chocolate. Two. Harry loves chocolate. Sit down. Tell us what you're doing."

Harry sat in an armchair across from the white-haired lady. Given her advanced age, Aunt Tally looked good. She was in her favorite wing chair with a heavy checkered throw over her legs, propped on a hassock.

"This snow will be off and on. I'll come back tomorrow, too. Without Blair here to do outside chores like this, you and Teresa will be stuck."

Aunt Tally waved her hand, still bejeweled. "Mim can organize all this. She'll drop by today. By the way, how about Reverend Jones selling the farm to Cynthia Cooper?"

"Be good for both of them."

"I like having a law enforcement person for a neighbor." Aunt Tally smiled. "Oh, Teresa, put the cups down there." She pointed to the coffee table, which Teresa moved closer to them.

"How's that?"

"Good." Aunt Tally smiled then turned to Harry. "Ordered spring seed yet? Seems far away but spring will eventually come."

Harry shook her head. "Prices are so high right now, I don't know if I can overseed. Maybe they'll drop by March or April, but I don't know. What are you thinking?"

"Same as you. Outrageous costs, but having lived here all my life, I want to keep it up. I'll find the money. Big Mim's been in charge of my estate for years. I have to admit my sister's daughter is good with numbers. So was my sister. You don't remember her, do you?"

"Not very well, I'm afraid. I remember she wore such pretty sundresses in the summer. I remember the colors. Speaking of memories. Pewter, the fatty, pushed books off my shelf. A picture of my grandfather was on the floor, too. I picked it up. He is sitting at his station in the destroyer. He was so handsome when he was young. I only remember him as an older man. Still good looking."

Aunt Tally leaned forward. "We were the same age. He might have been a year or two older. I was born in 1920. When the war broke out he enlisted right away. As I was sent to private school, the dreaded Miss Porter's," she giggled, "I didn't know him that well until the war was over." She paused. "You resemble him greatly. Bring me the picture sometime."

"Did he ever talk about the war?"

"Only to say he was scared when they were attacked but one does one's duty. Those were his words. He also mentioned that he would have felt better had he been firing an antiaircraft gun. Sitting down below deck with the radio and telegraph, he didn't know what was going on. He also said the noise was deafening. He had to press his headphones tightly to his ears. He was a brave man. They all were."

"Yes. I wish I had asked questions but I was too young to know much about that war, his life."

"Funny, I often wish I had asked my grandparents things, but I was too busy going to dances. The 1930s are always written up as being terrible. Not if you were young. There were parties, discovering life, listening to the big bands. Oh, I loved that." She sipped her hot chocolate. "You know, Harry, you are the only person who knows how much I loved your grandfather."

Harry thought a moment. "It was such a different time. Today perhaps you could be together. Then," she put down her own cup, "it had to be so painful."

"I never married because no man lived up to Larry. Forgive me. Old stories."

"I'm glad you can talk to me. And yes, you would have lost a lot of social status."

"Poof. I could have cared less, but my mother and my aunt did. They were keen to see me engaged to that ridiculous Chicago department store heir. An idiot, but a rich idiot. All I could think of was Larry. If I couldn't have him then I'd stay single. But you know, and I never told this, he taught me how to operate a ham radio. I had to take tests, learn Morse code, and get a license. Learning about radio waves did not thrill me. Talking to Larry did. No one knew because if anyone walked into my room, I'd quickly turn the radio down and say I think I've got someone in Washington. That's about one hundred miles. Two hundred miles was pretty much the radius. For a good reason."

"I think one still has to get a license. I wonder what happened to Grandpa's radio?"

Aunt Tally replied, "Your mother would never have thrown it out. It has to be packed away somewhere or your mother gave it away."

"I bet Susan's mother would know. They were best friends."

"Well, if you find it, consider getting a license. You might need to go to class, but if you find Larry's radio, you can talk to me. I still use mine. I like to listen to what's out there. People really talking, you know. Not like cellphones or such. It's different. Maybe once a month I'll sit in my little room off the kitchen and use the radio, gives me comfort." She put her cup back on the coffee table. "And it makes me think of him." She stopped.

"I'll try to find his radio." Harry heard the door open in the back.

Teresa had hurried to it. Within a minute Big Mim came down the hall.

"Harry."

"Mim, so good to see you."

"Come see my four foals. Born early January. Well, you would know. Your husband was there." She sat in a chair.

Big Mim, in her early seventies, wore a warm, wonderful Navy officer's sweater. The turtleneck kept her warm. This white sweater was over a heavy skirt, plaid, and a pair of knee-high boots. Her earrings sparkled, gold domes, her engagement ring after all these years could dazzle, given its epic proportions. Mim turned out, no matter the occasion. She was born knowing how to throw herself together. Harry so envied that ability, as she lacked it. Susan would occasionally dress her.

"I would love to see them. He remarked on the bright chestnut filly. Said you needed sunglasses to look at her."

Mim laughed. "She is bright. If she turns into a foxhunter instead of a running horse, no one will miss her." Teresa brought a cup for Mim. "Thank you, dear."

Aunt Tally commented, "Harry plowed the new snow."

"Oh, Harry, I would have seen to that, but thank you so much. This snow crept up on us. Watching the news, I noticed piles of snow pushed up in parking lots, even in Richmond. Watching the news I got an earful from Amanda Fields. You must have seen it. I heard you and Susan were there when Ned introduced his bill. Sensible, by the way."

Aunt Tally lifted an eyebrow. "What? What did Ned introduce?"

Both Harry and Big Mim explained.

"How extraordinary," came the response, then Aunt Tally grinned. "I do give her credit for hitting Aidan with her high heel. Evens up the fight."

Mim looked outside the window. "Getting darker and coming down heavier. Harry, where is your tractor?"

"In the garage."

"Leave it there. Let me drive you home. Tomorrow Fair can drive you here, you can get the tractor, and he can drive behind you as you go home. I don't trust the roads even with lights on your tractor. Aunt Tally, I'll see you tomorrow."

"Well, this is a short visit."

"Be longer tomorrow."

"Forgive me for not getting up, Harry. Do look through your mother's things."

"I will."

Big Mim leaned over to kiss her aunt, then she and Harry walked down the hall; Teresa already had their coats in her arms.

Once in Mim's new X5, Harry remarked, "The perfect vehicle for bad weather."

"Yes, it is. Too big for me but I'm glad to have it in rainstorms, snow, even mud. Is this enough heat?"

"Yes. Aunt Tally looks good."

"She's frail but she still has that sharp mind and energy. Before I forget it, you might mention to Ned, or tell Susan, that he needs to keep some distance between himself and Aidan, even though they have co-sponsored this bill. People who lose their tempers rarely do it just once."

"I never thought about that."

"Jim loves politics. How many decades has he been mayor of Crozet? He's been avidly following the ruckus. Quite fascinated with the red high-heeled shoe. He hopes Ned will stay in politics, rise. Fewer and fewer people seem to have restraint. They were both foolish, but Aidan did start it."

Big Jim was Mim's husband.

"She's very intelligent, this Amanda. I knew her as a news-caster. I guess we all did. Politics is so unsettling. I don't know why any woman would seek a career in it."

"Maybe that's why we should." Harry quickly added, "But I'm like you. I don't know why women would want to be dragged through it. Maybe the idea of power, even just a little bit of power, becomes a drug."

"It must be. I forget how long your driveway is." Mim pulled up to the house. "Thank you again for plowing my aunt's drive-way." As Harry opened the door, a gust of air blew into the X5. "Good to see you."

Harry dashed in front of the SUV, waving to Big Mim, who then turned around.

Opening the door to the kitchen, Harry was rapturously greeted by the dogs. Pewter, asleep on the sofa, opened one eye. Mrs. Murphy, stretched on the back of the sofa, lifted her head.

Harry hung up her coat, wondering where her mother would have kept G-Pop's old ham radio.

8

"Why did I think I could do this?" Harry complained as she sifted through a large tin cylinder of her mother's papers.

"*You can always stop,*" Tucker counseled.

Pirate nosed the top of the storage unit. "*Old paper.*"

Turning to her dogs and Mrs. Murphy, investigating a few stacked cardboard boxes, Harry looked inside one more time. "You know, my mother was the librarian. She saved any papers she thought useful. There must be fifty years of carefully pressed papers here, all in folders. I wish I had Mother's organizing abilities. All right, I was an idiot to open this."

Putting the top back on, pressing it down firmly, Harry sat on the old bench in front of the washer and dryer; another irritating possibility, doing the wash.

"*Matilda has one eye open,*" the tiger cat announced to her friends. "*She's mostly out of it. Boy, she really is big.*"

Matilda, the blacksnake, slithered inside for winter, going into a form of semi-hibernation called brumation. She had enough fat on her to get through the winter. Once spring arrived she would leave the basement . . . she had her ways . . . go outside, and climb the big walnut tree near the kitchen window. This way, if she felt like it, she could stretch out on a branch and watch the goings-on in the house. She could also terrify Pewter.

"Pewter," Tucker mischievously called up the stairs, "*your friend is here.*"

Sitting at the top of the stairs so she could hear, God forbid anyone say anything about her, Pewter called down, "*The giant cobra. I'm not going to save you. You shouldn't be there.*"

Pirate, in a rare smarty moment, called back up in his deep Irish Wolfhound voice, "*Last time you talked about her, she was a python. How many kinds of snake can she be?*"

"*Don't insult your elders,*" Pewter hissed back.

Harry, hearing the animal chatter, remarked, "What are you all talking about?"

"*Oh, Pewter's being delusional,*" Tucker maliciously said.

Tucker, usually a sweetheart, had a big fight with Pewter when Harry was over at Aunt Tally's. A worn-out two-toed sloth toy, ever so valuable to the animals, was snatched from Tucker, even though she kept her sleeping paw on top of it. Pewter yanked it right out. This awakened the corgi, who leapt up to grab her toy back. Pewter gave the low-to-the-ground dog a whopping smack on her tender nose. Hence the unkind reference to the fat cat's state of mind.

"Maybe in this closet that I rarely open." Harry opened the door, which squeaked slightly. She reached for the long hanging beaded light chain for the overhead light. The bright light flashed on. Aligned on shelves were boxes. "It can't be small. In those days anything like a radio was big, whether a regular radio or a ham radio."

She knelt down, as the larger boxes were on the lowest shelf. Tucker and Mrs. Murphy came in to sniff.

Carefully opening the first box on the left, Harry peered down at the top of a portable refrigerator. "I didn't think they had refrigerators this small. What were Mom and Dad doing with it?"

She folded the top back, as Mrs. Murphy kept sniffing, Tucker behind her. Pirate stood outside the opened door. Given his size, if he came in they would have been crowded.

Mrs. Murphy scratched a box in the middle, perhaps a foot and a half high and as wide. "Try this. Has a metal smell."

Tucker stepped up to inhale. "Metal. The other boxes are more papers, one is clothing."

"Wool?" Mrs. Murphy asked.

"Mostly." The dog also scratched at the box.

Looking at two trusted friends, Harry thought, "Why not?"

Opening the box, she stared down at an old ham radio from the late 1940s. "Here it is. Maybe I shouldn't lift it out. I'll have Fair do it. If I drop it, that's the end of the radio. You know, it makes sense that my mother would keep her father's ham radio. Look at what I've kept that was hers and Dad's. Not a lot, but things I can't bring myself to throw away, especially the papers and stuff. Oh look." She reached down, sliding her hand along the radio, pulling up an old dog collar. "Moosie. What a good dog. Was my grandfather's bulldog. I can't believe Mom kept the collar. Well, I can."

"There was a bulldog in this house?" Mrs. Murphy was surprised.

Harry pressed the collar to her heart. "I was little. Moosie seemed so big. He would come sit next to me, and follow me everywhere. G-Pop moved into Crozet proper. Was easier for him. He stayed fit. He'd come out here and help with farm chores. Moosie came with him. G-Pop gave the farm to Mom and Dad. Mom said he felt as married people they should have the house to themselves. He had so many friends. He liked where he was but Mom said he missed Grandma so much. Maybe he couldn't live in the house without her. I don't know." She hugged the collar again to her heart. "I loved Moosie. G-Pop must have kept the collar. Funny what you find out years later." Three intent faces looked at her. "All right. Let's go. I found it, so I feel quite victorious." The animals raced up the stairs in front of Harry.

"*Did you bring that monster with you? I hope she eats you alive if you did.*" Pewter, wild-eyed, sat on the kitchen table.

Harry carefully turned out the light, closing the basement door behind her. "Pewter, you're puffed up like a broody hen."

"*You all are lucky to be alive,*" Pewter replied in a loud voice.

"*Oh, Pewter, it's Matilda.*" Tucker brushed this off.

Mrs. Murphy halfway defended her cat friend. "*She is the largest blacksnake in the world.*"

"*I knew it! I knew it! A giant. A giant in our basement.*"

Pewter's fur began to go down now that she knew the snake was in place. "*She hangs from a branch in the summer. You've seen her do it. Dangerous. She opens her mouth and flicks her tongue.*"

"Pewter, pipe down." Harry walked to the wall phone as her cat rattled on and on.

Dialing, she listened, then said, "How you doing?"

Susan's voice answered back. "Okay."

"Your driveway clear?"

"Ned plowed it before he left again for Richmond. He wanted to outrun the snow. Fortunately, my drive is a lot shorter than yours."

"I hope this snow stops. It's light but it keeps falling, so it will pile up. Official spring is eight weeks away but it seems like it should be warming up a little."

"It will and then we'll be slammed with bitter cold again. Ned returned because he feels he should push Aidan for an apology, plus he wants to get more support from the party for his program. The snow should help that. Do you know, Aidan has a non-profit? Perfectly legal. It helps his career. It's to fund scholarships for young people who want skilled-labor training; you know, electricians, plumbers, even cabinetry. I have to give it to Aidan, he does try to help those in need. But still."

"Sounds like a good idea; training, I mean, but what we really need is housing for poor people and those who are damaged and can't work." Harry couldn't imagine living in a big city with people sleeping on the streets.

Seeing poverty in areas of Richmond was bad enough.

"The party will get around to that. Think how much it will cost. If Ned and Aidan are getting pushback because of snowplow costs, hiring people with equipment, imagine what housing will do? I really get being careful with taxpayers' dollars, but we have to provide something in winter."

"Which reminds me, I plowed out Aunt Tally's. The farm road was cleared from the big snow, but this snow is piling up, so I went over, got most of it done, and put my tractor in her garage to visit for a bit. She's doing great. So thin but otherwise fine."

"Happens with great age. Look how thin my grandmother is."

"Yeah. Anyway, while I was there, Big Mim came in. She told me to leave the tractor there and she took me home but what I really want to tell you is that Aunt Tally and I talked about my grandfather. She said she'd loved him and always would. Obviously people who have heard her history or knew her years back know she had a lost love, for lack of a better phrase, but she will talk to me about it. And strange to say, she told me he taught her how to use a ham radio and they would talk to each other. Nobody knew. Then she asked me, did I have it? Was it saved, and if so, would I talk to her? Anyway, I should have started this conversation with this, I found it."

"What?"

"I found G-Pop's in one of Mother's packed boxes in the basement. I'll have Fair bring it upstairs. I'm afraid I'll drop it and I don't want to lift it out of the box. Just in case."

"How about that? But you know, you can't turn it on and start talking to Aunt Tally. You have to take a test to get a technician's license. People who do this are passionate about it. Better than normal radio."

"Why? Because you talk to actual people? You aren't getting a corporate or government spin?"

"I guess. But you make friends. Didn't G-Pop Larry ever talk about it?"

"Not to me. Once or twice he talked about being the sparks on the destroyer."

"If it's still working, do you really think you'll go to class? Learn? I suppose you could learn on the internet, but being with a teacher or with other students is better, I think."

"Me too. I can't learn from those programs you get for the computer. Some are on thumb drive, some on old DVDs, and some you sign in, pay up, then log in. Can't learn a thing. Can't concentrate."

"Me neither. How could kids learn during COVID? You need a teacher, other kids, a classroom. Too easy to wander off if it's on a computer, which everyone is finding out. Our education scores are down this year, and we usually do okay as a state. Some of Ned's colleagues think summer school is the answer. Not me. Those kids need a break. I don't have an answer."

"I don't either." Harry reached into a cabinet, took out cookies for the troops. "Aunt Tally is lonely. When the roads get better, go visit. Little Mim and Blair won't be home until Easter. Same with their daughter."

"The third Mim." Susan laughed.

"Family names can be a pain. At least we aren't Louis the Eighteenth."

"Better to be the Eighteenth than the Sixteenth."

"That's the truth." Harry looked out the window. "The snow is really coming down. This weather has to clear up at some point."

"I need to find a new light coat, semi-dress. So when it does clear up, let's go look."

"You get to be in Richmond. You can't find anything there?"

"Not as much as I'd like. I was thinking about Horse Country, especially now that she has such a range of clothing."

"Okay. I held my breath. Thought you were going to say Tyson's Corner."

Susan laughed. "I'd never do that to you. You hate shopping."

"Not for farm equipment."

"I can see you now, driving your tractor while wearing a sparkling tiara."

"Don't start, Susan."

"All right. Will call on Aunt Tally. Talk to you tomorrow."

After hanging up the old phone, Harry gave everyone a special treat.

Pirate ate his with one gulp. *"Mom has her best friend. You are my best friend."*

Tucker gave the huge dog a suspicious look. *"I'm not giving you part of my greenie."*

"I know. You know a lot about humans. If our human and Susan are best friends, why don't they groom each other?"

"They do a little bit, but not like we do. Sometimes they dust off their friend's clothing if it's got straw or leaf bits on it. I suppose in a city they dust off dirt, no straw. Sometimes they share clothing, but real grooming, no. They take a bath or a shower. No need, I guess."

"They don't lean on each other either. No sitting close."

"Sometimes they do." Tucker liked that Pirate was becoming so observant now that he was almost an adult. *"Human men never do. They never groom one another either. It's a girl thing."*

"It feels good to lean on someone. I like leaning on Mom. I like it when you groom me."

"We aren't out of touch with our true natures. I think they are. Comes from their many weaknesses. Can't face it."

"You mean no fangs? The stuff we sometimes talk about?"

"Yes. Our humans are healthy, but even Pewter can outrun them."

"I resent that," Pewter grumbled, bits of crumbs falling from her mouth.

Tucker quickly replied, as she was not looking for a fight. "*You can climb a tree, see in the dark. There's lots you can do.*"

"*Don't you forget it.*" Pewter sat up straight, then unable to keep her mouth shut, she said, "*Bubble butt.*"

Tucker ran to the counter, tried to get up on it, which she couldn't. Harry, watching the growling and spitting, stepped back for a moment.

Mrs. Murphy prudently left the room.

Harry slapped her hand on the counter as she stomped her foot on the floor. The noise stopped the antagonists.

"That's enough. You two better get along."

"*Why? Humans don't,*" Pewter sassed.

Her insight would be amply demonstrated before the snow melted.

9

"Radioactive. Ha." Amanda laughed as Lucas pulled up a chair by her desk.

"That's what she said." He raised his eyebrows as if in disbelief. "So the Democrats realize they have a problem."

"Bless Aidan Harkness. He's making my job easier. Plus contributions are flowing into my reelection campaign." Amanda tapped her shoe under the desk. "Maybe this is the time to introduce my bill about parents' rights?"

"I'd wait." He could be direct with her. "You have women coming to your side. Let someone else do that. Stick to the state budget."

She reached under the desk, pulling off her shoe. "You're probably right."

"Milk this for all it's worth." Lucas pushed back a blond lock of hair almost the same color as Amanda's. "The Democratic women . . . not all of them, but most of them . . . are willing to meet next week. The men are nervous."

"As well they should be." Rubbing her heel, she grumbled, "Shoes hurt."

"You're the only woman I know who can make walking in high heels look easy."

"These are the lower heels. Thought they'd be okay at the office. I might as well pull my snow boots on; at least they fit. Okay, back to this meeting. No one from our party has called to complain or back out. Nor has any Republican male uttered one word. Now, that is unusual. The last thing to die on many of my colleagues will be their mouths."

"So true." Lucas laughed, his even white teeth adding to his attractiveness.

"Any editorial yet in the *Richmond Times Dispatch* concerning Aidan's loss of control? You know perfectly well they will elaborate on mine."

"The paper leans left, but they aren't righteous. I expect there will be a balanced one tomorrow. You know in all our years together I only saw you lose control once."

Amanda grinned. "The William and Mary game against UVA. Well, that jackass behind me screaming every time UVA scored a touchdown finally wore me down."

"Yes, that was a helluva right cross."

"Thank you." She took a deep breath and looked at her calendar. "There's a budget committee meeting next week. Any new figures on when federal monies run out for housing, eldercare, that stuff?"

"I have most of it, but you probably should talk to Belvidere Coles, head of Golden Years Aftercare. He'd be the most practical, I think."

"Good suggestion. This snow and cold weather is making me bored with my clothes. It's harder to look good in the winter. I say we go shopping next week."

"You can't go to New York. No time for that kind of trip until mid-March."

"I know. I've been cruising on my screen. I'll find somewhere. Also, I feel like getting out of Richmond for even a day."

The phone rang. Lucas sprinted to his office to take it. Then walked back in. "It's Ned Tucker. Will you take the call?"

"Of course." She picked up the phone and purred.

"Amanda."

"Ned, my favorite Democrat. What can I do for you?"

"You've sparked a whirlwind debate. Which I think you know. Was my co-sponsor wrong? Never mind, I'm actually calling to let you know I'm planning a meeting of Democratic men to discuss the unwitting ways we ignore or even downgrade women. You and my wife use the word *mansplaining* and I've seen that, but I miss a lot. Anyway, I called to thank you for forcing this on us. And while I have your attention I want to urge you to go over the figures on hiring people to clear the roads. Study them."

"I will." She paused. "You know I am dead set against a lot of new equipment, but this doesn't seem much better."

"All of it is expensive. And if we get pushed to buy or use EV's, it will go through the roof; plus, if you run out of battery in the middle of a blizzard and you're on, say, 64, plowing, how do you recharge?"

"That's a thought."

"If you need me, you know where I am."

"A question, will the Democratic Party censure Aidan?"

"It's under consideration. If you're asking me what I think, I believe we should, even though he and I work together. I feel from a political point of view it has to happen."

"I'm not being censured, but my knuckles have been rapped by the party chair. He's such a Virginia gentleman. He did it in the gentlemanly way, but if I do anything that stupid again I'll have to sit in the corner with a dunce cap." She laughed. "I'll deserve it."

"We'll get through this. We all need to work together, Amanda. The state of Virginia can't afford these drastic ideological battles."

"I agree. Leave that to Washington."

"Or Florida."

That got her attention. "You know, the duel between DeSantis and Disney fascinates me. Can a government give a corporation that kind of favoritism in a former administration, then revoke it decades later? I can really see both sides of the issue. Again it gets down to taxpayers' money, which is my bailiwick."

"I know. You and I have years, I hope, to argue over it," he teased her.

"We do, but remember I wear red high heels."

"I will never forget."

After a few more pleasantries, they hung up, each feeling better for the talk.

Lucas called from his tiny office, "Sounded sensible. What I could hear from here."

"Ned's smart. Then again, his wife is the granddaughter of one of our most successful governors. He's had a head start."

"Yes. He's steady. He'd move up anyway. Are you figuring out how to handle this women's meeting? And don't forget no one in the Republican Party wants to be accused of being a feminist."

"I can handle it. Leave that to me. We've got to use this . . . for us, I mean. For my career. So at the meeting I need to find a smooth way to sidestep culture stuff."

He walked into her office, all six feet of him. "Walk softly, forgive the pun. No need to throw around your power. Walk softly. Carry a big stick."

"Why?"

"Stick to the broad issue of women supporting women. As it is, your reelection fund has bumped up by close to seven hundred thousand dollars since you appeared on *Wake-Up Richmond*."

"Now you tell me?"

"The radioactive was too juicy. But I'm telling you now, stick to the issue of how women are dismissed. Not that anyone wants to hear what I say, but I think I know better than most women."

"One of the advantages of becoming male, I guess." She rubbed her foot again. "What I miss is swapping clothing with you. Not shoes, obviously, but blouses and earrings. We can't do that anymore."

"Was fun. Men don't do that." He laughed.

"I know."

"The good behavior rule, male or female, is drummed into our heads early. That's why this meeting of most of the women delegates will be interesting."

"You mean will we act like ladies?"

"Yes." He leaned closer to her over her desk.

"We'll see. I'll wear my Louboutins."

They both laughed.

Harry sat at the kitchen table with her grandfather's ham radio in front of her. She had no idea what to do with it. When Fair carried it up last night, it didn't turn on. Could it be fixed? Then again, how was she going to learn the skills and get her license? She knew Aunt Tally was lonely. She ought to make an effort. Maybe she could buy an inexpensive radio to learn. Harry realized this would be like learning another language.

As she expressed this, Pewter flipped her tail up. *"She's never learned ours. She should learn cat first."*

10

"The potbellied stove keeps it warm." Aidan zipped open his ski jacket, which he'd bought in Wyoming last year.

"My wife and Harry came over to fire it up. We've all been working on this school for three years now. This fall will be when we can open it to the public, share the history."

"So much light." Aidan admired the long high windows to accommodate the story-and-a-half frame building.

"In the beginning, there was no electricity. Only whale-oil lamps. But even when the three buildings could be electrified, the windows saved money. The floors, smooth from all those feet, have also held up."

Aidan looked down, slid his boot over the floor. "Are people still alive who attended this school?"

"Yes. We have a few in their nineties, more in their eighties, who attended the grade school in the late 1930s, early 1940s. The high school, those people are gone. You'd be surprised how many eighty-year-olds are hale and hearty around here. The oldest student we have is ninety-three, Tinsley Moon. Every now and then some of the students drop by to see the progress. Floods of memories."

Aidan ran his hand over a desktop. "Those seats, the attached ones, are uncomfortable."

Ned laughed. "I don't think our forebearers were too concerned with kids' comfort."

"Guess not." Aidan confidently stated, "That's when teachers could smack you with a ruler."

"Those days are gone," Ned mused.

"You might want to change the name from Crozet Colored School," Aidan suggested.

"The old students will put up a fight. This is their school. They've made that clear to us. They wanted it remembered for what it was."

"Won't work."

"Aidan, the schools throughout our state were overseen radically by Walter Plecker."

"Ned, no one cares about history. I know Plecker was our first registrar of the Virginia Bureau of Vital Statistics, in 1912. He made sure every baby born in the state received a birth certificate. He also instituted the one drop rule. One drop of black blood, called Negro then, and you were black."

"Right. So then you know he determined there were no true Indians, the name then, in the state. He declared the indigenous peoples were so intermixed with blacks, they all needed to be called colored. So indigenous people couldn't prove they were indigenous. No help in subsequent decades from the federal government. No help for anyone with African blood. He instituted a terrible thing that held for most of a century."

"Like I said, no one cares about history. You wanted me to see the school building and help you get a historical plaque. The buildings are impressive, but no one cares."

"It's important." Ned was shocked, which he kept to himself.

"Why risk your career on people in their eighties and nineties? Really, Ned, drop it."

"Aidan, you're telling me to disregard the wishes of those living black and indigenous people who want their history remembered. Cherished even. We've actually found the schoolbooks used over the decades. Jerry Showalter, the antiquarian bookseller, found them. He drove all over the state to find examples of what was used over the decades. The people working on this project have put their heart and soul into it."

"I'm telling you to protect your career. No one cares about history. They only care about their interpretation of it. Careers are made and lost on this. You have the chance for a big career."

"I don't want a big career. I want to serve my district."

"Very noble." Aidan walked to the pegs along one wall, placed there for coats. "Somebody was a good carpenter or cabinetmaker."

"I know a large developer is looking at this land, even though I don't know which developer. It's twenty acres. We're worried. A plaque would make buying and developing this harder."

"And?" Aidan folded his hands together.

"Use your connections and influence to help me block it. Our county commissioners, as well as certain parties in Crozet, are being coy. Your nemesis, Amanda, will be all over this if we can dig out the details. She'll declare it's a great opportunity for any district. More citizens, more taxes, especially if they come because taxes are low, or business is tax free," Ned predicted.

"She will. Those people give the rich all the breaks."

"My goal is to save our history." Ned had raised his voice a bit.

Aidan wiggled into a chair attached to a desk. "Snow's not melting. At least there isn't more forecast. To change the subject, anything about Amanda tires me."

Ned sat across from him. "Will you help me and Tazio . . . the whole gang . . . get a historic plaque from the state?"

"I don't know. Give me time. I'm not sure a plaque can save this."

"For someone who is so concerned about how things are perceived, why didn't you think when you called Amanda a bitch?"

"We've been through that. Y'all are drumming on me to apologize."

"Speaking for the party, it's better for all of us if you do. You look like a sexist pig."

"And she looks like a wing nut. My wife doesn't think I'm a sexist pig. She said she would have called her worse names."

"Aidan, that's your wife. Be reasonable. You have to apologize. This isn't helping our bill."

The sound of a big motor attracted their attention to Harry and Susan in Fair's big truck, two dogs and two cats in the seat behind the front bucket seat. The big windows brought the outside inside.

"Who is that?"

"Harry and Susan. Every now and then Harry borrows her husband's big dually. Brutes, those trucks."

"I understand why someone would need one out here, but in Richmond?" Aidan shook his head.

"Hi, guys." Harry pushed open the door, followed by Susan, Mrs. Murphy, Pewter, Tucker, and Pirate.

Aidan's eyes enlarged. "That's the biggest dog I've ever seen."

"Irish Wolfhounds are the biggest breed." Harry kept her hand on Pirate's collar as the other three animals raced down the center aisle. "They are very gentle but very protective." She leaned down to stare into Pirate's sweet eyes. "Leave him alone."

Pirate blinked. *"Okay, but I'd like to smell him."*

"Do you hear?"

"Yes, Mom."

She released Pirate, who ran up to the dais on which reposed the teacher's big desk.

"Mouse." Mrs. Murphy spotted a tail disappear into a small hole in the baseboard behind the desk.

All the four-legged friends crowded around it.

Pewter cooed, *"Come out. We have gumdrops."*

"Not on your life," came the squeak.

Aidan complimented Harry and Susan. "Y'all have done so much work."

"Tazio, our architect, knew exactly what to do." Susan filled him in. "We want to have a grand opening, maybe in spring. The surviving graduates will give tours and speeches."

"How many are there?" Aidan asked.

"In our county, about two hundred. We've sent out letters to as far as California, anywhere we could find a name and address. We don't have a head count as to who will show up, but we will. Big day of memory, you know, teachers, those who have gone on. The grade school, this building, was built in 1892. The next building," Susan pointed to the building next to it, identical, on the west side, "the high school, grades nine through twelve, was built in 1894, along with the building on the other side of that, which you can't really see. Looks like these two. That was for basketball, also a makeshift auditorium when needed. A smaller building was finally constructed for hand tools, mowers. 'Course, they were all manual."

"I had no idea educating our institutionally oppressed groups went that far back," Aidan remarked.

"Actually, black kids and some indigenous kids had access to religious schools as far back as 1735. But public education came much later. Roughly after 1865, then in the twenties things picked up a little."

"We're still struggling." Aidan watched the four animals check out every inch of the building. "Look at how test scores have dropped."

"True." Susan cared passionately about education. "Some of that is due to COVID. Not being in classrooms hurt kids. I don't know if they will get those years back."

"Honey, that sounds defeatist," Ned told her.

"What I mean is, if you were not in class for fourth grade, maybe you absorbed the material from Zoom. But you will never have the experience of fourth grade with your peers. I think it holds kids back in ways. And we won't know for some time," Susan explained.

"Our public school system is nothing to brag about." Harry got up to see what exactly Mrs. Murphy and Pewter were inspecting. "What are you two doing?"

"*Mouseholes.*" Pewter puffed up. "*I'm protecting you.*"

"*They're living here. Better than being in a nest outside. The schoolhouse is pretty nice even when the potbellied stove is not warming it.*" Mrs. Murphy thought the mice smart.

"Actually, our schools in Northern Virginia are among the best in the nation," Aidan corrected her. "The high school with the most graduates in the country going to Harvard is in Alexandria."

"Well, it's time to spread that excellence across our state. Think of who lives and works in Northern Virginia. Lots of government workers. People with advanced educations. Some powerful corporations, too," Harry countered. "Those people demanded good schools. And some with funds actually don't want to send their kids to private schools."

"Doesn't seem to be working for Richmond, having government workers improve the schools." Ned, like his wife, worried about young people getting a good start.

That good start was education.

"Well, we'll keep pushing." Aidan checked his watch. "I have to get back. I promised Faith I'd meet her on Cary Street for dinner. She found a babysitter. A miracle in this weather."

"I always thought it was a miracle no matter what." Susan laughed. "But I had the advantage of my mother and grandparents."

"That is an advantage." He smiled. "My folks are too far from Richmond and Faith's are in Phoenix."

"Oh, doesn't Phoenix sound tempting right now." Susan grinned.

As Aidan drove off, Ned told his wife and Harry, whom he had known for decades, "He's wimping out."

"What?" Susan uttered.

"Would like us to drop the school's name. Doesn't matter that some graduates will be here and they want things accurate. He thinks a plaque isn't going to help us if a developer makes an offer, as the city owns the school buildings and the land."

Harry leaned on a desk. "Chicken."

"We've saved this piece of history," Susan said. "Everyone should know how people were treated. And that despite it, some went on to success. Where is the pride?"

"Oh." Ned, weary, sighed. "His concern is his career. That's become obvious to me. I also told him he had to apologize to Amanda. In some way I think he likes the attention. He is probably trying to think of a way to be the victim." He sighed again. "I'm disappointed. Maybe I'm being harsh."

The two women looked at each other. "Honey, what she did was outrageous, but he provoked it. You have to realize we deal with that kind of smug superiority, the name calling, a lot," Susan said.

He looked crestfallen. "I think I understand women better than most guys."

"Oh, you do. But you'll never know what it is to walk down a street with some creep following you, because he likes the way you look. Or catcalling. It's not a compliment. I think you are wonderful. We're only saying you can't experience this."

"She's right. There have been times in my life when I would have gladly socked someone. You reach a breaking point," Harry chimed in.

"Well, I'll never know what it is to walk a mile in high heels either." Ned's sense of humor was returning.

Pirate, nose near the mousehole, uttered, "*Why do people wear high heels?*"

Mrs. Murphy answered, "*Mother says it makes your legs look better.*"

"*Makes her taller,*" Tucker added.

"Why don't we all go to Burton's? I'm starved and this way, my bride, no cooking." He stood up and kissed her on the cheek.

"I've got to get the herd home, plus I made Irish stew for Fair. Why don't y'all come home with me? There's enough for everyone. You know I make good stew."

"Better yet. I'll go home with Ned and get some French bread and Irish butter to bring. Bought a loaf this morning. What do you say?" She put her hands on her husband's shoulders.

"Nothing better than eating with friends."

As they closed up the school building, Susan hopped in Ned's car, Harry and the gang got into Fair's massive dually. Pirate took up a lot of the backseat. Along with the cats, Tucker had to be lifted into the back.

On the way home, as Harry drove carefully since the roads were packed but snow-covered, Pewter dreamed big. "*They'll drop stuff from their plates. Happens when humans talk.*"

"*You can always hope,*" Tucker drily replied.

Pewter was right. The dear friends enjoyed one another so much, along with the bottle of wine Fair brought home, morsels were dropped.

Pewter was in her glory.

11

Walking through the pasture behind the refurbished school buildings, Harry marveled at how white the snow remained, shiny. Flashes of color, depending on sunlight, created rainbow magic. Snow crunched underfoot. She stopped, as did the two cats and two dogs. About fifty yards away, a male cardinal alighted on the snow, pecked at something, looked up at the creatures standing still, then lifted off, landing in a large old Douglas fir. This tree was somewhat out of place here. Perhaps some former student had planted a tree after Christmas as a gift from his class. The school buildings faced north, which helped with the light but didn't do a thing to soften the harsh winds.

Starting up once the cardinal flew to his nest, or whatever he had in the Douglas fir, Harry reached the storage building, also the basketball court. Fishing out her keys, fingers cold once out of the gloves, she unlocked the door, cut on the lights, checked everything inside. The bleachers had been pushed back. The basketball floor, unused, was still protected. Old canvas tarps covered it, held down by bricks. At the other end of the room one riding mower sat. The small toolshed outside held the hand tools.

"We drained all the oil and gas out," Harry informed her charges, who pretended to be interested. "And the tires are off, the mower up on blocks. You'd be surprised how much work that stuff can be."

"We watch you," Tucker replied.

"All this costs money. We have so little. Time for another fund-raiser, I guess. Still things left to do." She looked around, imagining the room jammed with young people cheering on their team. For most, regardless of the group to which they belong or are told they belong, being young means you are bursting with energy, so desirous to be an athlete or a cheerleader, or whatever, in the old days, but just to be with other kids. To them, adults are tedium underlined. Harry smiled, remembering her junior and high school days. How silly they all were, but how wonderful those days were. That's when wearing the wrong color to school was the worst thing you could imagine.

She sat on the corner of a bleacher for a moment. The room was cold. No need to fire up the stove, she wouldn't be staying that long.

"You know," her hand fell on Tucker while Pirate dropped his handsome head on her shoulder, "it's what's in front of you that you miss especially when young. Looking back I think I can pick out the kids who went home to abusive or drunk parents. Parents who didn't care about those kids or ones who pushed, pushed, pushed, ruining what should be carefree days. I wonder how much I missed."

Mrs. Murphy, back from checking out the riding lawn mower, rubbed herself against Harry's heavy jeans. *"Don't fret. Everyone has to grow up, Mom."*

"Ha," came the noise from behind the bleachers.

Tucker lowered her head to see Pewter batting around a small basket that had fallen under the bleachers. "You didn't."

"*Cats don't need to grow up. Dogs, of course, do. You are so dumb to begin with.*" Pewter whacked the basket toward the corner where Harry sat.

"Don't." Harry pushed her hand down slightly on Tucker's head as the corgi was growling. "All right, let's lock up and check the other buildings."

The high school building was fine. The one difference between it and the grade school was one wall contained bookshelves. This served as the school library.

Closing the door and turning off the lights, she walked to the grade-school building. A cloud passed over the low sun. A chill passed with it and a sprinkle of tiny flakes began to twirl down.

"This wasn't on my weather app," Harry complained, opening the door.

"*Why watch them? I can tell you what's going to happen better than your phone,*" Pewter bragged.

Tucker, seemingly in agreement, said, "*They don't pay attention to their bodies. You do. You have a lot of body to pay attention to.*"

Pewter, stung, chased the corgi into the grade school, around desks, until slowing down. Her wind wasn't as good as it should be. If she lost weight perhaps it might be, but this was not going to be solved by the cat.

Harry checked the furnace. The ashes from their earlier visit were low. No need to clean the potbellied stove yet. A car sound drew her to the large front windows.

Opening the door she called out, "Tazio."

The beautiful woman got out from her trusty Subaru Outback, closing the door. She hurried to Harry, where the two women hugged.

"I just got back. Thought I'd check."

"How is your mother?" Harry inquired, for Tazio's mother had suffered a mild stroke.

Tazio spent five days in St. Louis, helping out. Fortunately her brother lived there, so there was no need to hire anyone. That would have been difficult, as her mother would have pitched a fit.

"She's pretty good. Thank God my sister-in-law was with Mom when she started slurring her words and stumbling. Got her right to the ER. Mom had had a small stroke. Now she's had every test known to humankind, and things look positive."

"What a relief. Glad you stopped by. Want me to start a fire? Only takes a minute. Ned, Susan, and Aidan Harkness, another state delegate, were in here a few days ago. I've come over each day, fed the fire to battle the worst of the cold. Helps keep the electric bills down. Thank God we didn't have to rewire the place, old as the wiring is."

"Those potbellied stoves are wonderful. Granted, now the bad news is they add carbon to the atmosphere but I begin to wonder what doesn't. One of the good things about architecture is that a lot of companies . . . whether selling heat pumps, lighting devices, stoves, refrigerators, so many things . . . now have computer readouts. They send information back to a central location. If your stove has a burner not turned off, the stove will make a noise. No response, it sends a message to a central location, which will alert either the fire department or a designated number. It's all very new, but the hope is for smarter, more energy-efficient houses."

"Well, computer chips won't work here. Anyway, we will never run out of wood." Harry stopped. "We will have some classes, but the students can't have the experience without the stove. The whole point is to live for a week as their ancestors did, most of our ancestors."

"I know. You and I can present information around the clock. Think what we've learned by rehabilitating these buildings." She pulled off her cap, placing it on the desk. "It's the graduates that will make the point when that time comes. No one really cares what we think, no matter what we've done."

Harry then told Tazio about Ned wanting Aidan's support to get a brass plaque for the school. Takes a fair amount of work for anything to be cited as historic.

"If Ned gives me a list of who might be able to help us . . . not just delegates or state senators, but people in the various agencies . . . we can start calling on them." Tazio paused. "Sounds like this Aidan fellow goes whichever way the wind blows."

Harry pulled her scarf tighter. "Most of them do."

Tazio sighed. "Politics. Never changes, really. If we want to have a big opening in spring, always a good time, have all the living graduates here, I suppose we'll have to grease a few palms in some way. It used to exhaust me. Now I figure it's the cost of doing business."

"Taz, you're a lot smarter than I am." Harry noticed her cats fluffing up their fur, as it was getting cold inside. "I don't really get politics. Susan does though. Even in school she was a whiz. President of our class."

Harry rose, walked behind the teacher's dais, pulled out two logs from the reserve pile there, and put them in the stove. She lit a match under the sticks of fatback. Fired up instantly.

Changing the subject, Tazio pointed to the inkwells in the upper right-hand corner of the desk. "You know, I never noticed the inkwells were on the right side. Of course, most people are right-handed. Bet it was tough to be left-handed." She thought a moment. "Can't make up my mind if we should use the inkwells or not."

"Those children had to learn not to spill them. Do we assume children now, say in fourth grade, are too clumsy to keep things intact? And the inkwell is sunken. You can't knock them over."

"No, but a kid can knock over an entire desk."

They both laughed.

Tazio said, "We don't have to make that decision right now but we should make one soon over lighting."

"From 1892 or 1945?" Harry quizzically raised her eyebrows.

"Right. Maybe for the opening we should mimic 1892. We can't have gas lamps, but we could have electric lights that duplicate the look and the flicker."

"True. Might be expensive. Would plain old lightbulbs from the thirties be cheaper?"

"Maybe not, Harry. Incandescent lightbulbs are harder and harder to buy. If we duplicate the 1892 look, it might be easier to keep them up. We won't have to swap them out, since some modern bulbs are designed to look old."

Tazio looked at the large wall clock, the type found in railroad waiting rooms. "You've been winding it." She then checked her own watch quickly, pulling her sweater over her wrist when done.

"My Monday morning chore when I run into Crozet to pick up a few groceries. Works. Old stuff so often does. I'll feed the fire but I let it go out once a week to remove the ashes. I like physical chores."

"Let me get back. Brinkley was glad to see me." She mentioned her yellow Lab, a half-grown fellow whom she'd found while walking around the countryside.

"Hope your husband was happy, too." Harry grinned.

"Yes, but Brinkley brings me presents. He brought me his orange Wubba. Paul never brings me a Wubba."

They laughed again, then stepped outside, Harry locking the door. Her animals dashed to the old truck.

"Hurry up," Pewter complained as Harry walked to Tazio's Outback.

"I'll keep you posted on what we will have to do, who to see, etc., for the brass plaque." Harry noticed a sparkle on the snow as Tazio opened her door, sliding behind the wheel.

"Okay."

Kneeling to examine the sparkle, she saw it was a bracelet. Picking it up, Harry held it out to Tazio. "Did this just fall from your car?"

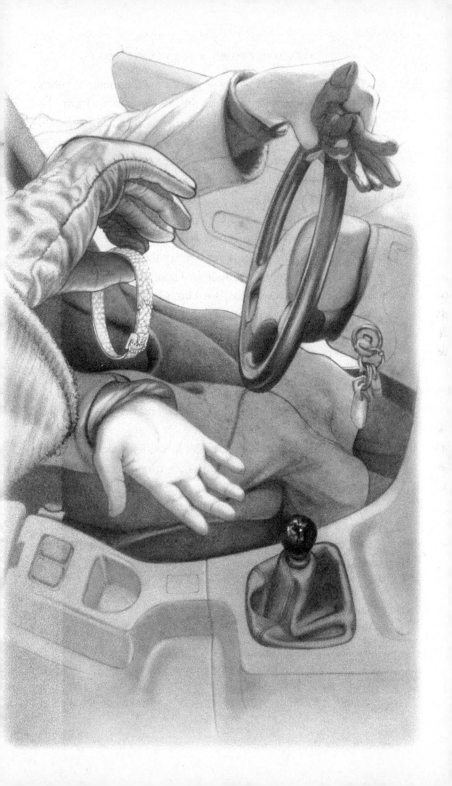

Tazio, pulling off her gloves as she started the motor to get the heat going, allowed Harry to drop the bracelet into her palm. "No. This is expensive. Heavy gold, and the clasp is diamonds. Unusual." She dropped it back into Harry's glove.

"Bet it fell out of Aidan's car. That's the only thing I can think of. You know the rest of us don't have anything like this. I'll give it to Ned. Good to see you."

As Tazio carefully backed out, Harry opened the door to her old Ford F-150, lifted up Tucker and Pewter. Pirate carefully allowed Mrs. Murphy to get in first. Harry then walked to the passenger side and opened the door for Pirate, who gingerly stepped onto the old bench seat. Easy for him, given his height. The cats grumbled, as everyone had to squeeze in. With chains on the tires, the vehicle proved reliable in the snow. Took a bit of time for the heater to fire up. The four-wheel drive had to be put into use by hand, but as Harry had done that the minute the snows started, the truck was fine. She loved this old truck. No computer chips. Easy, really. As the cab heated up, she took off her gloves, plucked the bracelet out of her coat pocket.

"Aidan must be making bucks. Bet his wife wonders where her bracelet is." She slowly pulled out of the front parking spot, such as it was. "You know, I think he married money. I dimly remember Ned mentioning something like that. This costs a bundle. I'd be afraid to wear it." She slipped it back into her deep pocket, slowly driving toward the farm, the tiny snowflakes hitting the windshield with a slight tap.

12

The next morning . . . temperature all of twenty-one degrees, Fahrenheit . . . Harry checked everyone's blankets, threw good hay into their stalls, and put two scoops of feed in some buckets; for others, their scoops had extra supplements due to their old age. Finished with that, listening to the munching, she walked into the tack room, closing the door behind her, glad for the small propane stove.

The dogs followed her in. The cats, who'd stayed in, slept on saddle pads.

Tossing her lumberjack cap onto a hook, hanging up her coat and scarf, she sat down to check the news on her computer. Brush fires had given way to avalanches in the west.

"I don't care where you are, something's going to get you," she announced to the dogs.

Tucker, while respectfully listening, laid down in front of the stove, Pirate beside her.

A sound far down the drive alerted the dogs. Both got up to stand by the tack-room door.

"*It's Susan,*" Tucker barked.

Hearing the tires on the snow, Harry knew it was Susan, as she had called her last night about the bracelet.

Within a few minutes, hearing the car door slam, the barn door open and close, Harry opened the tack-room door for her friend to step in.

"Bitter out there." Susan removed her gloves.

"It is. This is when you think spring will never come, even though you're closer than in December." Harry helped her friend off with her coat.

Pulling up a chair, Susan felt the welcome warmth. "That stove was one of the smartest things you did. Throws the heat and you don't have to clean out ashes."

"I don't really mind. I clean out the ashes at the school. But it's so much easier not to chop, stack wood. Fair spoiled me when he gave me this."

Susan said, "Okay, show me the bracelet."

Harry got up, went to her coat, fishing the bracelet out of the deep pocket, then dropped the weighty piece of jewelry into Susan's outstretched hands.

"Good Lord. This thing is a Harry Winston piece. Cost a fortune."

"Like how much?"

Susan felt the weight of the gold, the slight curve of each thick link, turning it around to the extravagant diamond clip. "It's a rough guess, but I'd say it cost close to $150,000, maybe $200,000? It's the diamond clip that puts it over the top. The gold is beautiful, but those diamonds pop the price. And look how clever. The diamonds are the clip, so not on top of the bracelet. It's both outrageous and understated."

"I knew you'd know. It's dazzling. There it was in the snow at the school. It had to have slipped out of Aidan's car."

Susan held the heavy piece in her hand, which she dropped into her lap. "Where would Aidan get the money to buy something like this?"

"Ned might know. Then again, Aidan's wife works. Faith makes money, plus I think she inherited some. You told me that once when I admired her dress at a fundraiser in Richmond."

"She has an eye, but this is . . ." Susan searched for words. "This is not something you'd expect the wife of a delegate to wear or have. I mean, those wives are well dressed and everyone has good pearls."

"Susan, it's the South, everyone has good pearls. I have okay pearls, but once a month I visit the ones I want at Keller and George."

"Harry," Susan, slightly exasperated, replied. "You have been looking at those damned pearls for over ten years now. Every year they get more expensive."

"I can't afford them. I need farm supplies. The cost for seed and fertilizer is rocketing up. I can't buy my pearls, and don't you dare tell Fair. You know how impulsive he can get about things."

"Every woman should have a man who wants to buy her jewelry." Susan said this with a flourish, having obviously been drilled by her mother and grandmother.

"Back to this piece. You give it to Ned, who can give it to Aidan. Maybe Ned can find out details."

"Mmm. It's entirely possible Aidan has no idea what this piece is worth, unless he bought it for Faith."

"He well could have. You know, for an anniversary, or to make up for a mistake. When men cheat, they usually accompany their apology with a major piece of jewelry."

Susan laughed. "Harry, you've been watching too much TV. First cheating men try to lie their way out of it, then they finally admit it and promise it will never happen again. I'm sure some buy a car, a ring, or whatever, but you have to have money for that."

"Well, obviously Aidan does. Or she does."

Susan rubbed her chin. "Faith doesn't strike me as the type of woman to buy her own stuff. Just doesn't."

"You know there are cats who wear jeweled collars." Pewter thought emeralds would look smashing against her dark gray fur.

"Dream on. You'd soon choke on it the way you eat," Tucker ungraciously commented.

"You've put on the pounds. Every winter your butt gets bigger and bigger," Pewter snapped.

"I'd never get a jeweled collar. My neck is really big." Pirate knew he was huge and getting even bigger.

"I'd rather have catnip." Mrs. Murphy quietly reached down to touch Pewter on the head.

The cats lounged on saddle pads on the saddles racks, one above the other.

"Gotcha." Pewter reached up to bat at Mrs. Murphy.

"Well, I'm afraid to have this in my possession. You take it."

Susan looked down at the fabulous object. "Okay. Ned can be forgetful. Maybe I should take it myself. But that drive to Richmond is such a bore."

"Better than old Route 250, the tension turnpike." Harry smiled. "That's what G-Pop used to call it."

"You told me the ham radio doesn't work. It's incredible you found it though." The mention of Harry's grandfather pushed Susan to change subjects.

"He loved it. I figured Mom wouldn't have thrown it out. I could try to get it fixed, but it will cost too much, plus I don't know how to use it. Then again, who would know how to repair it?"

"You promised Aunt Tally you'd talk to her on the radio."

"I know. I had no idea how difficult this would be."

"Buy an inexpensive one and take lessons."

"Susan, I don't have the time for this."

"You got yourself into it. Come on."

"Susan, I need to take a class, plus I don't really care about ham radio."

"It can't be that bad, and you'll make Aunt Tally happy."

"Do it with me."

A long, long silence followed this. "Let me investigate classes. To answer you, that's a qualified yes. Might be fun to talk to the kids on radio instead of cellphones. I don't know. Never thought about it."

Speaking of cellphones, hers rang.

"Would you carry a phone around?" Pirate asked Tucker.

"No."

"We don't need them," Pewter called down. *"But we could call for food. Harry jumps when her phone rings. Might be worthwhile."*

"What?" Susan's voice rose. She listened then clicked off. "Okay."

"What's going on?" Harry wondered.

"That was Ned. One of the pages has been found dead."

"A page? Good Lord."

"Reid Ryder. Ned said he was in an accident driving in the snow. He borrowed Ellis Barfield's car. That's all anyone knows right now."

13

Shocking and sorrowful as the page's death was, the budget crisis loomed before the Assembly. On an odd year, the Virginia Assembly is in session for thirty days. That can be extended to forty-five. On an even year, the Assembly sits for sixty days. As the session convenes the second Wednesday in January, there is pressure to get issues resolved. For one thing, not getting them resolved allows the administration to make more decisions, which creates havoc in the opposing party, the one that does not hold the governorship. Lawsuits are threatened. Cries of overreach fill the airwaves, the electronic media, and the newspapers. A clever governor sidesteps it, especially if large groups of voters receive some benefit from gubernatorial action.

The state budget, in place until June 30, 2024, had to be reaffirmed for 2023. Snowplows were the least of the contentions.

Harry, not as close to all of this as Susan, was far more concerned with her promise to Aunt Tally, outrageous fertilizer prices, and yet another leak that had been found at St. Luke's Lutheran Church, where she was in charge of building and grounds.

The church, graceful, simple in design, was built immediately after the Revolutionary War. The lovely, arcaded walkways off the main church building led to two smaller buildings, one at the end of each walkway. The Very Reverend Herbert Jones stood in the top floor of the men's wing as it was built for the men's meetings. Each arcade, forty yards long, ended in a right angle, then another thirty yards. The two smaller buildings at the end of the thirty-yard arcade were mirror images of each other. Simple two-story buildings with glass windows.

"There's not much that can be done with snow and ice on the roof." Harry pointed to the darkening trail from the corner of the room heading toward the floor.

"I guess not."

"We'll have to repair this corner inside. What I could do is take out part of the wall and try to close the leak from underneath if I can. It might be enough to stop leakage, but what will end the leak is replacing slate shingles. If you're willing, I can open this up inside."

He stared upwards then placed his hand on the darkening stain, which felt a bit damp. "Well."

"I know you never want me to do any work myself." She smiled at him. "You can't get used to a woman being in charge of build-ing and grounds."

"Harry, you take too many chances and you get on this roof. Cutting part of the wall doesn't seem to be dangerous. Some of your other escapades are." He smiled back.

She chose not to argue about the word *escapades*. "Does that mean I can open this up?"

He patted her cheek, as he adored her and she him. "All right. And I assume the dogs and cats will be with you?" He looked down at the animals.

This included his three cats; they were Lutheran cats, which was important.

"*We can do anything.*" Tucker was confident.

Lucy Fur, one of Reverend Jones's cats, sassed, "*Tucker, what you do is find our food and eat it.*"

"*Not if Pewter finds it first,*" Tucker slyly replied.

"*If I weren't at St. Luke's I would smash your nose. I'll get you, Tucker,*" Pewter hissed.

Cazenovia, another of the reverend's cats, raised her luxurious eyebrows. "*That's not Christian.*"

"*You have to be a Christian cat. I don't.*" Pewter defended herself.

"*No, but if you don't stop hissing, Mom will think twice about bringing us here to work.*" Mrs. Murphy loved prowling around the church.

After inspecting the site, the group returned to the reverend's office, a lovely large room overlooking the back quads of St. Luke's, viewing down to the old cemetery surrounded by a stone wall.

The secretary brought them tea.

"Thanks, BoomBoom." Harry took the cup from her high school classmate's hand.

"I'm here until we can find reliable help," BoomBoom explained. "You'd be surprised how hard it is to find someone who will work five days a week."

"Boom, I wish I could say I am surprised. Look at all the small places that have closed, little food shops, even some gas stations. I think it will be years before we know how much damage COVID cost us."

The tall high school prom queen nodded. "I think it takes ten years to get used to your age, then the next thing you know you're in another decade. Who knows how long it will take to figure out what we've lost. No one wants to think in years." Boom laughed. "Rev," she called him by his nickname, "anything else?"

"No thanks."

She returned to her area in front of his big office.

"Do we have enough to repair the roof if it comes to that?" Harry asked as they settled down.

"I have the rainy day budget. We should be okay for a small repair, but replacing a large section of the roof, no."

"One of the great things about St. Luke's is it was built to last centuries and it has." Harry admired those early people who designed and built the church. "We'll be okay. How is everything?"

"Apart from the snow being unrelenting, good."

The cats sat on the window seats at the large windows, looking at birds eating from the big feeders out back.

"Another blue jay. There should be a rule against feeding blue jays." Pewter sniffed.

"That will never happen." Elocution watched the pretty but very aggressive bird.

As the two friends chatted, Harry mentioned her promise to Aunt Tally and how she had no idea how much she would need to study.

"Do it. I go out to give her communion. She's doing well, considering, but she is frail and lonely. Mim visits her, of course, but one needs friends who are not family. At least I think so. When I go, she can't stop talking after communion. And give her credit, she can be quite fascinating."

"What do I know about radio frequencies?"

He considered her question. "When I was in Vietnam we always had a radio operator. While that wasn't my job, I was a backup. Snipers wanted to get the communications officers first. Without that soldier, it was hard to coordinate, and it was hard to rescue men left behind. The helicopter pilots needed information. And if a man in the field used a handheld talkie, then the enemy knew right where we were, because they had those frequencies."

"Did it take you a long time to learn?"

He finished his tea. "When you are that young . . . I was twenty-one . . . everything you don't want to do takes a long time. But learning about the difference between AM frequencies plus FM frequencies, I actually began to like it. And our company's sparks came home alive. I didn't need to fill in."

"Does the military use that stuff anymore?"

"Not as many servicemen are taught. We have better technology, but if all else fails, you can still use Morse code or even semaphore. I think the Navy uses lamplight between ships. That's Morse code. It is universal and so are regular ham radios. Millions of people sit down at night to talk to other people. The more expensive your radio, the longer the range. And think about it, if you call a drug dealer on your cellphone, law enforcement may be able to listen in, to get you. If you use a ham radio, eventually they might figure it out, but no one looks there now. Again, drugs are billions of dollars, pure profit. No taxes."

"It's a difficult thought. Taxation, I mean. It drives people to all manner of crime and excess." Harry felt nothing happens in a vacuum.

"So it does, but even if one were a drug dealer you could create a legitimate business, declare those profits, hide the others. If you aren't in the street shooting your competition, you might get away with it."

"Gross."

He nodded. "We live in interesting times . . . but then, every human being thought that. Take our General Assembly and the uproar about the budget. It is the oldest lawmaking continuous body in the Western Hemisphere. And in all those centuries, the budget is always a fight."

"Susan tells me that."

He smiled. "She grew up in politics. So here we are, centuries away from the summer of 1619, when we started the Assembly. The good thing is that every bad action happened here first. That's how I look at it. But did we learn anything?" He shook his head. "No. Same mistakes. Same hypocrisy. Now, are some of our elected officials decent and good? Of course. But so were some in

1619, in 1790, in 1858. The twin evils of politics are greed and power."

"I guess that will never end."

"What disrupts my sleep sometimes is that even the Lutheran Church suffers from politics. And the Catholic Church has been obsessed with power since Rome's glory days."

"Yes, but over two thousand years of consistent worship is awe-inspiring." Harry was impressed.

The reverend leaned forward. "That's one of the things I have always liked about you, Harry, even when you were a child you could see a bigger picture than most. And you are absolutely right. This is not a time for the differing sects of Christianity to stand apart from one another. We are all losing people."

"You're not."

"Well, my services are full. But there aren't as many young people as even ten years ago." He slapped his knee. "Forgive me. I don't mean to complain, but I am worried. Are churches corrupt? Yes, some can be, but it is still a strong guide for life and I still believe if you believe in Christ, He will bring you home, so to speak."

"People, so many now, would look at you as an unintelligent person believing what makes you feel good. We live in secular times. I keep my mouth shut. Not with you or my friends, but I can't see arguing as a way to help people find faith. You aren't going to think your way into it." Harry had thought about this, as she often thought about big questions while doing her farm chores.

He folded his hands over his chest, looking at this person he had known from the time she was baptized. "You're right, Harry, it's not about the mind." He leaned forward again, unfolding his hands. "I feel that we're failing. We are all failing one another."

"You have never failed us, Rev. Never. When my parents were killed in that car crash my senior year at Smith, you were there. You listened. You helped me find . . . well, you helped me finish college while you found people to take care of the farm. I finished my senior year. I can never repay that kindness. And you did some of that work yourself."

"We all love you, Harry. Helping you was a joy. You should have been able to finish your last year. You graduated summa cum laude. Your parents would have been so proud."

BoomBoom called from her office, as the door was open a crack. "More tea?"

"No, we're revisiting old times and current times."

"I can still sing an old song if it helps. Or a hymn."

Harry laughed. "There was a reason you didn't win the talent contest in high school."

"God will get you for that."

The Reverend Jones couldn't help it. "The girls," as he thought of them, made him laugh.

Mrs. Murphy asked the three church cats, *"Did you ever hear Boom-Boom sing?"*

"Yes. She's in the choir, you know." Cazenovia reminded them. *"She mouths the words, but doesn't sing. The choir director put her there to fill out the numbers, plus she's so good looking, people like seeing her up there. Especially men."*

Later, in the kitchen, Harry picked up the ringing phone.

"Ellis Barfield was questioned today concerning why Reid was driving his car. Ellis said he lent the page his RAV4 to drop off video film. The afternoons, especially during committee meetings, can be slow, so he gave him the key," Susan said.

"Bet he feels terrible." Harry imagined the guilt.

"What's so sad is it was only a few blocks away. The skid marks indicated someone bumped into him. Bad luck."

"You never know."

"Aidan picked this time to push for the bill about snow removal. Ned is furious. The roads are bad. To use this to promote their bill is grossly insensitive."

"It is."

"The body is at the medical examiner's." Susan paused. "Matter of course. Young people can have heart attacks. Some kind of service can be planned once the autopsy is complete."

"Maybe Ned can impress upon Aidan he shouldn't say anything, push the bill, until after the service."

14

"It's sleek. The dark fabric, the windowpane overlay is white, gives you options." Lucas, sitting on a low bench, watched Amanda try on clothing at Horse Country. "You can wear a white open-collared shirt, a cashmere turtleneck, options."

The front door opened, Susan and Harry hurried inside as a biting wind picked up.

Susan announced, "We're here."

Horse Country's Suzann, behind the counter, grinned. "Who would guess?"

"It's the weekend. Our only time to get away right now. The weather had us imprisoned." Susan immediately hovered over the glass case filled with glittery estate jewelry. "Oh, look at the diamond horseshoe pin. The perfect size."

Harry leaned on Susan to peer down. "Elegant. Your mother would wear something like that." Then she paused. "Or you. Too fancy for me."

"Harry, you could carry it off."

"You are too kind."

A patter of paws alerted them. The low swinging door to the cash register area opened, a just groomed Scottie stepped out. He evidenced an air of self-composure but then he had just been in a fashion show in D.C.

"Osmun." Harry knelt down to greet him. "You look like a star."

Marion Maggiolo, the owner of the store, beamed. "Did you see him in the fashion show? There's a video on the store website. Just went out yesterday."

"He had to be the star." Susan loved the Scottie, as did everyone.

"Here." Marion walked over, punched on her phone, and the video came up. "He had trouble getting up the steps so the model, all of twenty-one, bent over, scooped him up, putting him on the stage, and he walked across as her escort. The crowd cheered."

"That ham." Harry giggled, thinking of her dogs, although the true ham would be Pewter.

"He does have an air about him." A hint of motherly pride escaped Marion, not a woman to brag.

"That jacket, the one on the model, where did you find it?" Susan, a clotheshorse, swooned.

"England. You know how many suppliers I lost over the anti-hunting mess then COVID? Some are coming back, new people taking over. Anyway, I found this not in London, where you would think, but in a small store near the Quorn Hunt. You like it?"

"Fabulous." Susan was enthusiastic.

At that exact moment, Amanda and Lucas walked from the back fitting room to the front of the store, Amanda looking like a knockout in that very coat.

Susan, quiet for a moment but always the Virginia lady, held out both arms. "Amanda, you look like a movie star."

Neither woman gave off a hint of awkwardness. That was for the statehouse. It was time for girls to be girls, and both Susan and Amanda excelled at that.

Harry, hands behind her back, smiled, for Amanda did look incredible.

Marion knew the problem was between Aidan Harkness and Amanda, not Ned and Amanda. Although the bill was co-sponsored, Ned was in the other camp, obviously.

"Here. Look at this." Marion pulled up the fashion show.

Amanda and Lucas, practically joined at the hip, stared at the brief flash from the fashion show.

"The man, a true Scot, was a fun model. We did this for Friends of Scotland. The show's name was Dressed to Kilt, so clever. We did have a good audience. I think every Scot in D.C. came."

"I had no idea there is such an organization." Amanda bent closer to the brief video.

Lucas quickly pulled out a small Smythson notebook . . . his initials, LSD, embossed in gold . . . to write down the name.

Marion, missing nothing, touched his elbow. "I'll give you the information. Anything you want to know about the Scots, Scotland history, anything, they know it. Easy to work with. Delightful, really."

Amanda observed Osmun. "Now, if I had this fellow, everyone would pay attention to me."

Lucas laughed. "They do anyway."

"He has to say that. He's my aide-de-camp," she joked, using the military expression.

He nodded his head.

"This jacket calls to me." Amanda smiled as Lucas removed it from her, then quite carefully placed it on the glass-topped case.

"You'll dazzle everyone," Susan complimented her.

"You flatter me," Amanda responded. "I had to learn to dress. When you're on the air, people are hypercritical. You hear about your hair, your clothing, your voice. Thank God for my aunt, who once worked in Manhattan."

"I forgot my manners. Amanda and Lucas, have you met my childhood and still current best friend, Mary Minor 'Harry' Haristeen?" Susan introduced Harry.

"I have not, but I saw her sitting with you in the gallery on that infamous day." Amanda paused, held out her hand to Harry, then added, "This is Lucas. He was my sorority brother at William and Mary."

No one said a word. Susan knew but the others did not. Everyone behaved as though a sorority brother was common. No one asked questions.

"Delta Delta Delta, as I recall." Susan noted how warmly Amanda grasped Harry's hand, then Lucas followed suit.

"That's right. I was a few years ahead of you." Amanda knew a bit about Susan.

"We were all lucky to go to William and Mary." Susan loved her alma mater. "My daughter went to William and Mary. My son went to Dartmouth." A pause. "A wonderful school but I would have so liked him closer to home."

Amanda laughed. "That has advantages and disadvantages."

"Would you like to try on anything else?" Roni, one of the "girls" at Horse Country, emerged from the back. She'd been putting clothes in the changing room for Amanda.

"I want to try on everything. We got lost in conversation." Amanda started to walk to the back, then turned toward the group and Osmun. "Susan, out of the chamber, I say to hell with politics."

"I agree." Susan shoved her hand into her pocket. She fumbled around, bringing out the bracelet she had slipped there to give to Ned so he could return it to Aidan.

The diamond clasp caught the light, stopping both Amanda and Lucas in their tracks.

"I knew I forgot something." Susan held the piece of jewelry in her palm.

Marion walked over, plucked it out as Susan opened her palm farther. "How incredible."

Amanda, taking a moment to steady herself, also came back. "Susan, where on earth did you get this?"

"Quite by accident. Aidan Harkness, forgive me for bringing up his name, had driven out to us . . . well, to . . . Ned to discuss the snow bill and a large developer sniffing around one of our projects. Ned met him at the old schoolhouse we are restoring. It was found where Aidan had parked his car.

"I forgot to give it to Ned before he left again for Richmond. It probably belongs to Aidan's wife, unless Aidan is leading a secret life."

Picking up the bracelet, Amanda slipped it on her wrist, closing the clasp. "It's mine. See? It's a perfect fit. I've been missing it for, well, since the uproar in the House. I took it off back at the office. I thought I misplaced it."

It was a perfect fit.

Harry spoke up. "Is this something any one of us could buy?"

"I had it made by Harry Winston. I can give you all the year this was done and the person with whom I worked. He'll give you the price then and the price now."

"Amanda, no one is suggesting you are trying to steal this, well, work of art, it's just so odd. Such a coincidence."

"The odd part is, what was my bracelet doing in Aidan Harkness's car? It didn't get to your school by itself. I could throttle him, just throttle him. I never expected him to be a thief." Amanda's face reddened.

Lucas, the best person to defuse an explosion, calmly addressed his boss. "It's possible he found it. I, like you, don't think Aidan is a thief. Perhaps he found it in the hall or he came into your office and found it on the floor."

She said with an edge, "Or he came into my office where I stupidly left it and nicked it. Right now I have trouble finding much good about Aidan Harkness."

"He overstepped civility," Lucas again calmly interjected. "But don't think the worst. My suggestion is, Monday, back at work, call and ask him."

Amanda thought a long time. "All right. Fair enough. I mean, what is he doing with my bracelet unless he's supporting drag in new ways?" She laughed.

Harry laughed, too. "Oh, Representative Fields, every time I slip into an evening gown, I feel like I'm in drag."

They all laughed.

"Come on, Lucas, I want to try on those things. I have no intention of saving money."

As they retreated back to the fitting room, Roni in tow, everyone looked at one another, big smiles, not a word.

Susan leaned over the case. "Tell you what, don't sell this horseshoe pin without calling me first. Give me right of first refusal."

Marion nodded. "All right."

"Susan." Harry's tone said it all.

"Don't start, Harry. You have been visiting your eight millimeter pearls at Keller and George for years now. All I'm doing is asking for time."

"Well, you could put a down payment on a new station wagon for the price of this pin." Realizing she was working against a sale for Marion, Harry quickly apologized. "Sorry, Marion. You know I lean toward the frugal."

"Oh, that's a nice word for it," Susan sputtered.

"I'm not worried, Harry. That pin will sell when the right person comes in. It truly is unique, understated and beautiful."

"Just like me." Susan's good nature was restoring itself.

"Oh, you took the words right out of my mouth." Harry beamed then kissed Susan on the cheek.

Marion laughed. "Come on, Osmun."

The two best friends, one human, one a dog, walked back into Marion's office, where Osmun had a few select toys in his banana bed.

"Okay, you and I were going to look at clothes," Susan reminded Harry, which they did.

Driving back the three hours to home, thanks to traffic, the two women discussed the day.

"I know it killed you buying that Barbour jacket. You'll look good in it. Plus, you'll stay dry."

"So expensive," Harry moaned.

"It is, but it looks a lot better than your old raincoat."

As they drove past the car dealerships on Route 29 above Culpepper, Harry mentioned, "Odd about the bracelet."

"Is. What was it doing in Aidan's car?"

"I'm sure she'll find out." Harry laughed.

"I'd like for things to calm down," Susan wistfully dreamed.

"That'll never happen," Harry predicted. "You solve one problem, another pops up."

"Well, some of ours seem to be popping up all at once. And Aidan still has not apologized," Susan grumbled. "But he will."

"Why are you so confident? Because if he doesn't, Amanda will attack him as a drag queen, which will be worse to some of her crowd than stealing?"

At this Susan laughed, because it was true.

15

 "This is more than I expected," Harry dismally remarked.

Reverend Jones patted her hand. "It's easier than you think.
Start with this book. Things you need to memorize: the wave-
length of radio signals. Not difficult, but you need to know it.
Read. Then you and I can work with a radio together."

"You have one?" Harry noticed the sunlight passing over the
snow, turning rainbow colors on the back terraces.

"No, but Miranda Hogendobber owns a small one."

"My Miranda?" Harry had worked with the older woman in
the post office once she graduated from Smith.

"Yes. She'll surprise you. When you get familiar with the information, I can go over to Aunt Tally. Everyone can practice."

"Miranda never mentioned a ham radio to me. We talked about
her choir, her church, and her garden, for years. And she talked
about Mom and Dad, as she knew them so well."

"Mostly she uses her radio for choir practice. A few of the ladies in her choir are becoming old, it's harder for them to travel so Miranda gets them on the radio. They have practice, then the women are driven to Sunday services. Of course, it's hard to get that done in the middle of the week. But with everyone on their own radio, they can practice."

"So a few of them can talk at the same time?"

Reverend Jones nodded. "It's like a roundtable. You have to key in." He stopped himself. "I'm getting the cart before the horse."

"Can Miranda reach Aunt Tally?"

"Of course. You alert Aunt Tally. The great thing about the ham radio is that if communications are down or if it is a crisis, either weather or multiple car collisions or even political, you can help people. It's important and I don't think any young people are learning."

"Everyone thinks computers can do everything." Cazenovia walked into the room, so Harry held out her hand for the cat, who came over to the sofa.

"Where are the other cats?" Harry asked.

"Bible study." Reverend Jones laughed.

Harry laughed with him. "Thanks for your time. I'd better get back to the farm. It's Tuesday, delivery day for feed. The roads are good enough now. Not great, but good. Susan and I drove up to Horse Country on Saturday. Slowly. The roads were cleared, but I'm on the alert for black ice. So was Susan. Oh, and who should be there but Amanda Fields?"

"The newscaster turned delegate?"

"Yes. She's, mmm, easy enough to talk to. She's ambitious. Not that she's selling herself, but you can feel her drive."

"Ah. I've reached the point, Harry, where I can't watch the news anymore. I know who she is, know she's very conservative. That's about it." He turned as Lucy Fur and Elocution also came in.

"Come on over here. Did you read your Matthew?"

"No. We'd like to read 'Puss in Boots,'" Cazenovia said.

"I think that means treats." Reverend Jones got up, as did Harry.

"Thanks again." She hugged him and left as he filled a bowl with tiny liver bits, dried. Three happy cats dove for it.

On the way back from St. Luke's, Harry turned into Susan's driveway. Her friend's house was west of St. Luke's.

She'd texted before driving out of the church parking lot, so as she drove up the drive, Susan had the door open.

Closing the car door, Harry briskly walked to Susan.

"Hurry up. It's cold," Susan ordered her, quickly shutting the front door when Harry stepped in, greeted by Owen, Tucker's brother. "What's up?"

"Had to tell you face-to-face." Harry recounted Miranda using ham radio to sing with older, somewhat infirm members of the Church of the Holy Light choir.

"I had no idea Miranda was technical. Is there a better word?"

"I don't know, but her choir means the world to her. You have to give it to that church, the choir never falters, plus they have young people."

"They do."

Harry dropped into a chair in the modern kitchen. "Any word from Ned?"

"About what?"

"Aidan's apology."

"Aidan was railroaded into it. Amanda accepted. There's a budget committee meeting and delegates are wondering how that will go, since both antagonists sit on it, but the real news is, Reid Ryder had fentanyl and cocaine in his system. His parents declare their son never took drugs. They believe someone gave them to him. The other oddity was a Ball jar in the car had traces of liquor, illegal."

"How can anyone prove something like that?"

Susan turned on the hot water on the stove then sat down. "I don't know. But whether they can or they can't, it looks terrible. If the House isn't willing to cooperate, everyone looks irresponsible. But the parents swear their son never touched drugs. Ellis said he never saw Reid take drugs. The police checked the house where Reid dropped off the videos. Everything was okay there. The fellow at the house said he made copies for Ellis, who didn't have the time to do a good job. Oh, and he said Ellis told Reid he'd give him a few bucks to run errands. The kid was fascinated with video, so Ellis would let him in the room when he shot footage."

Harry frowned. "One hopes it's true that Reid didn't do drugs, but so many people are fooled by their kids. All this stuff is easy to get."

"Getting isn't taking."

"That's the truth," Harry agreed with her.

"There's more." Susan rose, as the water was boiling and the pot whistling. She pulled down two cups, poured the water in a ceramic teapot with a ball of expensive tea inside. Once that was on the table, a trivet under it, she sat down.

"Okay. Ned and Aidan were walking down the hall to their offices. Passing Amanda's, and she came out as they passed. Told them to stop. Lucas, apparently white as a sheet, trailed behind her. She walked right up to Aidan, who had apologized that morning, shoved her wrist under his nose, on which was her Harry Winston bracelet. She'd waited to put it on, obviously. She accused him of stealing it and said she had to use all her discipline not to nail him in the chamber when he was apologizing. But this was private. What was he doing with her bracelet? Why was it found in the snow at the school here?

"Aidan stood his ground and declared he found it right outside her door, picked it up, intending to give it to her the next day, then thought he'd lost it. It must have fallen out of his pocket when he came to Crozet. No sound, thanks to the snow. But he said, not realizing it had been found, he'd been going to replace it."

"That bracelet cost a fortune!"

"Exactly what Amanda said," Susan replied. "My husband

should have told Aidan you found it, and that I had returned it to Amanda.

"More unpleasant words. Lucas tried to calm her down, but couldn't. Aidan again said he'd been going to replace it, even if he had to sell his car."

"Pretty dramatic. Would he have sold his car?"

"I don't know," Susan honestly answered. "Then Amanda turned on Ned. He said I'd had the bracelet. I'd put it in my pocket and forgot about it. He was very apologetic. But she accused both of them of hoping to sell it. Ned got furious, but shut up and walked away, leaving Amanda and Aidan to bicker even more, and louder. Finally, Lucas managed to get her away."

"Aidan, bad judgment notwithstanding, isn't the type to steal bracelets," Harry posited.

"Well, I certainly hope not." Susan exhaled, pouring the tea. "It's crazy. Everything is happening at once. The wild weather. The fight in the House. My husband being dragged in. That poor kid with fentanyl in his system."

Harry turned all this over in her head. "What if there are drugs in the Assembly?"

Susan frowned. "Don't think of it."

16

Budget committee meetings redefined boredom. The various members droned on, reading from pages filled with numbers. Whether the numbers were true or not was another issue, but no one missed the opportunity to project future costs, which would be in line with their party's programs.

Amanda kept notes as others spoke, underlining with a regular one-foot ruler what she wanted to research or argue.

"And then you keep pushing the idea of a delayed budget." Aidan's voice filled the small room. "We all know that's a political trick to get Governor Youngkin off the hook. You refuse to even consider our designs for education and mental health. Given the wild number of shootings here and everywhere, mental health treatment for unstable kids is critical. We need some identifying system in our schools, or we need more teachers, counselors, therapists, and security guards. We have to raise taxes."

As he wrapped up his remarks, nothing new or unusual to the committee members, Amanda took the bait. "Look at Texas, Florida. You cut the corporate tax rate and business flocks to your state. If you want more services, boost the economy."

While she was speaking, Aidan rapped the table with his fingers. Rat-a-tat-tat-tat. It was noticeable.

"Productivity is the answer, not more taxes. Do you want to be like Illinois, New Jersey, or Connecticut? You drive corporations right out of your state along with wealthy residents. Boom. There go your taxes, with more people rushing for help from the government, which has made insupportable promises. Given the tsunami of rich leaving, the others need help. Less money. Less services. We can't do that."

The delegate from the Wytheville area spoke. "If we delay the budget, we'll not get the revenue information for the final quarter of the fiscal year."

Amanda smiled. "Exactly. So how can we make trade-offs between spending and tax cuts?" Rat-a-tat-tat getting louder. "We need information."

Rat-a-tat-tat.

Aidan then spoke up. "Whether you have all the numbers or not, you'll push your one billion dollar tax-cut plan. This is all theater."

She remained calm. "Well, if that's the case, Representative Harkness, my party and I will give you one. If taxes are cut, we can raise the revenue of this state by five percent."

"Impossible," Aidan bellowed.

She waited. "Are you done?"

"No. You want a one percent reduction in corporate taxes and a quarter percent reduction in individual taxes. The individual rate alone will cost us $333 million in the next year and $1.5 trillion in two years."

A silence fell over the room.

"Your figures are way off and designed to frighten people, especially the most vulnerable, to whom you and your party present themselves as saviors."

He kept tapping the table again, irritation rising.

"I'll make it easy for everyone on this committee. Instead of listening to me, I will bring in a tax specialist from the University of Virginia's Economics department, and another one from Princeton. They'll give you some hard facts. They may agree on the exact numbers, they may not, but what they provide for us will be free of the desire for career security or advancement. They aren't coming up for reelection on November 7, 2023. We are."

Rat-a-tat-tat.

Her self-control vanished. Amanda picked up her ruler, stood up, walked around the table, and smashed it on Aidan's hand.

"Ow."

"You have tried to deter attention from me. Next time, I'll break your knuckles."

He started to rise, but the chair quickly, firmly ordered, "Delegate Fields to your seat. Delegate Harkness, hold your hands if you must, because it is irritating."

As the meeting devolved into further disarray, Harry was bundled up, crouched down by the large tractor, the snowplowing tractor, blade on the front. The animals were with her, the cats on the tractor seat, little puffs of cold air coming out of their mouths.

Harry checked the large tires, all okay.

Then she swung up onto the seat, which meant the cats had to move.

"*Let me sit on your lap. It's cold in the snow.*" Pewter moved just enough so Harry could get in the seat.

Mrs. Murphy jumped down.

Harry turned the key, listened to the music of the machine fir-ing up. "There you go."

"*Go where?*" Pirate wondered.

"*She means all is well. The tractor started,*" Tucker translated.

Letting the tractor run for a few minutes, Harry thought about what she needed to carry to St. Luke's tomorrow. She wanted to open up the wall before another storm rolled in.

Satisfied the tractor was fine, she climbed down carefully, for the bottoms of her boots were slippery on the packed snow. Once safely on the ground, she grabbed the old thick horse blanket she had put to the side. Removing her right glove, she felt the engine.

Pewter carefully got down, then dashed for the barn. It was too cold. Warmth overcame nosiness. Mrs. Murphy followed, shaking out her paws from time to time.

"Gotta wait a minute." Harry walked across from the equip-ment shed to the smaller toolshed. She used to hang her tools in the big equipment shed, but over time thought they should be in an enclosed structure with a bit of heat if she wanted to work there. She and Fair built a twelve-by-twelve building with a fourteen-foot ceiling. Harry liked high ceilings. If she needed to do close work, she could. She walked back out with a small wrench. Picked up the blanket, drawing it over the engine hood. As it was high, this took some effort.

"Got it."

Then she checked the older, smaller 25 HP tractor that had been her father's. It, too, had a blanket on it. She pulled that off to fire up the old machine. A wonderful rumble greeted her ears.

"Love it. Just love it." She sat there while the tractor shook a bit. It was fifty years old, lacked refinement but not dependability. Her big tractor, the 80 HP, had a cab but was built before tractors were filled with computer parts. Thanks to the cab, she could stay out of the wind and rain. She had to open the sides in heat, but the cab was still a big help. Sitting there she dreamed of spring, pull-ing a drill seeder behind her. Overseeding made her happy. For another woman, buying spring outfits in those alluring pastels would make them happy. Cutting the motor, Harry repeated what she had done with the larger machine. Once satisfied with the hood's temperature, she pulled another old horse blanket over it, which was easier, as the tractor was smaller.

"Come on."

"We are," the dogs replied.

The crust on the snow kept the dogs from sinking in, although Pirate did occasionally break through, given his size and weight.

Once inside the tack room, Harry turned up the stove. The room warmed quickly, being a small space, plus the electric heat had been on enough to keep some warmth. The pipes in the washroom had heat tape wrapped around them, and the small washing room also had electric heat along the floorboards.

Removing her heavy coat, keeping on the sweaters for now, Harry sat down at her computer.

"Someone could sit on my lap."

Mrs. Murphy jumped up. *"I'll keep you warm."*

"I can do a better job." Pewter had to get on the desk using a small set of wooden stairs for the purpose of older animals . . . or, as in this case, fatter. She walked behind the computer, putting her head over it, looking at the screen.

"Nothing," Pewter announced.

She was wrong, because Harry was mesmerized by a news report, the kind that flashes on your screen. She read intently. Read it again, then picked up her phone.

"Where are you?"

Susan answered, "In the bedroom. Changing sheets."

"Turn on your computer to Channel 6."

Susan, having a small laptop in the bedroom, not a good idea, did that. "Oh dear. If they've interrupted the program for this, you know it's only going to get worse."

"You're right. Give the police credit. They got right on it."

"What's going to set everyone off is, after going through Reid's clothing, everything, they found a small bottle in his pants' cuff with traces of cocaine residue inside. They found no fingerprints on the bottle. They found his fingerprints on a ballpoint pen in his inside pocket, but nothing on the . . . I guess you call it a coke bottle." A long, long silence followed this. "Harry, what if this has something to do with politics?"

"That's a horrible thought."

"With no fingerprints on the bottle, you have to wonder. Harry, I liked that kid. I didn't know him well, but I liked him the times I spoke to him. He was bright, eager, loved being in the House, loved hearing the debates and ideas. A bright future for a bright boy. Gone."

"Well, a car could have sideswiped him, given the state of the roads, but maybe he was high? Not in complete control of the car?"

A burst of anger had Susan's voice raise as she said, "The world is crazy, Harry. Damn crazy. A good kid on drugs. People shooting one another like it's the Wild West. Bills floated in statehouses that make me wonder how long it will be before books are banned, our libraries come under siege? People arrested for teaching the wrong things or speaking out right or left or whatever. People pull their punches now. That's frightening. You don't know what someone really thinks and feels except for those trying to profit from advanced irrationality. Oh, this is just awful. I can see that boy's face."

"Susan, why don't I come over?"

"I'll pull myself together. You're good to . . . well, you know me."

"You have a soft heart. A big heart. But you know, I think the world has always been crazy. Some times are worse than others, and reason so rarely prevails." She stopped herself. "That doesn't mean we can't try."

———

As the two old friends commiserated, the news hit the delegates and state senators hard, and they knew some people would assume drugs were in the Assembly.

No one would dream of saying, "What if that boy's drug dealer was in the House?" Certainly not. Not one of them. What if someone sold him drugs? It was so far out there that few would countenance it. Ned wasn't thinking in exactly those terms, but a chill ran through him. Deep down he knew something was terribly wrong. Not just another blowup at the budget meeting, which of course he'd heard about, but something deeper, darker.

17

"You weren't there," Aidan defensively grumbled.

Ned, sitting in a comfortable chair in Aidan's office, agreed. "I wasn't, but I heard about it. Granted, there's so much else going on, I didn't hear about it until today. What's the matter with you? You aren't hurting her. In fact, you're making her look like a victim."

Aidan shifted in his seat. "I can make her lose her temper." He smiled. "Self-control is part of leadership."

"Then where is yours? You don't look overly mature rattling papers, drumming tabletops. Or calling her names. She gets under your skin."

"Well, I get under hers."

"We have a bill to get through the legislature. This isn't helping." Ned focused on work; emotions weren't part of the job for him. "Lose your cool and you look weak."

"I doubt there's a man out there that hasn't felt the same way."

"But he isn't a delegate of the state of Virginia," Ned calmly said.

"She doesn't look so good."

"No. But women can get away with more emotional displays than men. It plays to her fan base if you provoke her. It hurts you more than it hurts her."

"I apologized."

"For which I and the Democratic Party are grateful. We've co-sponsored a bill and I believe it can help our state. I don't have time for this, and you shouldn't either."

Aidan looked at the ceiling for a moment, his long eyelashes noticeable in profile.

"Aidan."

Aidan looked back at Ned. "I don't know why she gets under my skin." He paused then grinned. "I did get to her yesterday though. She smacked me with her ruler like a fourth-grade teacher in the old days, the days when teachers had authority."

"She's in her late forties. I'm sure she remembers." Ned couldn't help but smile. "Promise you'll ignore her."

"I'll try. I was stupid. Not so much about detracting from her performances. I consider her political statements performances. But I should have never picked up her bracelet. I saw the sparkle when I walked past her office. It was on the floor near the door. I went in, picked it up. I was going to leave it on the desk. You saw it. Worth a fortune."

"Harry Winston's stuff usually is," Ned confirmed.

"Anyway, I thought I'd give it to her or to Lucas the next day. Drove out to you, and one way or the other it fell out of my car. Thankfully your wife's friend picked it up from the snow. Amanda accused me of stealing it. It's back in her hands. I don't care what she drops or forgets in the future, I'm not picking it up."

"My wife was deeply impressed by the bracelet. Maybe if I save, I'll be able to afford one for our fiftieth anniversary. I've got time."

Ned smiled. "She's worth it, but what do you think that bracelet costs?"

"I called Harry Winston. Couldn't take the mystery. A year ago it was worth two hundred and five thousand dollars."

"No kidding?"

"It's the heavy weight of the gold, those overlapping links, and the diamond clasp is big with so many diamonds. Obviously, Amanda made a lot of money when she was on the air. Ron isn't poor, but nowhere near her earnings."

Aidan mentioned Ron Forman, Amanda's husband.

"Don't you wonder why she left TV?"

Aidan shrugged. "Forties is old for TV, even though people still look great. So she went out on top. She had the highest ratings in Virginia. Also, I think she always dreamed of a political career. She wants to be our state's first female governor."

"You know more about her than I do."

"If she's going to cross me, argue with me, smack me, yes, I think I'd better know about her. We all have cracks in our facade. I'll find hers. I'm sure she doesn't want to look older. A dig about age ought to rattle her."

Ned opened one hand, a gesture of resolve, not supplication. "Don't waste your time. You have career plans, too. Concentrate on getting legislation passed or working with other delegates. Then you can run for the state Senate. After that, well, depends on what you've accomplished."

"I'm not wasting my time, she'll do her best to bring me down."

"Maybe not."

Leaning forward, Aidan, voice low, lifted his eyebrows. "What do you think the deal is with Lucas?"

"He's her assistant."

"They're very close. Didn't your wife say he was in the changing room with her at Horse Country?"

"Uh, yes." Ned furrowed his brow.

"Pretty close."

"Well, they were sorority sisters once."

"Not now. What if they're having an affair? Lucas doesn't seem to date. How easy would it be to get away with an affair with your chief of staff, who used to be your best girlfriend but is now a guy?"

"Oh, Aidan, I don't think it's easy for anyone to have an affair if they're married. Amanda is married. Ron seems like a good guy."

"Well, I'm paying attention."

"You're too wrapped up in this. Amanda knows everyone and can get to everyone. And right now she has women stirred up. Back off."

"No. I'm not going to pick fights, but I'll be vigilant. Did you ever think maybe they slept together in college? That would rock the boat."

Back in Amanda's office, sunlight shone through the windows for a change. Piles of papers, tidy piles, covered her desk. A photo of Ron graced the right-hand corner. Lucas, notebook in hand, he probably slept with it, sat next to her. They were looking at her desktop computer screen.

"Seems like a regular medical examiner's statement to me," Lucas intoned, leaning closer to the screen.

Amanda played it again, pointing out the medical examiner. "Look at how stiff she is."

"Well, it's a sorrowful situation. A fourteen-year-old kid, gone. Fentanyl."

"Mmm." Amanda turned to face Lucas. "There's more."

"If there is, she probably can't say it. The parents are threatening a lawsuit. They haven't filed yet, but they will."

"The parents swear Reid never took drugs. They aren't yet

claiming statehouse irresponsibility, a possible drug dealer in our midst, but they will eventually."

"That's a far stretch."

"Not if you're a grieving parent." Amanda clicked off her computer. "Parents all believe their kids are the best, and in his case, he was a good kid. But people are completely irrational about their children. If I had them I'd be the same."

"Well, if the chief medical examiner is tense, it may be she doesn't want the department attacked. Then again, they do the finest work. People know that. The parents haven't hinted that there's been a slip in the autopsy."

"No." Amanda picked up Lucas's hand, pressing his finger on her desktop. "Look."

"My fingerprint on your shiny desk." He whipped out a handkerchief to rub it away.

"Wait a minute. Look at how clear your fingerprint is. So my question is, why were there no fingerprints on the cocaine vial, the stuff mixed with fentanyl? Not the tiniest smudge."

"Right."

"That doesn't mean Reid was murdered. But my question is, is there someone in the statehouse selling drugs?"

"Don't say that out loud." Lucas was adamant.

"I'm saying it to you. If there is, who? And if someone, say another delegate or just your average nutcase, had it in for anyone, they could plant a vial of the stuff in their office, car, you name it, then call the police with their suspicion."

"Yes."

"We'd best keep our eyes open. I have riled up a few people, but especially Aidan."

"Amanda, get over him. He isn't going to plant drugs in your office or car. He pisses you off. He is disrespectful and arrogant."

"How do I know he doesn't want to cut short my career?"

"Oh, I think he'd be thrilled to get rid of you, but I don't think he's a criminal."

"But you do think he's a rival?"

Lucas stroked his beard lightly, hummed, then replied, "Uh, I do. You two are the most attractive new people in the game. You have the advantage of being known. He has the advantage of being a rising star in the Democratic Party. He appeals to the young. Those who are naïve about politics, he'll promise them anything. They'll learn, of course, but he has time. Should he become our governor, however, then he'll have to deliver. Still, now he can complain about how hard he is trying, and how people like you block his noble efforts. He backs all those issues." Lucas inhaled. "Some of those issues I care about, too."

"Well, I certainly care about women's rights." She took the handkerchief from his hand, rubbing out the fingerprint herself. "Not that I'm going to lead the charge, but I . . . well, you know what I believe. If nothing else, dammit, Aidan and his kind are going to take me seriously."

"Then don't let him set you off. Your reelection fund is growing, thanks to the send-up, but back off. Don't lose your temper. He hasn't seen the worst of your temper, and I don't think anyone else should either." Lucas paused. "You might be the right person to lead the women's charge, a middle ground between hard-core feminists and mothers and working women. But be careful. You really could do this. Would cut the Democrats off at the knees." He pointed his wagging finger joint. "No temper tantrums."

"You're just saying that because when we had a fight back at the sorority house, I sewed together the legs on all your underpants. Took me half the night. You never even knew I took them." She pointed back at him.

A broad smile crossed Lucas's face.

They both laughed.

18

"Good leather." Tucker chewed on an old Timberland boot left by the tack-room door.

"May be good but you know she'll wear it until the boot disintegrates," Mrs. Murphy accurately predicted.

Pirate, standing over the corgi, sniffed. "Smells good."

"Anything she wears smells good. Every human has their distinctive scent. Mom's smells like fresh dirt and grass." Tucker bit through the leather up high near the ankle.

"She'd have a fit thinking she smelled like dirt." Pewter giggled. "Showers. Remember she takes showers to remove scent."

"Doesn't work." Tucker happily gnawed away. "You can always smell a human plus the dirt is fresh. Wonderful. You know some dogs eat dirt."

"Figures. Only a dog is dumb enough to eat dirt. I, myself, prefer mouse tartar."

"Pewter, you've never caught a mouse in your life. Too fat. You have no idea how they taste." Tucker insulted her.

The gray cannonball launched off her perch on the saddle high on the rack, a direct hit on Tucker. The two rolled around, the Timberland work boot sliding to the side.

Pirate went over to it as those two screamed. "*I don't get it.*"

Mrs. Murphy said, "*Good thing.You are so big one bite and the boot would be destroyed. She loves her work boots.*"

As Pewter and Tucker rolled around, vile talk filling the room, the tack-room door opened.

"What are you doing?" Harry rushed to pick up her boot.

"*I didn't do it.*" Pewter hurriedly jumped back up on the saddle covered by a thick saddle pad.Tucker, guilty, looked up then down.

"*I couldn't help myself,*" the adorable dog confessed. "*It smelled like you. I miss you.*"

"*Oh bull, Tucker. She's only been gone for fifteen minutes.*" Pewter prayed the dog would really be punished, like no treats.

Mrs. Murphy, on the desk, defended her corgi friend. "*She's sensitive about Mom.*"

Pirate sat by the desk, as he'd figured out, even when a puppy, that the tiger cat was usually the voice of reason.

"I've worn these shoes for fifteen years.They fit perfectly.You're a bad dog."

"*I missed you,*" Tucker repeated, eyes downcast.

"*Lay it on.*" Pewter reveled in every minute of this.

"Oh well." Harry exhaled loudly. "The soles were wearing and I did have a couple of holes in them, but really, when you get shoes or boots that fit, it's not a big deal if your feet get a little wet."

"*We wouldn't know.*" Pewter sniffed, as Harry pulled up boots and prices on her computer. A sign of defeat.

"Here's a pair. I like the light natural leather, a hundred and fifteen dollars. Six inches high. Wow, here's a six-inch pair for a hundred ninety-seven. Tucker, this isn't going to be cheap. But then, if I buy cheap boots, I wear them out in a year." She scrolled, cursing under her breath. "I'm not buying anything on Amazon. I'll have to go to the store and try these on. It's too much money to take a chance."

"*Now you've got her obsessed about money,*" Pewter groaned.

"*No, I didn't. She always worries about money.*" The small herding dog pointed out the obvious.

"*Yeah, but even if that's so, she'll be in a bad mood,*" Pewter rejoined.

"*We can get her out of it. Just wait a bit.*" Mrs. Murphy peered at the screen.

Pirate could easily see this from the floor, as his head was near Harry's shoulder. "*They sort of look the same.*"

"*Some are lined. Some are unlined. The lined ones keep her feet warmer,*" Mrs. Murphy told him. "*She can wear socks, and she does, but boot-makers can put stuff in to fight the cold. Humans get cold feet.*"

"*Even in bed, she can get cold feet.*" Pewter thought this odd.

"I'm not going to look anymore." Harry reached for the power button on her desktop computer, then stopped, and started punching the keys. "Over a thousand dollars! I can't believe that, even though I know it."

"*Work boots over a thousand dollars.*" Tucker was aghast. "*I never meant to cause that much trouble.*"

"*You didn't. She's looking at high heels.*" Mrs. Murphy watched with fascination.

"*A thousand dollars?*" Pirate wasn't sure about money, but listening to the others, he knew this was bad.

"*Right. High-heeled shoes like spikes with red soles.*" Mrs. Murphy detailed the images.

"I can understand spending money on jewelry. That lasts. But shoes? Why not just burn your money?" Harry reached for the old phone to call Susan, telling her about the chewed boots and her re-examining the Louboutins. She'd checked them out after the fight between Amanda and Aidan.

"It is crazy, but they are unique," Susan replied.

"Would you wear a pair?" Harry was incredulous.

"Well, maybe when I was younger. I can't wear heels like I used to," Susan confessed.

"You never wore heels that high."

"No, but that doesn't mean I wouldn't have, given the chance. They do look terrific and Amanda Fields can carry it off."

"Oh, I think she likes the noise they make on hard surfaces. The delegates should be thankful there is carpet in the chamber itself. You know, she must be really rich."

"She is," Susan confirmed. "She had high ratings, the highest for the six o'clock news for years. She made bundles."

"Well, she's obviously spent bundles, too." Harry thought a minute. "It's funny. She is pretty outrageous and sometimes she's to the right of Genghis Khan, and yet I like her."

"I doubt few of these people on the fringe believe in what they're saying, although I do believe she cares about women's rights. But if there's one thing a TV personality knows, it is how to get attention. Then again, she's not totally on the fringe. I'm being judgmental."

"I guess," Harry predicated. "What does Ned really think?"

"He thinks paying attention to her plays into her hands. That's why Aidan is such a fool, plus it hurts the party."

"Sure seems like a lot of work."

"It is. Look what we've all gone through rebuilding the school. If we didn't have Tazio, I doubt we could have done this. We had to raise money, as you know only too well. The damn county wouldn't give us a cent. They got out of our way, though, for which I am grateful. Still, no money. When those living graduates went to an open meeting and lambasted them for denying black history, indigenous history, that's when things changed. All of a sudden commissioners became cooperative. That was a wild meeting."

Harry laughed. "Seeing our elected worthies called out is always a good show. But it's hard to top this feud in Richmond. She keeps losing it, and yet it works for her. Fascinating."

"If you think about it, she knows the people of our state better than we do, despite us being born and raised here. She knows what grabs people's attention and she is dead-on about women being blown off, belittled. He walked right into it. Really, this is crude, and my mother would smack my mouth, but Aidan is an ass."

"He is," Harry agreed.

"You at your big computer?"

"Am."

"Okay. I'm sending you today's latest. One of the pages took it and handed it to a few friends. Now that kid will get into trouble if the delegates rat on her. One of the girl pages. Those poor pages. There's enough going on, but I am glad she did it. Sit tight. You'll have it in a minute."

Harry watched, listened for the beep, then brought up the piece. "Oh good Lord," she exclaimed as Mrs. Murphy looked at the screen.

"What's going on?" Pewter and Tucker wondered.

Mrs. Murphy, at the computer, relayed the video. *"A pretty lady in high heels, the one Mom was looking at is walking down the long polished hall. You can hear the click click click. Behind her is a man who is imitating her walk. He's swinging his hips. Behind him, moving fast, is Ned. He grabbed him by the shoulders. When he did, the pretty lady spun around, figured out he was mocking her, and cussed him out. Now people are out of their offices. She's tapping her heels, one heel on the floor. She's mad. She practically stuck her boobs in his face, she's so close. Her face is red. His is, too. Running down the hall is a blond fellow. He takes her arm and leads her away. Click click click. The rude man is now surrounded by other men and some women, too. He's pulled into an office and the door is slammed."*

"She pushed her boobs in his face?" Pewter was curious.

"She was mad. She shook her finger, too," Mrs. Murphy continued.

Pewter laughed. *"Humans only have two boobs. How bad could it be?"*

"Bad enough." The tiger cat watched as Harry played this again while talking to Susan.

"I suppose we should be glad humans only have two. If they had six or so, think

how many bras they'd have to buy, and that would be one more thing for Mom to worry about. Poor things." Pewter sniffed.

Tucker, in a moment of clarity, said, "They don't have litters. They don't need lots of boobs."

Mrs. Murphy added, "They do have litters, some of them. They have them one at a time over years. Still a lot of mouths to feed."

As the animals were discussing human anatomy, Harry remarked to Susan, "Hope the page doesn't get into trouble."

"Ned will cover for her."

"You know, it is funny. I mean, to see an elected official mincing behind another elected official, a female. Maybe Aidan could get on RuPaul's show."

"Not enough makeup."

Harry laughed. "He could learn. He'd have to buy his own pair of Louboutins."

"He'd better make more money."

"Susan, he's not poor. No one can be poor and be in politics."

"True. That's why it will never be truly representative. But we do the best we can. The cost of elections I find destructive. If the Canadians can have a six-week election period . . . don't know what it is for the Brits . . . we can, too. The amount of money wasted on elections is a sin. Ned and I have drawn a line. He's leaving if it spirals upward. His life is already jammed with fundraisers. Who has time to govern? He's in his second term. Our district generally turns out. Some people are swayed by what I call anger politics, but most really want good roads, good schools, job opportunities, affordable housing. Sensible. But again, we have drawn the line. You can have all the rights in the world, but if you can't eat, what good are they? That money now spent on elections should go to county food kitchens."

Harry let that settle in. "You're right, but what I think drives a lot of today's anger is status anxiety. How do you like that word?"

Susan laughed. "Coming from you, very impressive."

"People don't want to lose their place. They want to move up the totem pole. Granted, I'm not much for politics, but people don't change. We're the same as we were millennia ago; we now have central heating, running water, we don't have to walk to the well, but nothing is truly different, just easier."

"Nuclear weapons are different."

"They are, and we can all go up in smoke, but if you think about it, in every age there was some new military development that scared people."

"We are over the edge now," Susan firmly stated. "In a way, a strange way, that's why this absurd feud distresses me. The huge problems in the world, well, perhaps the Virginia statehouse isn't going to fix them, but we have things we need to do for our state. Having two representatives waste time needling each other doesn't solve a thing."

"No, but it brings them both to the public's attention. And I bet it gets people giving to their election campaigns. To change the subject, I am not buying a new pair of work boots unless I can try them on. I'll keep you posted."

"No you won't. You'll drag me with you. Now, my opinion would mean something if you were buying those red-bottom heels. Timberland work boots? Maybe not. You'll look like you always look, whether in an ancient pair or a new pair."

"That's not very flattering. I'd like to think I'll look better."

"You will." Susan laughed. "Maybe you should look at a pair of inexpensive heels, so next time we go to Richmond you can click down the hall. People will think there is competition for Amanda."

A long pause followed this. "I don't think she's ever going to have competition. Okay, back to it. I'm going over tomorrow to check on Aunt Tally. I know she's all right, but given the weather, she can't get out. Teresa could drive her somewhere, but walking her to a restaurant or, say, Talbots is not a good idea. Slick. And given the nights, frozen until more salt is put on the sidewalks."

"You're right. I'll make scones. Aunt Tally has always liked my scones."

"Me too."

"*They're talking about food.*" Pewter's ears perked up.

"*Scones.*" Mrs. Murphy cited the food.

"*I'll eat scones.*"

19

Teresa brushed crumbs off the table, brought in Aunt Tally's old ham radio, plugged it in.

"Thank you." Aunt Tally turned to Harry and Susan. "It's simple once you learn the etiquette."

"Such as you have to identify yourself?" Harry had been doing a bit of research.

"You have a call name or call letters. You are registered. Here, let me tune in."

"This is a newscast?" Susan asked, listening.

"No. It's one man's opinion. He lives in Berryville. For shows and newscasts, one uses regular radio, a different frequency, of course, and remember they have big budgets. This radio is for people, not stations. That's what makes it so interesting. To me anyway."

"Do you use it a lot now?"

Aunt Tally looked from Harry to Susan as she leaned back in

her special, expensive desk chair, one that gave her support. "No. Every now and then I'll get curious, but I have heard most political views, personal adventures. There isn't a lot new out there for me except rudeness being accepted. Is it rudeness or not being taught manners?" She exhaled. "Maybe it's the same."

"Times change," Susan simply said.

"People don't," Aunt Tally countered. "Fashions change, what is acceptable changes up to a point, but the human animal remains driven by the seven deadly sins. We all have a bit of it in us, but we learn control and I hope as we age we can see the other person's point of view."

"I'd like to think so, but the last few weeks have shaken my hopes." Susan pulled her chair closer to the centenarian. "I've spent a few extra days down at the statehouse and the people are rude, thoughtless, you name it."

"At least in the old days when they insulted one another, they did it with style." Aunt Tally laughed.

As the humans discussed the feud between Amanda and Aidan, for Aunt Tally didn't know much about it, Mrs. Murphy, Pewter, Tucker, Pirate, and Owen lounged on the floor, the carpet being thick. Mrs. Murphy snuggled next to Bitsy, Aunt Tally's ancient dachshund. Bitsy slept a great deal but liked the cat cuddles. She began to snore.

"Is Bitsy as old as Aunt Tally?" Tucker wondered.

"Close, I think. Human years are different than ours, but close enough," Owen replied.

Owen, like Harry's friends, had spent time with Aunt Tally and Bitsy over the years. Everyone knew everyone.

"Harkness." Aunt Tally considered the name. "Isn't the fellow raising money for scholarships? Some for trade schools, too?"

Susan answered. "He gives speeches. No one has complained about conflict of interest for now. Where monies get dicey is with reelection campaigns, stuff like that."

Aunt Tally turned off her radio. "If a politician wants to dip into funds, believe me, he or she will find a way. But young people need our support."

"They do. Try finding a plumber." Harry laughed.

"Supposedly this administration will work to create more trade schools. More scholarships to college as well," Susan posited. "Keeping track of income and expenses is complicated."

Aunt Tally nodded. "That's what people always do when they don't want you to know what they're really up to. Complicate it. I've watched this for over a century. Of course I didn't pay attention until my early twenties. It's an old trick. That's what made Cicero so formidable as a lawyer. He could figure all this out."

"Plus his sense of humor destroyed his opponents in the Senate." Harry loved history.

"Nothing changes. Truly." Aunt Tally turned her chair and rolled the wheels back to the small table, as they were in a window-seat area off the kitchen, large enough for a table. "Susan, I have to have another scone."

Back at the food, more tea from Teresa, they talked about the weather, their friends, and when it might be time to plant.

"Aunt Tally, before TV, how did you get the news? Not everyone could read."

"Susan, not everyone can read now. We had a morning paper and an evening paper, each representing a party in the editorial page. I promise those reporters were good. I learned a lot and I read every word."

"I forget literacy can't be taken for granted." Harry glanced back at the ham radio; it was so big.

"Right now the schools are a hot issue. What is taught. How it's taught." Susan broke a scone for Aunt Tally, then buttered it, slathering on some divine homemade jelly, raspberry.

"Honey, maybe that's a good thing. Our schools have been in the shade for so long that this dustup at least is getting people's attention, including the people who don't have children."

"A lot of this would be solved if schools taught civics again."

Harry was positive. "You can't really be indoctrinated into anything if you know civics, the Constitution, and the Bill of Rights."

"Oh, Harry. Some people can always be indoctrinated. There are humans who need answers, need a framework to hang on to whether it's true or not, but I agree, if civics were back in the classroom, there would be fewer suckers, for lack of a better word." Aunt Tally couldn't help it, she licked the raspberry jelly off the spoon; she knew better, but the taste was too sweet.

Also, when one is old, one can get away with a lot.

"My grandfather used to quote P. T. Barnum and say, 'There's a sucker born every minute.'"

Aunt Tally laughed. "Larry Beaufoy did not suffer fools."

"Boy, my grandfather did." Susan shook her head.

"He was the governor. He had to. You know, your grandfather was one of the smartest men I have ever known. He operated on the principle 'Praise a fool, and you may make him useful.'" Aunt Tally laughed.

"Ugh." Harry grabbed a scone for herself. "It's funny, though, what you remember. Mostly I wanted to be outside. I didn't care. Now I actually can recall some of the things Mom, Dad, G-Pop told me. It's funny what sticks."

"It is." Aunt Tally turned to Susan. "You know that Harry's grandfather and I were close. I'm so old now that I don't care anymore, and secrets are burdensome. My memory is sharp. I have forgotten very little. But Harry's grandfather and I were two peas in a pod until my family broke it up. I tell you this because it is why I learned to use the ham radio. When I learned it, you had to learn Morse code as well. That took some doing, but Larry told me the secret is not to write it down. No dots and dashes. Will take so much longer. Try to recognize whole letter sounds, plus the seven second pause between words. So I did. We did talk but if something was close to us, emotional, we used Morse code."

"No one uses that anymore." Susan listened intently. "Knowing it makes you valuable."

"Some people still learn it. There are soldiers, sailors, people in the corps who must learn. In a dire emergency it may be all we've got. But now you can get your ham radio license without it. I'm wandering off. Sorry. Once we no longer could see each other we would talk via radio."

"That had to be painful." Susan was sympathetic.

"Eventually the pain subsided. And he married." She faced Harry. "Your grandmother was a good woman. Larry wanted to have children, a family. Obviously that was impossible with me. I often wonder what would have happened if I had defied the family and run away. Could we have made it?"

"You probably would have had to leave Virginia." Harry raised her hand. "Too many people knew your family, Aunt Tally."

"Yes," she simply answered.

"Maybe you could have moved to the West Coast. Back when the film industry was new, sound coming in. Bet he could have found a job." Susan remembered Harry's grandfather well.

"I was too young, I gave in. I haven't had a bad life, perhaps not the one I wanted, as I didn't have Larry, but in other ways it's been full. My sister married well, obviously. She had a lot to offer. We weren't poor. I helped raise Big Mim. She was a bright child. I enjoyed that. I find I look back more now. I can understand things I couldn't understand then." She stopped, and sighed. "Well, I'm nattering on."

"We love hearing it." Both women nodded as Susan said this.

"You flatter me. But back to this uproar in the statehouse. I've received mailings from Aidan Harkness for his foundation. I think the trade school idea is good. I hope a bill for that passes, but since it would mean the state coughs up more money, I wouldn't bet on it. So I sent a check."

"The woman he's fighting sooner or later will start a foundation," Harry filled in.

"I haven't received any mailings from her for anything, I'm not on the Republican list."

"She is growing ever more powerful, thanks to Aidan's stupidity." Susan leaned toward Aunt Tally. "As my husband has co-sponsored a bill with him, I care. I don't want Ned dragged down by this."

"Of course not," Aunt Tally agreed.

They talked, thought about spring, compared garden notes, until finally it was time to go.

As Harry walked out, she clucked to her pets, as Susan did to Owen.

Mrs. Murphy patted Bitsy, who opened one eye then fell asleep again.

Driving back to Harry's, Susan said, "Can you imagine what it's like for Aunt Tally? No matter where she goes, she is the oldest person in the room. There will be no contemporaries."

"Maybe a few people in their mid-nineties, who remember her as a young woman, but you're right. Who knew your parents' friends? The events you shared. It has to be lonely."

"It does. I don't know if I want to live that long."

"Don't say that, Susan."

"Do you?"

"I figure I'll take what the good Lord gives me."

Susan smiled. "Now you sound like your mother. See, we're contemporaries."

Harry noticed droplets falling from tree limbs, as the temperature hung in the low forties. Seemed warm, given the last few weeks.

"We share a lot. Actually, we share a lot with Aunt Tally, too, although we aren't her contemporaries. We don't know life without her."

"It makes me think of that good kid, Reid. Dead at fourteen." Susan frowned. "A long, long life compared to a short one."

"You never really know, and I think we're better off not knowing."

20

Agreeing on the state budget pressed the lawmakers, as time was running out. Lucas hunkered over his desk, piles of paper on the floor, the desk, and one chair. The blue light from the computer flickered a bit. He pulled out papers from the pile on his desk, double-checking numbers one more time.

The door to his small office was open. Amanda languished in a meeting with the Republicans, regarding cultural issues. She fiddled. She wanted to get the budget nailed down. As to cultural issues, she didn't think she could add anything to it.

Lucas looked up as Keisha Simmons rapped on the door frame. "Mr. Dennison?"

"Come on in. Here, pull up a chair. Just put the papers on the floor." He smiled at her as she followed his instructions.

"I've brought the papers from Representative Gibson." She placed them on his desk, then sat down.

"What can I do for you?" Lucas had a soft spot for young people.

"You went to William and Mary." He nodded, so she continued. "I know this is a little early, but I'm trying to figure out what would be best for me. In two years' time I'll be filling out applications to colleges."

"William and Mary will give you a sound education."

"And I'm an in-state resident. Can save money. But I'd like to go out of state. See something different. And then come back and go to William and Mary's law school. Because if I live here and eventually run for office I will have made good contacts at William and Mary. But I could also go to UVA's law school."

He settled back in his chair. "Law school is one step closer to employment. And it never hurts to go to a powerful law school or the best in your state. Most every elected official starts as a state official, which you know. William and Mary is the oldest law school in the nation."

"Yes, Sir. But Mom and Dad don't have much money. They want me to go to undergraduate school in Virginia and then go to law school out of state on a scholarship."

"It makes sense, but Keisha, you'll get scholarships floating down upon you like confetti. Where would you really like to go?"

"Howard."

"Ah." He smiled. "A history of outstanding graduates."

"I've never been in a situation where more people look like I do than don't."

"You're right. Perhaps it will help you concentrate more on your studies. Will you be more relaxed, you think?"

She nodded. "And if I do okay, then I can apply to law schools here."

"You can. If you plan on a career here, and there's time to figure that out, I strongly vote for William and Mary. But then, I would."

She sat a bit awkwardly for a moment. "Reid wasn't a druggie. I want you to know that. I . . . I . . ." She hesitated. "I trust you because you're different."

He smiled. "That's the truth. You know I'll listen to you. My issues were different than those of many, but growing up is a challenge no matter what. I didn't fit in, but I tried."

"Yes, Sir."

He smiled again. "I didn't mean to focus on me. Let me ask you a few questions, just between us."

"Yes, Sir."

"Is everything else in your life okay?"

"No, Sir."

"Can I help you?" His voice was soft.

"I don't know, but I want you to know that Reid wasn't a partier. Never. It upsets me."

"Do some of the other pages take drugs? You don't need to give me names . . ."

"I don't know. I'm not popular. I mean, I get along with everyone, but I'm not . . . oh, cool. So I never saw anyone doing anything like drugs."

"Have you ever suspected a representative or someone working as staff supplying drugs or taking them?"

"No, Sir, but sometimes people act crazy. Some of the delegates get, uh, they talk too much after lunch."

"The famous martini lunches." Lucas pursed his lips together. "Has anyone approached you? Made improper suggestions?"

"No, but I believe someone put that vial in Reid's pants' cuff." She waited a long time then came out with it. "He would never be that stupid. We were, uh, going out. I know he would not jeopardize his future. He had his career planned out a lot better than I have mine." Her eyes filled up.

"Don't worry about careers. They change. But you are right. He was a focused and organized young man."

"We were busy the day he died. Sometimes Reid and I might have lunch by ourselves, sometimes with others. He whispered to me that he had news. Important news. He'd tell me later. There wasn't time then." She grabbed the seat with both hands. "Mr. Dennison, I think he found out something."

"Something that could compromise an official or someone in the administration?"

She nodded her head. "I believe he was set up."

A long silence followed this.

"Do you feel in danger?"

"I'm afraid because of what happened to him, but I don't know anything."

"Don't tell anyone else. If you tell your parents, be prepared for them to take you out of here. They want to protect you. You have to decide what you want to do, but don't tell anyone else. Just go about your business as if things were normal. Be glad he didn't tell you. That would be a harder burden to bear." He stood up, walked over to her, and put his hand on her shoulder. "I will not reveal this conversation to anyone. If anything or anyone frightens you, come to me. If your parents take you out of here, don't worry. It's not going to hurt you for recommendations to college. Really, don't worry. If you drop out of page work and enough time goes by, I will see you get a good job working for someone in the administration. You're in school. It will be part-time, but you'll keep learning. The process of government is exhausting."

"Yes, Sir. Thank you, Sir."

"If anyone wonders why you were here for a little extra time, tell them we were talking about college and I'm trying to get you to go to my alma mater."

"Yes, Sir." She stood up, smiled weakly, and left just as Amanda walked in.

"Good meeting?"

"Ha," Amanda replied.

"You missed a good conversation about our alma mater. I gave Keisha the pep talk."

"She'd fit right in." Amanda plopped on the two-seater sofa along the wall. "I think I'm becoming a saint. I listened to everyone. It was beyond tedious. We are all Republicans. We all want fiscal restraint. We aren't looking to cut critical services but if we don't receive cooperation, then yes, our budget will slash tons of fat." She smirked for a moment. "How will that play in those holier-than-thou districts?"

"Pretty much as it always does. You will be the spawn of the devil." He laughed and she joined him.

"Why can't we get that information about the revenues in the final quarter of the fiscal year? Then everyone, even the Democrats, will know what they're talking about concerning numbers. I'll be damned if I'm going to offer trade-offs without facts. I do know our economy generated $3.6 billion in added revenue. We can make beneficial choices."

"Quite right. Do other people in the party want to cut services?" he asked.

"Yes. They aren't twisting arms hard enough yet. There are a few who want to cut all social services. Politics is a rough game. But blowing smoke over numbers, I'm going to work. We'll dig in, as you know."

"Right." He thought of Keisha, a bright, bright girl obviously excited about politics.

One might have the brain for politics, but do you have the stomach?

"In the 2022 budget deal, the Assembly agreed to reduce taxes by four billion dollars, taking effect July 2023. You know that. Everyone in the Assembly knows that. There is a conspicuous silence. I sit on the budget committee. I have got to push our party members on the committee. Others I have to restrain. Be precise. Offer a trade-off for any social spending. I'm not opposed to alleviating rents for the poor. What do we gain by people being thrown on the street? But if the state offers relief, then it has to benefit with work. No money without work."

"Well, it once worked for Clinton." Lucas recalled national politics.

"Lucas, no one specifies the work. And some of the people who can't pay the rent, much less have it raised, are single women with children. That's why I need a speaking schedule. I need to go out and push for women. See what you can line up. Anyway, I am ready to tear my hair out, but I just got it colored."

He lifted his eyebrows. "Looks smashing."

"The other thing. Someone must have talked about us being in the changing room together at Horse Country. I fielded a snide remark from one of our party members . . . that's right, not that jerk Aidan, but one of our members . . . about inappropriate behavior, my being in a changing booth with a man."

"Oh, Amanda, go for it. If you're going to be hung for a sheep, be hung for a wolf." He laughed.

This stopped her for a moment. "Do you think Susan Tucker would blab?"

"I don't know her that well, but she doesn't strike me as a cheap gossip. We don't really know her friend though."

"Harry? Yes, Harry, that's her name. She's kept her figure. Susan is putting on a little weight. I digress. Do you think anyone at the store would have called us out?"

"Amanda. I doubt anyone at Horse Country is interested in playing politics, plus we kept the door open . . . not wide open, but definitely open."

She shifted in the seat. "You're right. God, I'm tired. Tired of being the coxswain. I push and push. Do these people think things are going to happen just because we now have a Republican governor? They need to wake up. Of course, everyone pays attention to money."

"Yes, they do."

"All right, now I'm hungry. Let me get a sandwich."

"I'll order your favorite salad. Be here in a flash. Really, you shouldn't eat processed meat."

"You are so fussy."

"We are fussy about different things." He smiled. "Does the changing-room story mean we will again be accused of having an affair?"

She clapped her hands as he rose to call a close-by restaurant they often frequented. "I love it. It does make us exciting, doesn't it?"

"At least unconventional. I loved you in college and I love you now, but I never wanted to sleep with you. I mean, that's like sleeping with your sister, truly your sister."

"Yeah." She was calming down. "On reflection, I think some of our sorority sisters were sleeping with one another. Think about Babsie Rogers and Paula Finch."

"Um, maybe."

"Want money?"

"For what?"

"Lunch."

"No. But look at the papers on your desk. Keisha dropped them off."

"Should I give her the rah rah about William and Mary?"

"Maybe in a week or two. Let it percolate." He walked into his office, called for food.

Amanda sat there, unwilling to get off of the sofa, which was more comfortable than her desk chair. She slipped her phone out of her pocket, punched in the account number for her reelection fund, gave the password, and checked the numbers. The money was rolling in. She was beginning to be thankful to Aidan. A big smile crossed her lips.

21

A smattering of fresh snow brightened the undulating terraces at the University of Virginia. From the rotunda to the statue of Homer, the lawn, now white, was bounded by redbrick one-story buildings on each side. At regular intervals, a two-story building—formerly living quarters for professors and their families—was beautifully cloaked in snow. Proportion, restraint, a sense of organized space welcomes whoever might be walking along, regardless of season.

Harry, Fair, Susan, and Ned hurried down to Old Cabell Hall, which was directly behind Homer. The cold spurred them forward. A stream of people moved in the same direction, with each individual happy to be inside out of the cold. Old Cabell Hall . . . built in 1898, designed by the extraordinarily talented Stanford White of McKim, Mead & White . . . could accommodate musicians, speakers, and panels. The auditorium seated 851 people, treating them to amazingly clear sound.

Tonight's program started at six. Already dark, the light inside
the auditorium enlivened people. The ground of UVA, not awash
in bright lights, necessitated watching carefully where you stepped,
especially in winter. Seated close to the front, in part thanks to
Ned being the county's delegate to the Assembly, the four removed
their coats, laying them across their laps. People kept streaming in.
This was a packed house, filled with students as well as townies.

A few minutes after six, the program started. The head of the
Political Science department introduced Lucas Dennison. Late-
comers leaned against the back wall. The school administrators
tried to keep count. No one wanted to run afoul of the fire department because the room held too many people.

After the introduction, strong applause was mixed with boos.
If Lucas was upset, he didn't show it. Looking into the audience,
he recognized Ned and Susan and smiled.

He spoke of the state system of government and how he found
his way into it. When he mentioned being a student at William
and Mary, there were a few boos, more as a rival than animosity.

"Remember, we were founded on February 8, 1693, and you
were founded on January 25, 1819," Lucas teased them.

He outlined briefly the larger issues facing the Assembly now
as he harked back to greater issues in the recent past, most especially the admittance of black men and then the admittance of
women. Both actions provoked a dramatic drop in alumni funds,
which eventually evened out. People got used to it, plus the new
students proved outstanding. He also indicated those issues, gender and race, affected William and Mary, as well as every other
university and college in Virginia.

He encouraged young people to participate in politics. For
those going into law school, he urged high performance. They
would be hired at powerful law firms or clerk for imposing
judges. There was a lot to learn.

He briefly addressed studying at William and Mary, enjoying
the friendships but never quite feeling right, never feeling he fit

in. Finally, in his mid-twenties, he knew he had to make a drastic change or he'd live a miserable life.

He praised his best friend, Amanda Fields, for sticking by him. A few hisses followed this. He repeated how good she was.

"No one knew exactly what would happen, how long the process would take. And it did take time for both of us, for my family. My mother cried that she was losing her daughter. My father was confused. My brother was okay. My sister took more time because she liked having a sister, so she said. I want you to know you can be who you are. It may not be easy but it's worth the process. Once I was able to live as I truly am, so much fell into place. My best friend, Amanda, got elected and chose me to be her chief of staff after I ran her campaign."

He paused, then said, "All eyes were on her. Not that many people focused on me as her campaign manager. But a few did. She handled it, saying I was the best and she trusted me.

"That's how I came to the Assembly. I love my work. I encourage you, any of you, to go for it if you have an interest in politics. Being in the middle of it is very different from looking at it from the outside. One has to get things done. Being ideologically pure, unable to compromise, is an impediment, not an advantage. We can agree on the big issues, such as the state of Virginia lags woefully behind on affordable housing. Richmond alone easily needs one hundred thousand units. There has to be a way, and some of you know my boss is fiscally conservative. She's tight with the budget but she's willing to work on private-public funding for low-cost housing. She won't vote to raise taxes but she is willing to cut taxes as an incentive for companies ready to help, like construction companies. Delegate Fields can be creative. And I would be remiss not to call your attention to your district's delegate, Ned Tucker, a stalwart Democrat. We can work together." Lucas held out his hand to indicate Ned, who slightly rose and bowed to the applause.

Susan beamed as she whispered to Harry, "He is the best. Really, the best."

Harry smiled back. After all these years, Susan was more in love with Ned now than the day she married him. Harry thought to herself, "When it works, when love grows, everyone wins."

The speech was not overly long. The questions bounced from respectful or issue-oriented to an attack on Lucas for not being a "real" man since his DNA was female. Quite a few riled people up, and those opposing hissed, booed. Then Lucas got grilled for not making identity politics the center of his political life.

In other words he was attacked for being trans by some, and attacked by others for not being trans enough.

Throughout all this, Lucas's self-composure was impressive. He kept returning to what we can do, what you can expect to do, and he said his boss was not a one-issue woman and he was not a one-issue man.

The speech ended at seven-thirty to cheers as well as boos.

Lucas walked out one of the doors; there wasn't an easy back way. Ned, Susan, Harry, and Fair followed, as well as the chair of the Political Science department. People crowded around Lucas. Little by little, the people broke off to go to their cars. As no parking is close to the lawn at UVA, those walks proved long and cold, for the mercury had dropped even more during the speech.

At Lucas's car, a Mazda SUV, students stood talking with him. Some were quite earnest about their problems, others wanted more career advice, and a few asked personal questions about his body. That made Harry wince.

As they approached him, Ned and Susan insisted Lucas come stay in their guest room. It was dark. The roads were bad. The morning would be better.

"You can sleep with Owen, our corgi." Ned smiled, then laughed. "Once you're at the house."

———

"He has lovely fur," Harry informed Lucas as she and Fair joined them at Susan's.

Chatting drew them closer together, and once Harry and Fair left Susan and Ned's, Lucas went to bed more exhausted than he could have imagined. Speaking took a lot of energy. Owen slept snuggled under his arm.

22

"Are you sure that clasp is good?" Lucas asked Amanda as she shook her wrist.

"It is."

"Okay, but don't take the bracelet off. You were lucky you got it back."

"I was."

Lucas had talked about his speech at Cabell Hall. He mentioned how lovely and homey Susan and Ned's house was, plus that he'd slept with Owen.

"Owen?" Her eyebrows raised.

"Their corgi."

"Oh." She smiled. "You said you had some boos and hisses. I hope I don't get that at my speeches."

"You aren't talking on cultural issues. You are talking about the budget." He paused. "Childcare. I suppose that could be contentious, but the statistics are that if women have childcare they will make more money."

"That's why I think childcare should be available like libraries are available. If corporations provided childcare, communities wouldn't need to contribute as much. It can be affordable for state and county budgets. Again, one still has to tighten budgets, re-allocate funds, but it's not out of reach."

"Be easier if churches, temples, and—"

She interrupted. "Lucas, they're losing people, not gaining. How are religious groups going to help?"

"There is that," he agreed as Keisha knocked on the door frame.

"Delegate Fields, Mr. Dennison, I wanted to thank you for helping me." She looked to Lucas. "My parents are taking me out of the Assembly, so this is my last day as a page."

"I am so sorry," Amanda responded.

"Is this because of Reid?" Lucas asked.

She nodded. "The threat of the lawsuit upsets them as well as the gossip. And they are afraid someone might slip me drugs."

"I'm sorry, too." Lucas meant it. "You have our number here. You can always call. I'm happy to talk about colleges, and so is Delegate Fields."

"Of course we are happiest talking about William and Mary." Amanda smiled. "You have plenty of time to narrow your choices and I'm sure whatever university you choose will be lucky to have you."

After her goodbye, the two sat quietly for a moment, then Amanda groaned. "Is this ever going to end, and how will it end?"

"Who knows, but it is . . . well, uncommon."

"Do you think someone will try and slip fentanyl to a delegate, if in fact that's what happened to Reid Ryder?"

"Anything is possible. I think it's far-fetched, but it is possible. You can die from an inhale. That's about all I know about fentanyl, except deaths are up something like 260 percent since 2016. If that isn't accurate, it's close." Lucas rubbed his temples.

"Don't worry, I won't quote you. What I need to do is line up meetings with big corporations to discuss lower taxes if they provide special service like childcare or, say, being responsible for a public park in their district.

"Be a smart move for one of our big corporations, especially a tobacco corporation. Think about that. We aren't encouraging smoking or vaping, but they can be the model both for their workers and the public in general. The point is to get publicity and campaign donations. If one big corporation starts the ball rolling, I think others will join. And with careful positioning, this can be a critical factor in reelection. Our terms are so short. You get elected, you start campaigning again almost immediately. I'll push for state funding, private-public deals. There's time to work it out. Again, I can never go to the state government with a plan to tax."

He exhaled loudly. "Right. It's going to take a lot of figuring, visits, talk, and what are we willing to barter, more or less?"

She stroked her chin for a second, then switched to a stray lock of blonde hair, which she twisted with her forefinger. "I believe you trade lower taxes for public service, as I said. Not that I would put it in that language, but if we save corporations and small businesses money, that means they'll make more money and provide some agreed-upon services. To us it would be significant. To them hardly a drop in the bucket, but so much good publicity."

"True. But we have to step carefully and move quietly."

She cut off her cellphone, which had begun to ring. "All I ask is a minute's peace." She smiled as she looked over to Lucas. "Let me put on a little makeup before going into the Assembly."

"You look great."

"Sometimes I have to work harder at it."

"And don't play with your bracelet. Just in case."

"All right. All right."

"Look at the camera in there. Remember, we need to create a vlog just for you. Ellis Barfield is ready to create one. Although we can't use him. Conflict with the Assembly, but he does shoot you a lot. I'll get him to send us to someone good, and I'll think of a reward," Lucas said. "He'll be upset obviously, but he'll still get footage of you. He always does."

"Good, and don't worry. I'll keep my hands still. My bracelet hidden."

"Don't lose it."

"Yes, Dad."

Miranda Hogendobber sat next to Harry and fired up her ham radio. Harry watched everything.

"Memorize the steps," her old friend and former work partner at the post office told her. "It's like anything else. Break it down into small steps. Do it often enough and you don't think about it."

"I never knew you were in the WACs."

"I mentioned it once or twice, but I didn't dwell on it. Serving made me feel useful. Okay, now you turn it on and listen for the repeat."

Harry went through the motions that she'd seen Miranda doing.

"There. You've got it."

"Do you ever talk to Aunt Tally?"

"I never knew she had a radio," Miranda replied. "All these years I've known her. So when I was in my teens, she was already way beyond me. I signed up for the service the minute I was old enough; Tally, older, ran her farm. Most of the men were gone."

"I rarely think about that," Harry honestly said.

"I know, and there are fewer and fewer of us every day. But we did all the work the men did, whether it was in steel mills, law offices, the corner store. The only men that were left were old or young. Fighting-age men still around usually were involved in something critical to the war effort. Maybe a man in his forties ran a giant corporation or was a chemist with special skills. Back then, forty was considered old." She smiled. "Times change. Forty is nothing."

"Well—"

"Harry, you're in your forties now. You know I never forget your birthday. Do you feel old?"

"Some days I do. When I think I've heard something before or seen a story before. I can get bored."

"You walk without a hitch in your giddyup." Miranda laughed. "About the ham radio, here's what I suggest. You have a lot to learn. People learn in different ways. Read the book you have. Then come back to me and we can go over all this again. Only then will you do it without me."

"I hope it doesn't take a long time."

"Come back here. I know how you think after all the years we worked together. You'll pick it up."

"Miranda, this is generous of you."

"I miss our time in the post office, but that's changed, too. Rules, rules, rules. When we were there, all we had to do was sort the mail, sell stamps, and talk to whoever needed us. Now you have to answer questions about any package being sent, and you have to push a button on the machine, looks like a credit card machine. We knew everybody. Now when I go to the post office . . . rarely, I confess . . . I hardly know a soul."

"We got out in time. When they built the new post office, all the charm of the old disappeared. I don't think it was that much easier to work in; but then, I was so accustomed to the old. Not being able to take the cats and dog did it for me."

"I'm grateful for my pension."

"You earned it. It's really your money." Harry couldn't help herself, she thought of the years the government had to use the social security taken from her paycheck. She wondered if she would get social security and she worried about people in their twenties. She kept it to herself. Seemed no good to worry people.

"I suppose. When George was alive, we had a lot of fun in the post office, but it was a different time. Anyways, when home, I'd get distant people on this radio and he'd be entranced. Then when I managed to convince some of the choir girls that we could sing if they got radios, well, they did. And we still sing together." Miranda focused on her radio.

"How is church?"

"Good. Okay, you talk to Tally. She might not want someone listening to her conversation. If she's fine with it, then you can practice here."

"Did you have to learn Morse code?"

"I did. The Army taught me. Few people know it today. Your grandfather did."

"I have a photo of him in front of his equipment in the destroyer. There are so many things I should have asked him."

"Everybody feels that way about those that are gone. Anyway, get back to me."

"I will."

"Kiss the dog and cats. And now the big dog, too."

"I will."

Driving back to the farm, Harry realized that no one really knew about Aunt Tally's ability with the ham radio. She'd kept it a secret but seemed fine now with Susan knowing about her skill. To think that all these years the woman had kept it to herself . . . but then, she'd also kept her love affair to herself.

Pulling up to the barn, the dogs rushing out of the house, the snow still on the ground, she wondered if she could ever keep a secret like that. Then again, she couldn't imagine needing to do so.

Secrets have an odd way of coming out.

23

Click click clickity clickity stomp.

With that announcement, Amanda moved past Aidan's office. He refused to look up at her, but she'd achieved her objective. He knew she was there. She need not say a word.

Turning to walk back to another colleague's office, a member of her party, she hastily moved to the side as two police officers, along with one statehouse guard, walked past her.

She watched their receding figures, then popped into Frances Whitlock's office. "What's going on?"

"I don't know."

"I was out in the hall, two cops breezed by with a statehouse guard."

"Well, who knows?" Frances didn't focus on the officers. A mistake. "How are you doing with your budget work? I expected you to sponsor a bill by now. You know I'll support you."

"I do know that, and I'm grateful. I'd like a few more numbers. Shouldn't take me long, and if I can't get them I will identify the departments not forthcoming. I don't care who heads them." Amanda looked out the door again. "Gone."

"Give me an example."

"Eight million dollars have been set aside to help put more resource officers in schools. Good. But which schools?"

"Underfunded or overfunded?" Frances asked.

"That's it. We don't know. Does Fairfax County have the same need as Bedford County? I'd like it spelled out."

"That means the counties will fight it out as well as falsify their needs?" Frances cynically replied.

"If I have accurate information . . . not just a broad budget number, but allocated funds . . . then I can put forth a bill with realistic numbers."

"Amanda, my advice is to get a bill on the floor. You can be specific over time," Frances affirmed.

They could hear sirens outside.

"What the hell is going on?" Frances asked, standing up.

Ten minutes passed while they listened with one ear while discussing how to handle the cultural hot spots that neither one thought would bring in the number of voters they needed.

"Cultural issues bring in the hard-right base. They'll vote in the primaries." Amanda heard a door slam.

Frances remarked, "Someone is angry."

Amanda said to her, "I'd better get back to my office. Lucas will know what's going on."

Amanda crossed her office threshold. "Lucas."

"Here."

"Do you know what's going on?"

"No. I'm searching on my computer screen for a news flash."

"I heard sirens, then retreating sirens. Oh, and a door slam."

The phone rang. Lucas picked it up. "Delegate Fields's office, Lucas Dennison speaking." He listened. "Yes. Thank you for informing us." He put the phone back. "The guard. He said Ellis Barfield, seeing two officers, ran out the door before they could stop him. The police didn't want to shoot. They wanted to question him, hence the lack of danger to others."

"The parking lot? He ran to the parking lot?"

"He was cornered and he ran out of the building. That's all I know."

"Anyone know why the police want to question him?"

"No, but Reid *was* driving Ellis's car. Crashed, sideswipe most likely according to police. They kept it for a day. Obviously, he has it back."

"Maybe they found dry residue. Not drugs, but maybe a wipe on a seat turned up something later." She wrinkled her nose for a moment. "It had to be something incriminating. Why else would he run?"

Lucas thought a moment. "I don't know. Maybe he has a past record. Thinks he won't get fair treatment and panicked. Possible."

"At this point, I believe anything is possible, but all of this is a distraction. Don't forget that." She picked up a pencil. "I'm sorry that page died. I don't know why Ellis ran. It's not my job to find out. Since this has happened here at the Capitol, the news will be all about it."

"True." Lucas grimaced.

"The eleven o'clock news will have interviews. Everyone on the state payroll has to make sure they did their job correctly, and if they didn't, they have to sound as though they did to whichever reporter is grilling them. I say that while being on the state payroll myself, for the princely sum of $17,640." She walked to the sofa, dropped down. "You know, when I got elected I thought I knew a lot about how government worked. I did compared to most, but I never imagined the cowardice of people. The first rule of any elected official, any appointee, truly is 'cover your ass.'"

24

"One, two, three." Miranda blew C Major on her pitch pipe, then repeated, "one, two, three."

The girls sang.

Over the ham radio, Harry listened to the beautiful voices. She was not alone. Others had asked to listen to the Church of the Holy Light choir practice, some not members of the church. The voices, so pure, drew people to the choir practice. Miranda's short solos sometimes interspersed into one of the hymns were, as always, heavenly. She had sung with the choir all her long life, starting as a child.

"Amen," everyone said in unison.

"Well done, ladies," Miranda praised them.

Harry heard a slight crackle, then a deep alto voice said, "Miranda, will Conner be the organist Sunday?"

"He will."

"Good," came the reply.

"Anyone else have a question?" No questions, so Miranda then said, "See you all at 7:30 Sunday. All right, La La La," Each La was a full note, followed by a quarter note. "Fa Fa."

Six other voices then sang the same notes, "La La La Fa Fa."

There was a short silence, then Harry could hear microphones turning off.

Miranda shut down the radio. "I think this cold weather, February hopelessness, provokes us all to want to sing to get everyone feeling brighter."

"So when the practice is over, you just turn off the ham radio?"

"We all said goodbye."

"I didn't hear anyone say goodbye."

"We sang it. Shortcut. You can shortcut so much with a ham radio."

"Miranda, you're losing me."

The older woman turned her chair to Harry, smiling, and sang, "La La La Fa Fa."

Always happy to hear the older woman's ravishing voice, Harry said, "Is that goodbye?"

"No, it's 88. Well. Two 8's. That's a shortcut for hugs and kisses. We just sang to one another, 'hugs and kisses.' "

"Numbers?"

"It's so easy and saves time. For instance, 73 is 'best regards,' and 33 is 'love sealed with friendship.' "

Harry brightened. "How do you say 'I love you'?"

Miranda laughed. "That's 143."

"That's quite something. Who would have thought of numbers for emotions."

"Back when so many operators used Morse code, numbers were easier than words. At least I think they were . . . are. Then it became a way of doing things, so even though we aren't pressing a Morse code key, we use the shorthand. Speaking or singing."

"So you could say 88?"

"Sure. We like singing it, using the code for numbers. Think how important this was in World War I and World War II." She stopped a moment. "Actually, the telegraph was used in 1861 through 1865 by both sides. The problem is, it's easy to intercept."

"Where did you learn all this?" Harry looked at her old work-mate with new eyes.

"I was a child during World War II, but wide awake for the Korean War. I became interested in communications, I suppose because the only news we received was by newspaper. I wanted more."

"Did you get it?"

"I did. Of course, one had to be careful. Even then our government was watchful." She took a deep breath. "I understand that military information needs to be carefully presented, but I wanted more. And I wanted it fast."

"Anyone ever come knocking on your door?"

"No."

"Well, what about other languages. Can the Japanese use Morse code?"

"Again, I was too young during World War II, but I know we broke their code. They had it tied to basic symbols, which are letters in a way. I'm not sure, but Larry . . . he was so smart . . . told me the British broke their code, and then we did."

"My grandfather?"

"Your grandfather was a highly intelligent man. I wonder if we will ever know what he really did besides operating the radio and telegraph on the destroyer. His mind was so quick."

"I had no idea." Then Harry corrected herself. "I mean, I knew G-Pop was smart, but I had no idea about something like this." She hesitated, then added, "But I can understand why numbers could substitute for emotions as well as information. Quick. One probably doesn't have a lot of time in war."

"He, as well as any other man I knew via survivors who served in the wars, they all say the same thing. You are ready to perish of boredom then the battle comes, and you may well perish, period. Everything is happening at once."

"Your choir, do they know all this stuff?"

"Everyone knows numbers. We all sang 88. And remember, we're all long in the tooth now." Miranda laughed. "When we were children, there were still survivors from the war of 1861 and the Spanish-American War. They were probably as old as I am now, but they seemed so old. Well, I am old, I guess. Lots were from World War I. And the boys from World War II, when I was in my twenties, they were in their thirties. The officers were older, usually. Men that served in that war were born in the teens or twenties. I was born in 1939, as World War II began." She sang "La La La Fa Fa."

Harry knew her well, so she sang it back to her.

"See, you're getting it."

"I have a lot to learn."

"We all do, Harry. We all do. But keep reading your books. Drop by Tally's perhaps more often until you can master this technology. I'll be your mentor. In ham talk, I'm your Elmer."

Harry laughed. "Okay, Elmer."

"Okay. You can say 'FB.' "

"FB?"

" 'Fine Business.' As I said, drop by Tally's more often. Let her show you things."

"Miranda, do you go out there?" Harry asked.

"Not when the roads are bad. I can still drive, thankfully. My eyes are good. My reflexes are slower, not awful but slower. Still, I'm not taking chances. I want to be here as long as the good Lord allows."

"Me too."

"Harry, you're not wet behind the ears; you're still young."

"Speaking of young, how about that page getting killed on the road? Susan said people are taking their kids out of serving. As he had cocaine and fentanyl in his system. The parents are frightened."

"I would be, too." Miranda took a breath. "There's so much excitement being in the middle of things."

"No drugs when I was in school. Well, weed, but that was it," Harry remarked.

"Obviously, none for me. If you smoked a cigarette, you were racy. The boys would drink sometimes on weekends. I'd hear about it. I don't understand what is happening to our young people."

"I kind of do and I kind of don't. Seems to me they have no purpose, except for some who want to be famous but have no mastery over anything. They just want to be famous."

"Well . . ." Miranda thought for a bit. "The Gabors. They were famous. Well, let me amend that, they could act and they certainly were beautiful, but they did court fame."

"Maybe they were more direct about it. You know I read somewhere that they escaped Hungary, their mother leading them out. They were Jewish. They never discussed it."

"That I do understand," Miranda said with feeling.

"Thanks for letting me sit in. I am learning slowly. Very slowly. Sort of like a centipede who can't decide what foot to pick up."

Miranda laughed. "You'll be fine. Tell Fair I hope he is well. Susan, before I forget, she's spending time in Richmond?"

"More than usual. Ned can't afford a dedicated secretary, a person just for politics. Hope I'm saying this correctly. Anyway, his secretary in the law office serves more than him. He can't take her away. Susan goes down to help. If he runs again, I think he'll find a way to have a secretary for his representative duties."

"I hope so. Yet Susan does know a lot about how things work down there. She must be so useful."

"She is. Thanks again, Miranda. I have to go and bring the horses in before it's dark." Harry got up, leaned down, and kissed her friend on the cheek. "You're good to me."

"Oh, come now." Miranda smiled broadly. "Tell Susan to be careful. Ned too. Something's not right in Richmond."

25

"Did you look at this?" Aidan strode into Ned's office, holding a piece of paper in front of him.

"No." Ned pointed to a pile of papers at his desk corner. "Not yet."

"This is making the rounds of the GOP. No one has presented it as a bill yet, but they will. It's a proposal for drug testing for pages. Daily."

"Oh, come on." Ned rifled his pile to find it, but Aidan handed him the paper in his hand.

Ned carefully read it.

"Well?"

He looked up at Aidan. "It won't work, but it might pass." He motioned for Aidan to sit down and rose from his desk to sit in the chair next to him.

"If we're going to have drug tests, then we'd better have alcohol tests, too."

Ned smiled. "Given the average age of delegates and state senators, that's a more prevalent failing than drugs. Then again, we
don't know how many prescription drugs people are on."

"Oh, any one of us can get a doctor to write a covering prescription."

"Really? You think so?"

"Sure."

Ned folded his hands, said, "I think we can get a prescription
faster than the average person, but I'm not sure we can get an illegal one."

"It doesn't have to be illegal," Aidan answered. "It can be an
opioid painkiller, a mood elevator. When you again look at the
average age of who is in here, it's not such a far-fetched idea."

"If an eighty-year-old delegate takes an illegal painkiller, why is
it of interest? Anything that helps someone do their job. Eighty, I
wouldn't give a fig. Thirty-five, yes, I might. You can get hooked
for the rest of your life. How much life is left at eighty?"

Aidan couldn't help but smile. "For some of these guys, quite a
lot, I think."

They both laughed.

"Maybe they're pickled. Didn't the Navy pickle Nelson to get
him back home?"

Aidan snorted, then really laughed. "Nelson was a genius aside
from being wildly brave. Our pickled people don't qualify."

"Ah, but Aidan, they think they do, doesn't matter the party.
And you know, those guys who have hung on for decades are
special, even if so often they're obstructionists. They slow us
down. But sometimes we need it."

"If this thing passes, we'll all be slowed down."

"What you read to me is focused on pages."

Aidan nodded. "Which is exactly why we have to make the
modification I suggested."

"I'm not so sure the party will back you on that."

"If I bring it up on the floor, then they have to speak on the floor or to the press, because they will all be pressed for comments."

"They will." Ned patted his thigh, a moment of nerves. "If this focuses only on the pages, isn't it age discrimination?"

"Since we are threatened with a suit regarding Reid's death, I guarantee you any lawyer will be praying for an excuse to create more business, so to speak. Age discrimination it is. Hmm." Thinking, Aidan rose and walked around the room, finally returning to his seat, where he dropped like a stone. "So what do we do?"

"We resist and say it is age discrimination."

"We'll be accused of not taking drugs seriously."

"Let them have their moment." Ned was sly when he had to be. "Then we come back with a compromise ensuring everyone's safety. Hence everyone is tested. Off the hook, plus we look good."

"What makes you think the party will go for it?"

"Some will. Some won't. But most will when we put forward the compromise."

"Which is?"

"What we've talked about in general. We need testing for drugs and for alcohol. All drugs, not just illegal ones. Here's the provision that makes us look good. Any drug legally prescribed is not made public, as it involves a delegate's health. We must trust if someone is currently facing a critical illness, they will tell us. Think about that. We've got everyone over a barrel because you know a reporter, even a blog person, will root out the legal drugs a delegate is taking."

"It won't pass."

"Of course it won't, but we'll have demonstrated that we are concerned and thoughtful about this. Which I am, and I assume you are. But if this is going to be thrown in our faces, best you and I come up with something. Let those of our party oppose, since the original idea did come from the Republicans, and rejoice that it's now a Republican problem. Not ours. They can accuse you and me of overreach, but for a good cause. We did our best to submit to the will of the majority. How good is that?"

Aidan crossed his arms over his chest. "Pretty good. You were understudying Governor Holloway."

"No, I truly wasn't. I admired him. He repented of his mistakes, which was honorable. The good he did Virginia in attracting business, keeping taxes low, trying to provide services, remember he was governor over forty years ago, was farsighted. He saw that we would grow. I didn't decide to run for office until last term."

"Why did you?"

"Disgust. I became so disgusted with the paralysis and posturing that I thought, 'I'm going in there to see what I can do. If I can improve things, even in a small way, I'll keep at it. If not, I'll leave.'"

Aidan tapped the arm of the chair. "You'd make a good governor."

"I don't want to be governor. I just want us to work together on what we can, and I do think we are going to have to accept higher taxes. We have twice the people in this state as there were when I was born. Some of them can't take care of themselves. With more people, we need more roads, more schools, you name it. All of it costs money to build."

"That's Amanda's argument about taxes. Bring in more business with lowered taxes and you will have more money."

"I don't know." Ned raised his eyebrows. "We have statistics that can prove either approach. What was it Disraeli said? 'There are lies, damned lies, and statistics.'"

"Some say Mark Twain, others Disraeli. Whoever said it, it's the truth." Aidan half smiled.

"Back to this. When do you think they'll present these ideas as a bill?"

"Soon. No later than the end of the week. The current gossip about Ellis's running away will feed drug stories, because it's easy. No one has proved a thing. And he's still missing. As he was the

cameraman for streaming, anyone can always say film people, ar-
tistic people, are prone to this."

"Oh, Aidan, that excuse is long gone. It's everybody."

"Well, if I'm asked for an interview, that's my story."

At the other end of the hall, Amanda was reading the same page.
"This isn't going to do a bit of good, but it looks as though we are
taking charge."

Lucas watched her read. "You have to promote this."

"Well, I have to vote for it, but I don't necessarily have to promote it."

"I think the press will come to you first. Are drugs rampant?
After all, you were on TV. You'll be asked what you saw when you
worked before the camera."

"The red light," she said.

"Don't be a smart-ass."

"Just with you. Of course I won't say that. I'll say drugs are
everywhere but I don't know if anyone here was taking any. I
never saw signs of coke or speed, or whatever the latest combina-
tion is. Speedballs."

"Those can kill you."

"Lucas, it can all kill you, but for some people they feel great;
they can think better until they finally go off the rails."

"I remember reading about Hamilton Jordan, Carter's chief of
staff, and Jody Powell, his press secretary, being accused of taking
cocaine." Lucas constantly read about mid-to-late twentieth-
century history.

Amanda threw up her hands. "You know that was a lie."

"Why?"

"If they'd been taking cocaine, they would have made better
decisions."

Lucas whooped. "You can be wicked. Of course you won't say

anything like that, but who would ask? We weren't even born then."

"I was toddling. Anyway, I will support this. Don't have much choice. And the party will get it out there tomorrow or next day. I guess our whip will present it as a bill. Maybe not. Maybe this should be someone from a difficult district in Richmond."

"Urban. Best chance. Most drug deaths."

"Gruesome."

"It is. The media feeds off of it."

"I've been thinking about a bill that will lower taxes, not a promise for the future but right now, and along with that will be a housing commitment. I've been investigating those tiny houses. We could put them up for about the same amount of money as hiring snow removal people. Obviously, you get the figures and we can jig them if we need to do so." She grimaced. "All this takes me away from the issues I find most important. I have no idea how to stop drugs."

"Don't present anything that way. You're having enough trouble with Aidan."

"Well . . ."

"Listen to me, Amanda."

"All right. All right." She gave him her usual comeback: "What else do I need to take a position on?"

"It's more what you don't need to take a position on. Follow the party line on most of the cultural issues. You can vote against something in the chamber that you feel strongly about, but you don't need to speak of it. You'll be asked after the session is over, but that will be fairly easy since whoever wins will get the bulk of the questions. All those dreary celebrations."

She picked up her wooden ruler, lightly rapping her other palm with it. "Where I'm vulnerable is the anti-trans stuff. I can't vote for it. You're my best friend."

Touched, he leaned toward her. "I appreciate that. Be careful. Right now it's an issue no one can win or make sensible."

"We have a few of those. What I'm thinking is, be silent on the hot-button issues, vote with the party except for on one or two. When I'm ready to run for governor, which won't be for at least four years, maybe more, many of those issues will have resolved themselves. I can say I learned from the process. Gets me off the nutcase hook."

"There have been so many nutcases in politics over the centuries. We never lack for them, but now we have non-stop media under no obligation to tell the truth. The days of objectivity, as best as a paper could do it, are long gone. The electronic media celebrates its lying by saying they aren't really news channels but entertainment."

She smacked her hand a bit harder with the ruler. "I got out in time."

"You did."

She glanced at the clock. "I need to go over to Chesterfield County."

"The composting lawsuit?"

"Yes. All those people who bought $400,000 to $600,000 homes in that subdivision . . . quiet, pretty . . . are furious about the natural composting business set to go into the thirty acres next to them. The county code doesn't forbid it, so something needs to crack this open. I'm in favor of the landowners. Granted, there are a lot of voters there and only three men who own Nature's Solution Composting. But even without the numbers, I'll do what I can. You build your dream home and spend your supposedly best years smelling manure. And the contractors want to build more subdivisions. So there you go."

"Turkey poop is the worst."

"And how do you know that?"

"Well, I don't, but that's what I've been told."

"Lucas, I could test that. I could dump some on Aidan's back lawn. You know, a scientific experiment."

He shook his head and laughed. "Go on. You'll be late."

Down the hall she walked, click click click. Then slowed in front of Aidan's office, his door open per usual. She executed a tap dance in her Louboutins. She came down with loud, long clicks, then she snapped her fingers like a Spanish dancer, busier taps. He looked up. She busted a few more moves, then blew him a kiss.

She sang the whole way to her car.

26

"She'll go blind." Mrs. Murphy watched as her human peered at the old typewriter in Ned's office in the Pocahontas Building.

Pewter, enthralled by the activity, lifted a paw. "She shouldn't take on jobs she can't do."

"She can't say no to Susan, plus she can do it. The lighting in here just isn't so good."

The small cubbyhole off Ned's main office suffered low lighting.

"Humans have bad eyes, especially in low light. Can't see in the dark." Pewter spoke the obvious.

"They hunt during daytime. So they can only see in the daylight. I guess they can see some things at night, but we're all animals designed for whatever it is we eat. Actually, that's an awful thought." Mrs. Murphy laughed.

"I prefer steak tartar. I told Tucker mouse tartar, and she was in such a snit. But raw meat is the best unless it's meat lightly cooked. That's okay." Pewter indulged in a moment of culinary reverie. "What are they doing?"

Harry, now standing next to Susan, who was sitting at a desktop computer, pointed to a line on the paper in her hand. "I've studied the numbers. They don't add up."

Susan took the page from her hand. "Put it down as written, then initial it so Ned knows you see the gap. He'll have to make up his mind about that."

"How can someone introduce a bill like this. Shouldn't they have accurate figures?"

"Yes." Susan swiveled to face Harry. "You can't predict accurate figures for the future. You can only give accurate figures for today."

"I understand that, but then why isn't there a graph to illustrate the value of money for, say, the last few years? Couldn't people then make an educated guess?"

"Up to a point. Here's what anyone in government soon learns: The one figure you can accurately foretell is that few costs will ever go down. So what's the chance of, say, a five percent rise in steel for the year? It might go down. But the bill is for the cost of a new government building, and if steel goes down, lumber may go way up. See what I mean?"

"I do." Harry returned to her typewriter and sighed. "Susan, I could never do this. I break out in a sweat trying to predict the next season's farming costs."

"Fortunately, you don't have to do this. As I told you, Ned needs to read and respond to other delegates' proposals, bills. Most want feedback. A few don't. Those just want to ram their ideas down our throat. A close reading unnerves them, but for the most part his colleagues appreciate a response. He is so overloaded, you and I need to trim it down."

"No, you need to trim it down. I'm typing up your condensation. Kind of like a cheat sheet."

"Harry, think of this as like those condensed versions of books we had to read in high school. I can still remember my *Silas Marner*. Mr. Janes saw the color of the Cliffs Notes booklet, yellow with black stripes. Gave me a detention for that!"

"I remember. No detention here. Poor Ned. Some of these are complicated. Anything wherein private property needs to be bought, that's complicated, but it makes sense for government offices to be close together. Doesn't do any good in New Kent County though." She sat back down.

"Do Ned a favor. If you've got a hot-button issue, say anything with drag queens, note if the sponsor has an, uh, entertainer in the family. It's in the paperwork."

"Okay. Does it make the sponsor more knowledgeable?"

"I think it does. They'll certainly fight harder."

"Okay." Harry returned to typing.

Susan heard a knock on the door frame, then Ned say, "Come in."

Amanda stepped in. "Heard your wife and her best friend are here being temporary secretaries. Thought I'd say hello, if you don't mind."

"Of course not." He pointed to the side room.

Amanda stuck her head in. "Hello, ladies."

"Amanda, come on in. You're wearing the jacket you bought at Horse Country. Looks terrific."

"Does," Harry echoed Susan, both now standing.

"There . . . well, here's a chair. Amanda, take a seat. I could use a stretch," Susan offered.

Ned walked into the room carrying a folding chair that was kept in the closet. "Here you go. It's more comfortable than it looks."

"Oh, thank you." Amanda sank into the surprisingly comfortable chair. "Cats."

"Don't rat me out." Susan scrunched down a little, as if to hide.

"It isn't her, it's me," Harry confessed.

"We are the only animals here. You all need serious help," Pewter bragged.

"And who is this?" Amanda ran her finger over Pewter's head as the gray cat rattled on.

"Pewter. She is opinionated." Harry smiled. "And this is Mrs. Murphy, who almost always figures out things before I do."

"Hello," Mrs. Murphy quietly greeted Amanda, who then petted her.

"Do you know if they're Republicans or Democrats?" Amanda laughed.

"I suspect they belong to their own party," Harry offered. "Smart cats."

Amanda smiled. "If we had pets here, I think we would have known about drugs earlier. Really, I do. Cats and dogs can smell things we can't. The more I think about what has happened, the more I think this has been going on for a long time."

Susan tilted her head to one side. "Me too. My shock was that it surfaced. Although I never thought it would be used by any elected official."

"Susan, why is this job different from others? All careers choke with stress, impossible deadlines, those people who would sell their mother down the river for career advancement. Sure, some people are good and decent, but most are looking out for themselves. Amanda's right. This has been going on for a long time."

Amanda took a deep breath. "Such a sorrowful assessment."

"My frustration is getting the better of me. I don't know what to think." Susan looked momentarily hopeless.

Leaning forward, voice lower, Amanda said, "Me too. It's not like I expected to be welcomed with open arms once elected. But I thought it would be easier to get legislation passed. Easier to talk about things. Denial is what really gets me. There's so much denial about drugs."

"Is," Susan agreed. "Then again, if I make a mistake, I'm not grilled on camera, torn apart in the papers, denounced on everyone's cellphone. Denial makes a kind of sense."

A long, long sigh followed from Amanda. "There is that."

"*I should run Virginia. Catnip every day. Fresh tuna,*" Pewter said.

"*What about the dogs?*" Mrs. Murphy's whiskers swept forward. "*Kibble.*"

"*Kibble and greenies. That's enough,*" Pewter compromised.

"They're chatty."

"Amanda, it comes and goes," Harry explained. "Sometimes I wish I knew what they were saying, sometimes not."

"Yes." Amanda drew out the word.

"Do you have dogs or cats?" Harry asked.

"Two wire-haired dachshunds. Ron, my husband, says if we ever part, he gets the dogs. He figures that will keep us together." She laughed. "I'd stay with him anyway."

They all laughed.

"That's a pile of papers, Susan," Amanda noted.

"Trying to condense each bill proposal into a sentence. Really."

Amanda thought about that. "You know I've always heard it said, if you're selling or pitching a film idea in Hollywood, reduce it to one sentence. Maybe that's not a bad idea. We complicate things."

"We do. But then again, you and my husband are standing before the entire state. You have to try to have some facts."

"Indeed we do. We know the residents of each county. We know the income averages. We know the average cost of a home. We know the condition of the schools and their graduation rates. We know the educational average of the citizens. We know the spread of professions. Hard facts for each county, which can be added up for our state. And . . ." she paused dramatically, "it's still not enough."

"What do you mean?" Harry was intrigued.

"We know how many children our citizens have. At least, the children that are born. We don't know how many women are pregnant. And we know little about parental hopes for those children. That's not a hard fact. It's those things that bring me up short, and it's where I think both our parties fail."

"I never thought of that," Harry confessed.

"Me neither," Susan echoed her best friend.

"Those aren't facts, but they drive people." Amanda tapped the crystal on her Schaffhausen watch. "I'd better get going. Having such a good time with you . . . and the kitties, of course . . . that I almost forgot my meeting."

"Your watch is stunning. A man's watch." Harry ogled it.

"Daddy's. Also, it being a man's watch, I can read the dial more easily."

They all laughed, given they understood that, and Amanda left, thanking Ned for allowing her to invade his office.

Mrs. Murphy watched her go. "*She's not happy.*"

Pewter didn't dispute that, as she knew cats could read human emotions better than humans could. Humans hid a lot of stuff.

The fat gray cat pondered this insight, then pronounced, "*Maybe she's hungry.*"

27

Rolling the small generator along the shoveled farm paths, snow-covered but packed down, Harry took a moment for a breather. She filled the generator up from the two huge, buried gas tanks by the big equipment shed. The generator used regular gas, cheaper than diesel. As a farmer, she could fill the huge, buried tanks put in by her father at a bit cheaper rate than gas sold at a station. She paid attention to the tanks, which had fortunately held up, no leaks, from the day they were installed when she was a child. The hand pump tested her, especially on a cold day, but she managed. Picking up the long generator handle, she pulled the yellow piece to the back side of the barn. Stopping behind the wash stall, she caught her breath. A snowflake fell on her nose. Looking up at the darkening sky, she grumbled. She carefully slid the cord under the window at the back of the wash stall, which she had opened a crack from the inside. The generator was under the generous overhang, so the worst of whatever weather was approaching wouldn't bury it. As the generator was a gas engine, it needed to be outside due to fumes. Opening the big doors a crack, Harry squeezed in, pulled the cord to an outlet high in the wash-stall wall. She cut the fuse box. She walked outside again, pulled the cord. The generator started right up. Good. Turned it off. She hoped the power wouldn't go out in the dead of night, because if it did, she'd need to come out, kill the fuse box, then start up the generator. No point running it all night as long as there was power. The last thing she ever wanted to face were burst pipes. Plumbing and electrical work cost way too much. She flicked the fuse box back on.

Back in the wash stall, she checked the outlet again, made sure the pieces of insulation were secure in the slight window opening. No cold would get in if she could help it. She made a note to cut a small square in the window frame so in the future she could put the cord through it without lifting up the window. She could stuff a tiny bit of insulation in that opening. Less wind. Finally, in the tack room, she fired up the propane stove. At her desk, the room warming, she checked her three weather apps on the computer. Were there thirty weather apps, she would have each one.

"All day and all night." She scrolled to other apps.

They were in agreement, although not as to when the snow would start or stop. A bark at the big barn doors drew her away.

She opened the big doors.

"Why did you leave me inside?" Tucker huffed.

"Come on, little friend. Guess the others are luxuriating in the kitchen."

"You should never be alone," Tucker forcefully barked.

Pirate, too big to get through the animal doors, the first one in the kitchen, the second in the door in the porch, languished in the house. He wasn't happy.

Sitting back down, Harry checked the news.

Tucker, at her side, listened as Harry gabbled on. Her brown eyes flickered with interest according to Harry's tone.

"Well, gas prices are dropping. Now, mind you, Tucker, they are down about fifteen cents a gallon. Good, but they are still sixty percent above where they were this time last year. Does our government think we don't notice? Ugh. Let me repeat that, ugh."

"You're right."

She leaned over to pet the sleek head, that wonderful corgi fur. "I've prepared everything in case this storm turns out to be bad, worse than just some snow. I say six inches. The news reports say four to six, depending on where you are. Well, given we're next to the mountains, maybe six for sure. Tucker, I hope I've got everything right. The house generator is hooked up. 'Course, we've got two fireplaces there, so we can keep things warm, turn on the generator when we go to sleep. I'm trying to keep costs down; they always spike in the cold. I hate bills."

"I know you do. You complain all the time, Mom."

"What the hell?" Harry read the news flash across the top of the screen.

She tapped the banner on the left. The story filled the screen. She eagerly read it. Picked up the phone, waited a minute. "Susan."

"I just saw it. Ned thought this would be introduced today."

"Testing for drugs. Pages. Is it . . . wait, let me start again, will it do any good?"

"Testing is done in small and big companies. I guess it works, but this is state government."

"Don't some drugs stay in your system? Even after twenty-four hours?"

"Depends on the drugs, but yes." Susan sounded tired. "There will be uproar. But here's what's fun: Aidan is going to say tests are a great idea, but everyone should be tested, including the delegates."

Harry yelped with glee. "Ha."

"That's what I say. At any rate, this will tie everyone up for weeks. Each angle will need to be covered. Interviews with corporations that do random testing. Sports teams' random testing for steroids. Even with that, nothing will happen. That's my prediction. Ned believes something heavily modified will be cobbled together from both parties so they look as though they are taking the drug problem seriously."

"How about attaching it to mental health? You know, no one takes drugs unless they are miserable. Their mother was mean." She giggled, because when in doubt, blame mothers.

"As a mother, I understand only too well."

"Apart from this drama, what are you doing?"

"I hurried to Harris Teeter this morning to buy eggs, milk, and coffee. Almost out. The place was packed. I called Ned and begged him to get home. Everyone else will be leaving the chambers, too."

"If he leaves now, it shouldn't be such a bad drive. I hooked up the small generator for the barn."

"I don't know if it will be that bad, but it never hurts to be ready."

"I called Aunt Tally this morning to see if she needed anything. Says she doesn't. If nothing else, I can organize my sock drawer if the snow keeps me in."

"How exciting."

"I have all these orphan socks."

"You have the horses to feed. Bring some in. Move them around, if needs be. Save the socks for spring cleaning."

"Yes, but if I do that, I'll have to pay bills today."

"You have to pay them anyway."

"Susan, that doesn't mean I can't drag it out as long as possible."

"If I didn't know you since infancy, I would think you're a bit touched."

"Right," came the sarcastic reply. "Hey, no sign of Ellis Barfield?"

"No."

"What drove him to run? Think, Susan. Drugs are too easy. They can be blamed for everything. He loans his car to a page, who was then killed in a snowy car accident. The page had a small drug bottle. Maybe he had nothing to do with drugs. Maybe that was a plant in Reid's cuff. No hard facts. Everything is an assumption. I mean, yes, there were drugs in the kid's system, but everything beyond that is conjecture."

Susan turned this over in her mind. "You're right, but it somewhat makes sense."

"Sure it does, but that doesn't mean it's true. Is there one day we don't hear or read a story about a famous person dead . . . coke, maybe heroin or fentanyl, found in their blood? Or gang kids. Either shot or drugged out. Non-stop."

"It is non-stop, Harry."

"I don't mean to sound like I'm taking it lightly, but Susan, if you think about this, you'll see what I'm saying. It's too easy."

"Whatever could it be, then?"

"I have no idea. Not one."

"If it's not drugs, then whatever is wrong in Richmond is still in place. I don't quite know how to regard this or explain it."

"What frightens me, Susan, is when we do get an inkling, it may be too late."

28

Lucas liked the snow. The offices were quieter, as some people stayed home. He could concentrate with fewer interruptions. He punched numbers from a paper in front of him onto a small calculator. A chunk of money had been withdrawn from Amanda's reelection fund, and he didn't know for what purpose. She had forgotten or neglected to tell him. One of his tasks was to check the books.

He ran his hand over his upper cheek. A light stubble informed him he hadn't done the best job shaving this morning.

Amanda walked into the office, and he called from his cubbyhole, "Tough drive?"

"They're slow clearing the roads." She stuck her head in his office. "How about you?"

"I'm in The Fan. Close. You have to come in from the suburbs. Hardly anyone is here." He cited a historic district in downtown Richmond.

"I noticed that. A couple of inches is all it takes."

"Makes me think about Ned's proposal."

"And Aidan's." She remembered she hadn't taken off her rubber snow boots, which were dripping on the floor. "Damn."

"Don't worry about it. I'll get it."

"Thanks." She walked to her office closet, removed the boots. She couldn't wear heels in snow boots. She was in flats, but had carried a small leather bag of her famous shoes. If she was called out, she'd put on those signature heels. At her desk she counted four piles of papers, the most pressing being closest on her right. Sighing, she pulled the pile over, flipping through each page.

Lucas appeared in the doorway between the spaces; kneeling down he wiped up the slush with an old towel. He was the organized type, keeping a small stash of towels for cleaning emergencies. Paper towels wouldn't do the job. He also had a small bottle of liquid wax, a bit of lemon in it, which he would run over Amanda's desk. He liked the scent.

"You missed your calling." Amanda put a paper down.

"What? I should have been a butler?"

"No. You should have opened a cleaning service. Who has the time to clean anymore?"

"I'll bear that in mind when you fire me." He wiped harder.

"Why? What did you do wrong?" She crumpled the paper, tossing it in her large wastebasket under the desk.

"Nothing. I'm perfect. But in case you have a mood," he teased her.

"Are you casting aspersions on women's emotions? Are you telling me I'm moody?"

"No. Actually, you're not, but if you lose your temper again, how do I know it won't be at me?"

"Nah." She reached down and pulled out the paper, smoothed it. "I'm reviewing this drug-testing stuff. I shouldn't just throw it in the bin." She read the paper again. "Did you read this note from our party chair?"

"Did."

"And?"

"You know me. Had to do some research. Here's what made me laugh. One in twenty workers in America is high on marijuana. The food preparation business, waiting on tables, is the highest, but others are not far behind. Take your pick. Insurance. Car sales."

"Where did you read that?"

"'Daily Mail' had a graph."

"I assume there were no stats for government workers?"

"You assume correctly. Same for teachers. That will change. Teachers, I mean."

"The teachers union will squelch it," Amanda stated with finality.

"Amanda, I don't think much of this can be pushed under the rug anymore. People, those precious voters upon whom we depend, are disgusted. This testing the pages isn't going the way the party thinks it will go."

"You mean the other party's comeback?"

"I do. That's going to be hard to refute. What's good for the goose is good for the gander."

"Well, it's all optics."

"Yes. And the optics are terrible. You shut up. If the party votes against it, you take a pass. Don't vote. Yes, you'll get your knuckles rapped, the press will notice, but all you have to say is you don't know how this could work, especially for prescription drugs, and you feel you don't know enough to make an informed decision."

She folded her hands. "They can have my blood right now. I take nothing. Not even sleeping pills."

"You never did. But you can't counter the party. This will be a big, public fight, most especially since nothing has been resolved. There isn't even a suspect if Reid really was set up, and as for Ellis, where is he? His apartment has been searched. Not much was found, except for Ball jars instead of glasses. And a list of shout-outs to small businesses."

"You know, this is getting grim."

"Grim and highly political. Whatever happens here will make national news."

Slipping her feet out of her flats, she rubbed them together. "This is a distraction from the budget."

"You can't say that. A missing person, fentanyl, grieving parents. This is going to take over. It's emotional. The budget is dull to most people until they get a new tax bill, and then it's too late."

Frowning, she got up, padded to the closet. "Hmm. Thought I had some old towels in here."

"I have most of them."

"Bring me a big one; heavy, if you have one. My feet are cold. Want to put the towel over them. Nylons do not keep your feet warm."

He went to his closet, pulled out a slightly torn but heavy towel, and returned to her. "Sit like you want to sit."

"Huh?"

"I'll wrap this over your feet."

"Oh, thanks. Sometimes I take a chill."

"Think we all do in this weather."

She looked up at him, then stroked his left cheek. "You missed a spot."

"I know. My beard doesn't grow in the same direction. I have to shave down, shave up, shave across my face. The chin is the worst. That's why I have a beard on my chin. Then I wash the shaving cream off, dry my face, and put on moisturizer because my face burns. One has shaving rituals."

"Ah. The trials of masculinity," she tweaked him.

"You have no idea how I suffer." He laughed. "Back to the drug testing. Say nothing."

"I can stick to needing to do more research. That's safe, and I do. It's not a subject for which I have had much interest. Same with alcohol. If you want to destroy your life, that's your business."

"But they destroy other people, most especially if they're behind the wheel of a car."

She sighed. "I know. On the other hand, Lucas, I suspect state-mandated compassion. This will reek of it before it's all done."

"Just shut up. Allow those who need to be morally superior their preening. The truth is, there is no answer. But if people vote for tests . . . and I have a hunch that after one helluva fight, they will . . . they can live with the results, which will be that this is not a group who will endanger people by drink or drugs. Perhaps one or two, but as a group, do they need to be monitored? No."

"After a session they do. A couple of our esteemed colleagues hit up the bars, including their own, before going home."

"That's true for everywhere in the world, I guess. Oh, maybe not Saudi Arabia." He shrugged. "Seems to me the human animal has a propensity for self-destruction. And that includes opening your mouth at the wrong time."

"Point taken."

He looked at her feet under the desk. "Warmer?"

"Yes, thank you."

"Before I forget, you withdrew fifty thousand from your re-election account, but you forgot to tell me."

"I did. I was going to put out full-page ads in the papers, as well as a brief ad for the three networks. I changed my mind. I'll put the money back."

"Ads for what?"

"Calling on women to support women. We need to be heard. That sort of thing. Not coming from the party, but from me. Given the shift concerning drug testing, I decided now's the wrong time."

"When you're up for reelection next year, that's a good time."

"I don't think so, Lucas. I think I need to firmly establish my-self before the election, because then I'll be accused of pandering. I'll wait. Drugs really do sweep other issues off the table." She paused. "And I guarantee you, Aidan Harkness will use the drug issue to make himself look ever so wonderful."

Lucas exhaled from his nostrils. "Yes. But don't bite." Then he added, "Given what's going on, don't bite anything you aren't sure about. I doubt anyone will put drugs in your food or smash a drug-soaked rag under your nose, but I would be careful. Until we really know what this is about, some care is in order. It may be bad luck. The wrong partying. The wrong toot. Let's hope that's it, but we don't know."

"Oh, Lucas, this can't be politically motivated."

"Maybe not, but there are many reasons to kill. Love. Money. Revenge. Hate. Even religious fervor."

"I don't know."

"More people have died over religious differences in history than just about anything else."

"It was used to cover the lust for territory and power. That I believe, but I will exercise some caution." She rubbed her temple for a moment. "I thought today would be a good day to work. I didn't consider self-preservation."

Shoveling snow, Harry worked up a sweat. She knew Big Mim would see to the road being plowed, but she thought she could clear snow around the house for Aunt Tally. Whoever would be doing the plowing might not think of that. The cats were in the truck. The dogs followed her as she scooped up the snow. Being in shape didn't make the job more appealing, but it wasn't difficult. As she tossed another load of snow, heavy, to the side, she did think of all those people who would be suffering heart attacks.

Reaching the back door, she cleaned off the steps then knelt down to brush the snow to make sure no ice lurked underneath. She carefully wedged the flat shovel blade under the packed snow, lifting it up in sections once she dug off the top snow. Wiggling that blade took effort, but she finally reached the wooden surface underneath.

Twenty minutes later, the steps and small landing were safe. Kneeling down again, she brushed off bits, chunks.

Returning to the truck, she opened the door, lifting out Mrs. Murphy and Pewter. Then she picked up the photo of her grandfather.

"Come on."

Pewter picked up each paw, shaking it as she followed.

Tucker and Pirate sat at the back door as Mrs. Murphy walked a few paces in front of Harry. Once inside the back door, in the small space for shoes, coats, lots of straw baskets, Harry again knelt down, this time to wipe off each animal's paws with an old bandana she'd stuffed in her pants pocket.

"There."

Hearing a voice, Teresa reached the door leading into the hall. She opened it. Everyone walked in.

"She's in the living room." Teresa noticed the clean paws. "Bitsy is asleep in there. She can't hear too well, as you know, and I only heard you when you were speaking to the animals. Hope my ears aren't going on me."

"I called Aunt Tally. Don't want to make more work for you."

"She told me. Come along."

The group walked to the living room, where Aunt Tally beamed up at Harry then down at the four animals. "That dog is big."

"He is. He's sweet. I figured Bitsy needed company."

Bitsy, now awake, was thrilled for company, even the cats.

"You're right. Sit down. What do you have?" She indicated the framed picture.

Harry handed it to her. "Said I'd bring it by."

Holding the photo close to her eyes, Tally studied Larry. "Handsome. Handsome. Handsome." Then she added, "And brave. I have so few pictures of him. And I could never put them out. But seeing him at his station post brings back memories. The war took so many away from us." She put the photograph in her lap, the glass-front down.

"I'm here to tell you that I am making slow progress. Miranda showed me how numbers mean things, and she and her choir sang some. La La La Fa Fa. La La La Fa Fa."

"Never heard Morse code sung before, but that's 88. 'Hugs and kisses.'"

"Wow, Aunt Tally. You know your stuff."

The old lady smiled. "Had to."

"I'm impressed."

"Usually Larry and I could talk, but sometimes we used Morse code. We both had a receiver and a key. We called the receiver a sounder. But you never see those anymore."

"Did you ever use the shorthand numbers? Miranda told me some of them. Like 73 for 'goodbye.'"

"We did. We could say the numbers when we actually spoke on the radio. For more complicated things that we didn't want anyone to know or overhear, we used Morse code. Then came the time when the people so opposed to our romance were dying or dead. My parents' generation was going. So we eventually spoke less Morse code."

"How often did you check in with each other?"

"Usually every night. Once he married, he had less time. He loved your mother, and he did love his wife, your grandmother. He'd always wanted a family. I understood that."

"Mom loved him. I loved him."

"What else did Miranda show you?"

"Basic stuff. Really basic, like turning the radio on and off. I listened to her call in to her choir ladies. They sang together."

"Wonderful."

"I will learn the numbers first, since they're a shorthand for feelings or orders, like 92, 'deliver promptly.' "

"It's the easiest way, once you know the dots and dashes for each number and each number code, to hear it all at once. Don't sit there and write out what you are hearing. How did you hear 88?"

"They all sang it as 'goodbye.' Every single person sang 88."

"Could you hear it as one word . . . well, two numbers?"

"I could. Then Miranda made me sing it. Of course, as short-cuts, this will be easier than mastering Morse code."

"It never hurts to learn Morse code, but you don't have to do it. Recognizing the shortcuts is a big help. You can speak to me in numbers as well as words. No one cares now."

"I had no idea what I was getting into."

Tally laughed. "I can see that. But you'll be glad of what you learn. I won't be the only person with whom you will be able to communicate."

Aunt Tally was right.

29

The office being blissfully quiet allowed Lucas to bang out letters to constituents. He'd type them up, Amanda would sign them later. They determined the contents beforehand. She felt direct communication, especially a written letter that a voter could show to friends, proved more potent than emails. If someone made even a small contribution, they received a signed thank-you. Those who had written in with ideas about the budget or her mistreatment by Aidan also received a response, not a canned one but a reply showing a close reading of their letter. She also wrote to those who attacked her. She thanked them for their time on the issue although she didn't agree. She ended those letters with "That's what makes a horse race."

Lucas's line rang, the button lit up.

"Delegate Fields's office."

"Mr. Dennison, it's Keisha."

"Hello. We miss you."

"I wish I were there. Richmond is a lot more exciting than Staunton."

"I'll bet if you find someone to work with in city government or Augusta County, you'll find it can be exciting. And sooner or later, you'll wind up in Richmond, maybe as an elected official from Augusta County."

"I hope so." She took a deep breath. "Mr. Dennison, I thought of something. On the day Reid and I were going to have lunch, he said he had something to tell me and he would do that at lunch."

"Yes, I remember you saying that."

"He didn't tell me or give a hint. But I've thought about it. I think he *did* give me a hint. He told me he had some cash. Once the weather got better, we could walk along Cary Street. We could look at stuff. He'd take me to lunch." She paused. "Reid never had much money. His folks are poor."

"I see. Did you ever meet his mother and father?"

"Once. They came to the hotel to bring him a pair of pants."

"Did you like them?"

"Yeah. I think he told them we were sort of going out. They paid attention to me."

"Did he have a nighttime job? Something on the side, maybe there's a better word than that. Kids without much income often find ways to make money. When I was young, it was shining shoes at the train station. The airport was too far away."

"He didn't say. He didn't say how much money he had either, but it must have been enough to go to a Cary Street restaurant."

"Have you told anyone else?"

"No."

"This may be nothing at all. Then again, it could be a clue of sorts. Let me think about it, Keisha. You should talk to someone in law enforcement, but let me think of who the best would be. In other words, don't talk to a local cop. Not that they aren't good at what they do, but this is a Richmond problem. Remind me where Reid is from."

"Wytheville."

"That's right. Slipped my mind. Always special when we get young people from southwestern Virginia. Give me your phone number. I'll get back to you today."

She gave him her cell number.

Lucas returned to his correspondence task. An hour later, a fatigued Amanda clicked into the office, wearing her heels, and plopped down on the small, comfortable chair.

"Do you remember working with women?"

He laughed. "I do. I still work with women. I work for you, remember?"

A sly smile lifted the corner of her mouth. "Oh now, Lucas, aren't I better than that? I mean, do I do girly stuff?"

"You do. Let me count the ways, to borrow a line from Elizabeth Barrett Browning. Shopping for clothing. Conversations with your mother, who sets you off. Should you buy a new car? Should you allow your house to be photographed? Does that laugh line look like a wrinkle? The list goes on."

She threw her shoe at him. He ducked as he walked away.

"And you're a bad shot."

"Oh, shut up." She shook her head at him. "I was never sporty."

"Okay, what's getting you wrapped around the axle now?"

"Two hours of the same argument going around and around. The Democratic women want us to make a grandiose statement concerning diversity. We are talking about women, not other dismissed groups. And the Republican women want to concentrate on parental rights, job opportunities, plus no trans women in sports. We aren't getting much done. So I suggested that we go back to what we have experienced as political people. If that differs widely, we can address the treatment of women by party. We don't have to work across the aisle. If it's similar, we can make a joint statement. We might want to compare those statements before we make them, just in case, you know?"

"Sensible."

"I really don't think we can mix in other issues. Even if, I'll use the buzz word, *oppressed* groups receive much of the same treatment. Concentrate on what happens here. If women out there . . . and some men, I hope . . . see this occurring at the state level, elected officials, maybe it will get them thinking. And the last thing I want to do is get sucked into passing legislation. Big time waster."

"Yes." He sat in the chair opposite her.

"I don't remember you thinking like this."

"Amanda, I didn't." He added, "If you mean I didn't think like a girl, I never fit in."

"You did too. You were pretty, dressed well, were outgoing, and you got into Delta Delta Delta. But, well, do you have less tolerance for women now?"

"I can't say I feel much different. I don't see that men and women are much different about ego, but men show it differently. It's harder for a man to publicly admit he was wrong. Women are better at it."

"I'd like to think so, but I have a headache from that meeting." She leaned back in the chair, stretched her legs out. "Got stiff."

"The correspondence is on your desk for your signature. I have about ten letters left."

"Good."

"It's quiet today, so I got a lot done. Want to ask you something."

Amanda's eyes focused on him. "What?"

"Keisha Simmons called me. She's back at school in Staunton. Misses the excitement. She said she thought of something. She and Reid were to have lunch the day he died. They had no time to talk in the morning, no surprise, but he mentioned to her that he had a little money and he'd take her to Cary Street, when they had time to go. He wanted to take her to lunch."

Amanda found that uninteresting. "And?"

"He had so little money. His parents have little money. He was selected to be a page from Wytheville thanks to his grades and winning personality."

She became more interested. "Where did he get the money, and how much?"

"She doesn't know. He died before he could tell her."

"Good Lord, you don't think he was selling drugs? Or delivering them?"

"I don't know. She wanted to know what I thought. Should she go to the authorities? I told her to sit tight, I'd think about it, but definitely don't go to anyone in Staunton. Not that they don't have good law enforcement, but this isn't their backyard."

"Right." She sat thinking, then sat up straighter. "Call her back and tell her to go to the head of the investigation in the Richmond police. And to ask not to be identified publicly."

He nodded. "This is a lot to handle for a kid. Not that Keisha isn't capable, but it's possible the department will blow off her information because she's a kid."

"Not if she says straight up she may have something of interest on the Reid Ryder case."

"I would hope whoever is in charge of this won't grill a kid or identify her publicly."

"She has to be clear about that. And it is difficult. They'll treat her okay. She's hardly a suspect." Amanda said, "You have the name and number of the officer in charge of the investigation?"

"I do."

"We have to keep out of it. Those who can't stand me or the Republican Party will drag my name into it and try to make it look as though we're hiding something. 'Why didn't we say anything or prompt Keisha earlier?' Doesn't matter that she only now thought of it. Etc."

"I know. I'll call her. May not mean a thing."

"True." She rose, pulled off her other shoe, as he had picked up the one she threw at him. "Give me that."

"Yes, Madam."

She smiled. "Takes practice. All right, let me sign these letters."

Harry, at her desk, had a booklet of Morse code before her. Even though she'd been told not to write out the dashes and dots, she had to do it. Then she'd hum the numbers. Looking at the letters, all twenty-six of them, she decided she'd get there a long time from now. She wasn't going to learn Morse code, only the numerical shortcuts. She made some progress on her ham radio studies. This was a lot harder than she'd thought but she stuck with it.

Keisha did as Lucas instructed. The officer was helpful. When he hung up, he called Reid's parents in Wytheville. He had no email address for them.

Reid's father picked up the phone. He listened as the officer explained there was a possibility that Reid had had a little money, how much anyone's guess. Maybe he'd had an odd job?

Mr. Ryder declared he didn't think his son had had time for an extra job. They worked the pages pretty hard at the statehouse. He agreed to look around though. He had given the authorities his son's bank account number shortly after Reid died.

After the call, he told his wife, who was sorting out washed clothing.

She nodded. She had found a thousand dollars in her son's left cowboy boot, which he'd left at home.

"He must have brought it home the last weekend. So maybe he meant to pick it up the weekend he would have been home when he died." She leaned against the dryer.

"We can't say anything. They'll leak it out as new details. Someone will accuse Reid of doing something with drugs, enough to earn one thousand dollars."

"I know. But I wish we knew how he came by the money." Her voice was soft.

He wiped a tear from her face with his forefinger. "He didn't sell drugs, or take them. I know he didn't." She grasped his hand as he fought back tears himself. "It's a lot of money. He would have told us if he lived."

"I think so, too."

"We need the money," he sorrowfully admitted, and she agreed with him.

30

Harry regretted offering to help Susan with paper-work. Ned's avalanche overflowed all the way out to Albemarle County. Neither woman wanted to drive back into Richmond. For one thing, the weather, more variable than usual, cast doubts on what roads were open, and even if they were, how many lanes? The last thing the two friends wanted was to churn through Route 250, two lanes all the way to Richmond. While it might prove better than I-95, if anything went wrong they'd be stranded in the car for a lot longer. On the other hand, there probably wouldn't be multiple car crashes. At least one hoped not.

Ned agreed to give his wife bills, papers, correspondence to read, sort and in the case of correspondence, answer. With Ned's permission, Susan gave half to Harry.

Tensions ratcheted up at the General Assembly. Those in Washington, D.C., also heated to higher degrees. People teetered on edge. This is not the ideal decision-making environment.

Reading through some of the stuff, Harry wondered how anything got done. Everybody believed their problem was the most important. Setting priorities upset somebody's applecart. No way around it.

"You know, Ned has to be mental to take on this stuff," she said to the animals.

"*Give out the treats.*" Pewter opened one eye from her perch on a saddle. "*Bribery works wonders.*"

"*For you,*" Tucker sassed.

"*Ha. You can be bought off with steak bone,*" the gray cat fired back.

"*I can, but how often does that happen?*" Tucker put her head on her front paws.

"*Not enough.*" Pirate surprised the others with this retort.

Mrs. Murphy laughed. "*Someone is growing up. Getting worldly.*"

The big boy turned his beautiful eyes on the tiger cat. "*I could use a steak bone.*"

"I can't believe this." Harry smacked down a letter.

They looked at her; she swirled around in her chair to observe her little family.

"This is why you should be glad you are cats and dogs." She shook the paper, then read, "'Dear Delegate Tucker, I demand that you speak to the Department of Transportation. They have put up a green stop sign near Lafayette Crossing. Green, and next to it there is a tricolor sign. For what purpose I can only guess. Stop signs are red.'" Harry saw she had everyone's attention. "'Beulah Boxter.'"

"*Maybe they ran out of red stop signs,*" Tucker said.

"*This has something to do with environmental stuff. They use green. Anyway, what's the big deal? Do you care if stop signs are red or green?*" Mrs. Murphy shifted her weight on the saddle pad.

"*No, but people are accustomed to red,*" Tucker replied.

"*A lot of humans don't like change,*" Mrs. Murphy then added. "*They think the sky is falling.*"

"*What?*" Pirate stretched his large frame before lying back down. "*Why would the sky fall?*"

Tucker told him the story about Chicken Little.

"*I have a better one than that.*" Pewter puffed up. "*There's one about a little girl who a wolf wants to eat.*"

"*Why eat a little girl?*" The Wolfhound was aghast.

"*Protein,*" Pewter said with no sympathy for Little Red Riding Hood.

"*Have you been rolling in catnip again?*" Mrs. Murphy lifted an eyebrow.

"*No. You got any?*" Pewter sounded hopeful.

As this discussion developed, Harry was oblivious to it. She picked out another letter. This one, neatly typed or run off from a computer printer, captured her attention. She reread it. No signature. At least Beulah Boxter had had the courage to put her name on her complaint. Then again, this wasn't a complaint.

Harry called Susan. "What are you doing?"

"Same thing you are," Susan answered. "Ned's under an avalanche of paperwork, plus the time pressure in the Assembly."

"Won't they extend the session?"

"They'll have to, but that's only fifteen more days. If there's a floor fight, it's more lost time. Everyone is under pressure. How you can run a state with such a short Assembly time, I don't know. Then again, running a state while paying people seventeen thousand, plus a few dollars more, is ridiculous. And working people can't serve."

"But if our Assembly went on for, say, the same amount of time as the House of Representatives in D.C., it would be more crap. Sorry to swear, but I don't see that anything more would be accomplished."

"I do. It's unwise to rush everything. Some issues need deliberation."

"You're right. I am disenchanted, and now that I'm reading these letters, I'm even more so."

"You'll get some nice ones. People really do have good ideas, but that's another problem. There isn't enough time to consider the ideas or go visit the people who proposed them, or call them to the statehouse. It's like my grandfather used to say, 'People on the ground see the problem first, and they often have the most practical solution.' He knew a lot."

"Yes. Well, here is an unsigned letter." She began to read. "'Dear Delegate Tucker, Concerning the drama at the statehouse. What if this death has nothing to do with drugs? What if there's money involved from other sources? Or what if someone's political career is imperiled? Drugs blanket our country, I realize that, but so does trafficking people, usually for domestic labor or prostitution. A page probably isn't involved in trafficking, but that doesn't mean the boy couldn't have unknowingly delivered messages to delegates who are taking trafficking money under the table. Could be for housing development. Cutting through paperwork. Arguing against established development laws. I bring this up because if anyone makes you an offer too good to be true, it is.'" She put the phone in her other hand. "Does someone out there know something?"

"It's possible," came the slow reply. "But I can't see what could be at stake other than a career. Someone is on the rise, and then they fall because they were pulled over while driving under the influence. That kind of stuff."

"This sounds like something organized. It's not a threat. More like a warning."

"People like to make themselves sound important. Could be a crackpot." Susan wasn't worried yet.

"Could be, but why send the letter to your husband?"

That got her. "Well—" Susan thought. "Buying adjacent land to extend one of our state parks. Or what about Delegate Linwood Cove pushing for far less oversight for eldercare, in some way more oversight over stuff like COVID. Belvidere Coles, who runs the Golden Years houses statewide, had been working with him. Each of those activities generate private profit using state resources or intelligence. Well, that's enough. Each is complicated in its own way and can rile vested interests. Any tip-off of future development, like if our schools get bought off, creates danger. Why do some corporations and businesses get taxed, but others don't?"

Harry said, "Well, it wouldn't hurt to scrutinize the bills Ned is sponsoring, or perhaps there is an issue the party is pushing. I don't know. I called you because I find it peculiar."

"I do, too."

"If you think of anything, will you call me?" Harry asked.

"Of course. You too," Susan replied.

31

Standing over the wood-burning stove, Harry rubbed her hands. "They're so cold, they hurt."

"You shouldn't have taken off your gloves," Pewter reprimanded her.

"She couldn't check the bolt on the under carriage without taking off her gloves. Had to use the wrench. She gets clumsy with gloves," Mrs. Murphy informed them.

Clumsy might have been better than touching metal on a cold late afternoon. Harry could be pigheaded. Like at St. Luke's she was sure she could fix most problems and save lots of money. Sometimes she could. Other times she made it worse.

One of the old riding lawn mowers stored in the basketball court building had a half-dropped blade. An old nut had rusted out, broke, so the blade hung lopsidedly. Apart from giving an uneven cut, it could be dangerous. Hence the repair. She had a much-needed tool kit in that building. It was on rollers, locked under the bleachers. Once the building was used again in warm weather, she'd take it out to the shed, where all could be safely secured. But for now, keeping stuff in the third big building made it easier. No walking to the shed plus one could fire up the stove in that building, which was a replica of the other two. She hadn't thought she'd be in there that long. But as usual, she'd underestimated how long it would take to ascertain the damage, much less repair it. She was now in the lower school building.

"Oh, this stings."

"*It will stop,*" Tucker commiserated.

Pewter's sympathy ran out as she thought she heard a mouse scurry. She trotted to the back of the raised teacher's dais, her belly fat swinging to and fro. Pirate watched in fascination but wisely kept his mouth shut.

Tucker ran to the door, barking. "*Susan.*"

Given the sensitivity of dog ears, the crunch of the tires on Susan's Audi was clear, but couldn't be heard by Harry until Susan parked in front of the lower school building. Harry heard the door slam. Then the building door opened.

"Awful out there."

"Come stand by the stove," Harry invited her. "I didn't expect to see you."

"Feels good. What did you do to your hands? They're bright red."

"I stupidly took my gloves off to work on the old riding mower in the gym. Kept them off too long. So I came in here, started the fire, and my hands are better. They really hurt. Warming up, they hurt then they improve. Sometimes I forget how brutal cold can be."

"We need a new mower."

"We need a lot of new things. But I can keep it going. We have to conserve money. Once we open the school and have a celebration, I think there will be more gifts. We'll get help."

"I love you like a sister, but sometimes, honey chile, you're a dreamer. Oh, everyone will come to the big party, including the

TV station. The former students, still living, will make a great impression. Then it will be over. And everyone will forget."

"Sourpuss."

"I resent that," Pewter half hissed.

"Where is she?" Susan knew a hiss when she heard one.

"Behind the dais. Dreams of glory. Slaying mice."

"Ah."

"You'll be sorry when this place is overrun," Pewter replied.

Tucker started to say something, then stopped.

"Let's pull these desks over. We'll stay warm." Harry helped Susan remove her coat.

"Even in winter light, the sun fading, those big windows create such an ambiance." Susan looked around. "I bet many a child spent study time daydreaming."

Harry looked outside. "Bet you're right. All the research that's been done, especially by Tazio, indicates that most of these kids lived good lives. They were institutionally oppressed, but they were a community. Do we ever give people credit for the emotional work of those times?"

"No." Susan's jaw jutted a bit. "Unless someone makes money, shows off, they're brushed aside. I'll take someone who has created a good family, works to help others, over some rich asshole."

"Well, that's something. You hardly ever swear."

"Harry, I came over because Ned called me. Not texted or emailed, called. He said Thanatos Construction has made noises about buying the school and the twenty acres. The county owns it. Paid no attention to it until we began restoration. And I got all the paperwork."

"I remember."

"Remember the corporation that bought all the land around Secretariat's birthplace, that wonderful farm? The state fair was put across the road. They decided people would live up there. Close to Richmond. A twenty-minute drive. Well, they want to build a huge housing development there. Upscale. It's being fought, but the delegate and state senator from that county are undecided. One says it's all historic. The other says it means a better tax base for Caroline County. It's a mixed blessing. I think this is Thanatos's model."

"Did it compromise Secretariat's place?"

"No. But any development will change the county. More roads. More services, including firemen and law officers. Look at where our school land really is. We drive to it, but we miss those adjoining properties out of view." She pulled a detailed map of Virginia from her jeans back pocket, unfolded it, smoothing it out on the top of the desk.

Hearing the crinkle of paper, Pewter returned. After all, sometimes paper had food wrapped inside.

"You're all safe. I terrified the mice," the gray cat boasted.

"I feel better already." Tucker lifted one side of her whiskers.

Mrs. Murphy jumped on the map, face peering down.

"Murphy, come on." Harry picked her up, placing the tiger cat in her lap.

"Want me to tell you what's on it?" Pirate volunteered, since he could see.

"No. Thanks. *I like to sit on paper."* Mrs. Murphy was polite. *"I find paper restful."*

"Why?" Tucker thought it odd.

One could chew paper, carry newspapers, or demolish a book, but why sit on paper?

"I don't know. I don't have to understand it to enjoy it," the cat sensibly replied.

"Okay. You see the red circle I've drawn? Put my compass point on the school. Then drew what I figure to be how long it takes to drive to Charlottesville. Then how long to Richmond. And remember Richmond is developing to the west. This distance will narrow a lot in ten years' time."

"We're on the very outer edge," Harry observed.

"Thanatos has been buying up land for the last four years. The

COVID problem halted any development. But that's gone, and we now have a different administration. Not that the current administration is going to wave a magic wand over every development but I expect construction companies, businesses . . . you know, like a trucking service . . . will receive a better hearing."

"I don't know." Harry peered again at the circle. "I think every Virginia governor wants to attract business. We rely too much on federal money."

"We do. But then, we *are* next to D.C., and we have Navy ports, military installations, you name it. The national government wants a satisfied neighbor. Maryland, Delaware, and southern Pennsylvania make out all right, too, but we get the lion's share."

"Okay. Tell me what this has to do with the school?"

"If the land can be bought at an enticing price from the county, it can sit here until Richmond expands even farther west, which it will do. Then they'll build."

"The uproar will have died down. People will have forgotten. They might have protestors here when those excavators show up, but it will be too little, too late." Harry wasn't necessarily political, but she knew how the world worked, and she knew people were overworked. They didn't have time to protest. Although the young did.

"My question, Ned's question, is why here? They must have found out. Not that we were hiding anything, but it's certainly inconvenient timing." Susan blew out her cheeks. "I distrust Thanatos to the marrow of my bones."

"Ned will find out more. We ought not to publicize this or panic."

"No, of course not, but you and I, Tazio, Jerry, our husbands, are the hard core. I wanted you to know even before I call Tazio."

"Thanks. I can go with you if you want to see Tazio face-to-face."

"She's on a project in Keswick. I think I should go alone."

"Of course."

"And another thing Ned told me is that tractor dealers have offered Thanatos discounts. As have lumber dealers, and trucking companies to move heavy equipment. It's becoming cozy. It usually is, but this is an early start, I think."

"Sounds well planned."

"It does." Susan's expression saddened. "One of the arguments or bribes to the county will be all the millions that they will pay . . . and it will be a pittance compared to potential profits, the property taxes, and that the money can be put to use for schools, for low income housing, fill in the blank." She scratched Pirate's ear. "The history of this place is negligible compared to that."

"Preserving history can make this a good fight."

"Whose history?" Susan's voice had an edge. "The buy-off will be scholarships for black youth, indigenous youth. Something of that nature. They don't care about black history, indigenous history."

"We can put up a good fight if it comes to that." Harry felt a surge of excitement, as a good fight enlivened her.

"I hope." Susan sat quietly while Pirate leaned his head against her shoulder.

"Brownnoser?" Pewter curled her lip.

"I'm not brownnosing. She's upset."

"Pirate, humans can get upset if someone wears the wrong color shirt. You can't take them seriously," Pewter said.

Susan blinked. "I almost forgot. The police found Ellis Barfield in Westminster, Maryland. He didn't put up a fight. He had over one hundred thousand dollars on him."

"That's a lot of cash. I wonder, did he always carry that much?" Harry exclaimed.

"So far he's not talking. He'll be brought back to Virginia, so maybe our people can find out what he was doing."

"Maybe." It was Harry's turn to be quiet.

"It's awful. The whole thing is awful."

"What if he wasn't selling drugs? Would a videographer have that kind of money? Maybe he shot expensive videos for other people. Sold some drugs on the side."

"If he did, no one has spoken about it."

"Pornography."

"Good Lord, I never thought of that." Susan blanched.

"It's a multibillion-dollar business. Not even millions, billions. He could have been shooting other high-end things. Even stuff like antique cars. It's also possible that wherever his work took him, there were rich people with drugs."

"Uh, I have to think about that."

"I do, too, but my gut tells me that whatever it was, it wasn't legal." She reached out to touch her friend's elbow. "And I am also willing to bet that whatever this is somehow intersects with political people, with power."

32

 "Jeez." Harry grabbed the Jesus strap inside Fair's dually.

"Sorry, honey. The road is slicker than I thought."

"Bleak. Another bleak day." She sighed.

"'O wind if winter comes can spring be far behind.'" He quoted Shelley.

"Right."

The backseat of this big truck easily accommodated the animals.

"How long? I know I sound like a child."

"Traffic is light. I guess we can thank the roads for that." He glanced at the time on his dash. "A half hour." Then he checked the rearview mirror. "Glad I tied that heavy table down. Putting rubber pads under the feet helped."

"Why couldn't Ned have just bought an old farm table in Richmond?"

"He could, but it would cost so much more, plus I had this stuffed in the back of my office. Might as well have him get use out of it."

"True."

"How are you doing with your lessons with Miranda? Haven't had much time to catch up with you. The Thoroughbreds are finished foaling, but others are starting. It's a little flutter. Won't really fire up again until it's truly spring."

"Living with you makes me appreciate OB/GYN doctors."

"Those new lives arrive at such inconvenient times. I remember one night when I had to deliver four foals, all at Mim's. This was years ago. Anyway, I'd thought I could fall asleep in the tack room, would shut my eyes between deliveries. One thing about being an equine midwife is, my patients weigh so much. If I delivered humans or had to move the mothers, would be easier."

"What about performing a Cesarean?"

"I've done it on horses. I suppose if I had to, I could do it on people. When all else fails, a veterinarian is better than no medical help at all."

She smiled. "Only if it's you."

He grinned. "You've been humming. Hear you in the barn. Hum me some stuff Miranda has taught you."

She hummed a full note, a quick little note, then another full note.

"What's that?"

"K. Just K. It can mean 'go ahead' or 'okay.' Miranda has such a memory for sound. You know what she did? She actually hummed every letter in the alphabet. I have some numbers. Here you go." She hummed three short notes and a space. Then a short note and a full note. Another short note and a full note and finally a full note and two short notes.

"What's that?"

"I love you. Number 143."

"Well, I love you, too."

"This has given me even more respect for my grandfather. I am learning to use Miranda's ham radio. She's taught me this number shorthand. Quicker communication. You know, only one or two percent of our population uses ham radio."

"I would have thought it was more."

"There are so many ways to communicate. They aren't secure, but no one seems to care. Fair, what is really cool is that people can be honest on ham radio. I don't think you can do that anymore. Not on the electronic media," Harry informed him. "Too many people getting into your account."

"Computers and cellphones make communication easy. What makes me careful is if an owner asks me to email a diagnosis and medication suggestions."

"You think people can listen in or see it?"

"Not so much, but the recipient can use my email to check with his or her friends, other vets. And if they aren't knowledgeable about horses, it's a worry."

"Funny, I never thought of that. I think of *cancel culture*. Another buzz word."

"It is. But careers have been ruined by people asking reasonable questions. Plus, so many things aren't easy to answer. Anything medical has nuance. Same for politics. Stuff can get twisted, misrepresented. So I'm careful. But if the animal has an untreatable problem, I'll say so. If it can be treated, I try to give the steps, the possible outcomes, and the time this will take."

"I couldn't do it. Like reading the letters and emails sent to Ned. I could never do what he does. And this is our district. Can you imagine if you held a national office?"

"You'd have a sense of the percent of nutcases in our country." He laughed.

"You don't have to look far for that," Pewter announced.

Harry turned to look in the backseat. "What's up, pussycat?"

"Nothing. Just commenting on human behavior."

Fair pulled up to the curb. Parking often was easy in The Fan, if you hit the hours right. This was late afternoon and Fair could back into the open driveway of a house with a big downstairs apartment that Ned rented. Occasionally people would park and block the drive, but today it was fine. Snow was still pushed up in areas of the city streets. The snow here had been shoveled away, although a pile of it by the next house's drive refused to melt quickly.

Fair cut the engine, dropped the tailgate to swing up in the truck bed. The animals stayed in the truck. Harry got out.

"If you untie it and get it to the edge of the tailgate, I can steady it. The two of us can do this."

"Why don't you knock on the door to see if Ned's there."

"I texted him. He'll be out."

"Okay." He knew better than to argue, but given the state of the sidewalk, the front walk to the lovely simple house, he didn't want her carrying any weight or steadying the table so he could lift it down.

Ned, as if hearing the conversation, stepped out of the front door. A goose down coat kept him warm.

Pulling on gloves, he reached the back of the truck.

"We can both lift it out if you slide the table to the edge. Looks nice." He could see it was heavy.

"It's hardwood," Fair warned, as if reading his mind.

Harry, gladly giving up the opportunity to balance then carry the heavy table, walked toward the front door, calling over her shoulder, "I'll hold the door open."

The two jiggled, joggled. The table was now perched on the edge of the truck bed, which fortunately had a bed liner or the thing would have slipped off. Fair jumped down, hurrying to the other side, reached up.

Ned counted. "One, two, three."

They grunted, managing to slide the table halfway off so the weight was in their hands, then they walked back a step or two and the one end moved off the bed.

"Let me get that, and I can hold it while you maneuver the other end down," Fair ordered.

Ned, knowing how strong his friend was, did just that.

Finally the table made it slowly to the ground, with significant grunts from the two men.

Mrs. Murphy, watching from the back window, exclaimed, *"They did it."*

Tucker, also on the backseat, commented, *"Fair could lift a house off its foundation. He's so strong."*

Pewter, not one to laud human abilities, had to admit, *"He probably got that strong dealing with horses. You know, lifting one up a bit off the ground."* She leaned onto Mrs. Murphy. *"There's a car parking in front of us. Tight in the city. Bet people have fights all the time."*

Lucas quickly got out of the car, trotted to the two men. "Ned, I can help."

"Good."

Lucas took the other back end so he and Ned were on one side, Fair on the other. Ned and Lucas together equaled one of Fair. Ned, not weak, was nonetheless grateful. Working with Fair reminded him of what a specimen the vet was.

Ned and Lucas walked backwards, careful not to slip, as Harry stood flat against the door, holding it open.

The men maneuvered the unwieldy table through the hall, with Ned giving directions. They stopped, stepping through the opened living room double doors.

"Leave it here for now."

"Better tell us where you want it," Lucas sensibly remarked. "You've got the manpower now."

"I know. But I need a brief breather." Ned looked around. Before the Haristeens had arrived, he'd cleared a space along a wall with an old handblown paned window.

Harry called out, "Honey, I'm going for the animals."

"Fine."

By the time the small squad trotted into the cozy apartment, the men had the table placed under the window.

"Natural light." Harry liked the placement.

"Not bad. I needed a bigger desk though. I'm running out of room," Ned said, then turned to Lucas. "Good timing. Hey, let me get everyone a drink . . . hot, cold? This was such a help. You shouldn't have." He smiled at Fair. "But I'm glad you did."

Everyone elected for hot chocolate when Ned mentioned that. "Harry, you know where everything is. Lead them to their seats, the ones that are comfortable."

"What I'll do is make the hot chocolate, and you fellows catch up. No offense, Ned, but I can do it better than you."

He smiled, nodded, leading Fair and Lucas to chairs.

"What a surprise to see you," Ned told Lucas while Pewter, none too subtly, checked Lucas out.

Pirate sat by Harry in the kitchen while the two cats investigated everything in the living room.

"Ned, I'm closing the bedroom door. I don't trust the cats."

"*What an insult*," said she who would happily shred a pillow, especially needlepoint.

"I was driving home and I thought that was you with part of a table on your shoulder."

"Glad you stopped." Fair smiled. "Haven't seen you since your speech at UVA. My wife comes down to Richmond more than I do. It's good to see you."

"You too. I haven't forgotten our adventure at the university."

Harry brought in a large pot of hot chocolate, then returned for a tray of mugs. The aroma of chocolate filled the room.

"Is it ever going to warm up?" Harry plopped down after pouring. "Ned, I didn't find cookies or anything."

"No, this is it. I go out to eat. Really, I only have eggs for breakfast. When Susan comes down, she grocery shops. I don't have time, plus my wife has spoiled me."

"She has," Harry agreed. "But she swears you are worth it."

The men laughed.

"Harry, thank you," Lucas said after enjoying his first sip.

"What are you doing on this side of town?" Ned asked.

"I live two blocks over."

"How good. The Fan has always been my favorite."

"Mine too. When Amanda got elected, I knew I should probably leave our district, except for a small room, and get a bigger place here. Pretty much I'm the twenty-four-hour guy."

Ned complimented him. "She's very lucky to have you."

"I like the work, although the workload can be overwhelming, as you know. She's becoming so popular, she really needs a second secretary, advisor, what have you."

"She'd need to be careful," Harry shrewdly said.

Her husband, not terribly political, lifted his eyebrows. "Why?"

"She can't flaunt her wealth but so much, honey," Harry replied.

Lucas nodded. "That's true, but I'm not telling tales out of school when I say her ambitions are big. If she kept a secretary in her district, that would be less noticeable. Her appeal to women is taking off. And she's just bought a beach house on the Outer Banks. She's keeping it quiet. Life is good for her right now."

Ned shifted in his seat. "It is."

Harry just blurted it out. "Well, you've somewhat restrained Aidan. His appeal is to those who will oppose her."

Lucas, stroking Pewter, who felt she should be the center of attention, shook his head. "Ned, Aidan is working with you on that bill, and he's sponsored other bills. He's not lazy. But bringing up the work of Otto Spengler in the Assembly room? No one wants a lecture."

Ned simply agreed.

"*The Decline of the West?*" Harry asked.

Lucas stared at her for a moment, then Fair said, "Smith College."

"Ah." Lucas smiled. "He was showing off, mostly attacking our party, saying we were devotees of Spengler, that we thought our country was going to hell in a handbasket. No point reviewing his argument. Hearing it once was enough. He went out of his way to irritate Amanda. She didn't bite, for which I was grateful. But he often makes distracting noises if she speaks."

"Personality clashes make trouble, no matter where they appear." Fair watched Pirate stretch at Harry's feet.

Lucas noticed, too. "That dog is huge."

"*I'm a good boy.*" Pirate's tail thumped the floor covered with a think carpet, welcome on a cold day.

"He still might grow a bit," Harry replied. "But Tucker is full size. Named for Susan and Ned, as Susan bred the litter from which Tucker comes."

"*All ill-bred. I'm the only Virginian here from good, old blood,*" Pewter puffed.

"*Pewter, no one likes a blood snob,*" Mrs. Murphy chided her.

"*Jealous. They are all from the lower orders.*" The gray cat sniffed.

"*What's a lower order?*" Pirate asked.

"*I'll explain on the way home,*" Tucker promised.

Ned finished his chocolate, placing the cup on the saucer. "Aidan took a page out of Amanda's book. He tapped his foot against the leg of his desk. Not the same as those high heels, but it was distracting. He has some good ideas. Maybe he needs to grow up a little."

"Not too long before this session ends." Lucas's voice sounded hopeful. "Like you, Ned, I need another desk for all the paperwork, but it's an exciting time to be in the House of Delegates. At least I think it is."

"I do, too." Ned smiled. "Now if we could just get a football stadium in Northern Virginia. Wouldn't that be the best?"

"I'd buy season tickets." Fair perked up.

Harry informed Lucas, "He was captain of our high school football team. After the Super Bowl, we have a slight drop in energy in the house, then he revives."

"The fight will be over where it will be located, which despite being a huge boost to the economy will offend others, especially those who have already made a good living. They don't need the jobs a stadium will provide, and they would lose their minds with the traffic," Ned wisely noted.

"I still hope we get one." Fair allowed Mrs. Murphy in his lap.

"Me too," the other three echoed.

"Harry, I can't thank you enough for coming down here to help me. Susan has dragged you into it, but as Lucas has confirmed, we are all digging out of an avalanche of paperwork."

"I like it up to a point. The city would be easier to negotiate in better weather."

"True, but for a state capital, it's reasonably easy to get around. I first considered living on The James in one of those restored buildings. They have parking, places for your bicycle, views of the river from most of the apartments. It is a wonderful view, but I fell in love with this older section of the city. It's quiet, the houses have such charm, some are painted, others are brick, sometimes the brick is painted. The Federal style feels right. And I like walking in the neighborhood." He smiled. "I can easily get to the Virginia Museum of Fine Arts or the Museum of History. Love them. The state library isn't far either. I rarely get time to go out, but when the session ends I'll be so glad to soak up Richmond."

"Amanda will keep you working." Ned wryly smiled.

"She will. She's worried I'm not dating and I'm middle-aged. She doesn't want to admit she's that age, too. Anyway, I'm not going to meet anyone in a bar, but whenever I go to the museums I see interesting people. Often the people who work there are, well, intriguing. But," he glanced at Ned and Fair, "you two are more robust than I. I'm not sure I'll catch a girl's eye."

Fair, always kind, leaned toward Lucas. "In the horse world, you'd be called weedy. Thinnish. Not skinny, and you're not overweight. Don't worry. The right girl will come along."

"Honey, these are non-binary days," Harry quietly said.

Lucas beamed. "Thanks, Harry, but Fair is right. I'd like to meet an interesting woman, and I figure she'd be in the museum. Every time they change an exhibit, I go."

"Good thinking." Ned smiled. "Fair and I were lucky. We knew our wives from childhood. I'm a bit older than Susan, so I can't say that I noticed her until I was twenty-seven and she had graduated from your alma mater; see, I remembered your speech. Then I noticed. We clicked. Could talk to each other about anything. Still can. Time will sort this out."

"Thanks for the encouragement." Lucas was grateful.

"Any more hot chocolate?" Harry asked.

"No. Thank you," each man answered, so Harry picked up the cups and saucers, took them to the kitchen, then returned for the pot.

"Harry, don't wash them. I'll put them in the dishwasher," Ned called out.

"I'll put them in."

Pirate peered into the dishwasher as she opened it. *"We don't have one of these."*

Pewter, coming to the kitchen, said, *"Harry doesn't like dishwashers, microwaves, stuff like that. She doesn't really like the washer and dryer either, but there's too much dirt. She has to have them."*

"Why?" asked the big dog.

"She tries to keep the electric bill low. She thinks a lot of this stuff is wasteful." Pewter thought Harry was silly. Why not make the job easier? Then again, she didn't have to wash dishes, so if her human wanted to do a lot of chores by hand, fine.

As Harry returned to the living room, Lucas was on his feet, saying his goodbyes. Harry kissed him on the cheek.

When he drove away, Fair and Ned turned to her. Fair asked, "Do you think women find him attractive?"

"Sure. He's six feet. He is thin. Dresses well. Has a good haircut and beard. Maybe if he had time, he could hit the gym, but he looks okay."

"I can look at Chris Hemsworth and see he is good looking. But I don't think men look at men as women do."

"And vice versa." Harry grinned at them. "Sometimes the magic hits. Sometimes it doesn't."

Lucas turned right at the corner, to drive the two blocks to his street. A black two-door Jeep followed him. The windows were tinted. As he turned, keeping to the right since his rented house was on the right, the Jeep revved up, swung around, then turned toward him, ramming him hard, pushing the car onto a snow-covered lawn. The driver's door was crumpled. So was Lucas.

33

The click of Amanda's heels reverberated down the long highly polished hospital corridor. She checked in again at the nurse's station, then paced back. The large round clock on the wall read 7:22. As she turned to go to Lucas's room, she heard footsteps. Ned Tucker drew alongside her.

"How is he?"

"In the operating room for two hours." She looked up at him.

They walked together to Lucas's room; private, with a large window.

Amanda sat as Ned pulled up a chair next to her.

"I had no idea. Susan saw it on the news, called me."

"How did you find him?"

"Called VCU, as I figured that hospital would be closest. Gave my name, rank, and serial number, so they informed me where he was."

"Virginia Commonwealth is careful. His parents are on the way from Florida. Retired." She stopped. "They don't get along with him. They speak but . . . well, anyway, they are coming up. I'm glad you're here."

"What's the damage?"

"Four broken ribs on his left side. One rib punctured his lung. That's the biggest problem. His left hip is slightly cracked, but not broken, so he won't need a replacement. No internal damage. He had on his seatbelt. No head damage, but I bet his neck will be sore. Everything will be sore." She stared at her old friend. "Hit and run. No one got a license number."

"Even if there was black ice, he wouldn't have been hit like this."

"As to the driver, I think this was thought out. That car is probably in a shop, bent fenders being pulled off and replaced. A different license plate put on and the car will probably be repainted or put in a truck, covered, and driven to another state."

"A business. Cars used to kill people." Ned shook his head.

"One of the things about being a reporter for so many years is that I learned a lot about organized crime, as well as disorganized crime." She paused. "The difference is brains."

"Why hurt Lucas?"

"Just for being trans," she simply said.

"It's hard for me to believe people are that crazy. I might face sporadic violence as an elected official, but there are people who face chronic violence, if that's a term. One doesn't think about it if one doesn't face it."

Her features reflecting her exhaustion, she nodded. "I never gave it a thought until he transitioned. He really has never looked back, but I do."

Ned studied Lucas's face, which was manly. He was handsome . . . slight, but handsome. He walked like a man, talked like a man. Again, Ned hadn't thought about it until forced to, but he realized all that stuff was learned for the most part. Yet when he thought about it, women often had a swing to their walk. He quite liked it. It was confusing. Was it sexist? Insensitive? Best not to think about it at this moment. Best to think about how to help someone he had grown to like.

"I take it you've talked to the surgeon or surgeons?"

"Yes. They were patient, explained everything, pulled up X-rays for me to see for myself. Dr. Yancy, the lead surgeon, told me Lucas should be able to walk, but whether with or without a cane will depend on the pain the crack causes. Sometimes that's not horribly painful. Sometimes, Dr. Yang, the other doctor, said, he'll feel it with every step. Often soft-tissue damage takes longer. He also said Lucas was lucky he turned away, as it probably saved his shoulder. He said there will be pain there from bruising. For one thing, his body will be out of balance. I didn't think about that."

"You mean, to compensate for the injuries?"

She nodded. "He'll be stiff. He might favor one side over the other, which is how Dr. Yancy put it. He also said Lucas will be on painkillers for three weeks. He will be slowly weaned off. Oxy-Contin. His assistant did say that some people do work while on painkillers."

"And . . . ?"

"He said Lucas will heal faster if he isn't in terrific pain. He's not going to feel great, but he won't be doubled over in pain."

"Thank God we have painkillers. In the past, it was alcohol. Can you imagine being wounded in the Revolutionary War? Any war before the late nineteenth century? Things began to improve then, but no wonder people grabbed the bottle."

"Childbirth might be another reason." She half smiled. "Our ancestors faced so much." She touched Lucas's hand, outside the covers. "He should sleep throughout the night. That's another thing he needs, sleep. He'll want to work right away. We'll see."

"That will be difficult for you."

"I'll manage. He's stubborn. You know, I've only been to his house a few times. The heat was good. He needs heat. Not hot, but he can't sit in a cold room. It's so cold right now. I hope it doesn't seep into his house. He'll need a nurse for a few days. If for nothing else, someone has to help change bandages."

"Amanda, this crash may have nothing to do with transphobia. What if Lucas found out something about Ellis? Or Reid? Was it drugs? Selling drugs, or was it something else?"

Her expression darkened. "That's a terrible thought."

"We've had terrible things happen."

"If he found out anything or had an idea, he would have told me."

"Maybe. He stopped at my apartment when he drove by. He saw my friends from Crozet, Harry and her husband, unloading a heavy table for me. He parked and got out to help. We all visited for a brief time, but I guess if he had a thought about Reid or Ellis, he wouldn't have mentioned anything in front of them. He might have called you when he got home if he did know something."

"How could he have set off his attacker?"

"That we won't know until we find out what this is really about, but sometimes a person makes an offhand comment to the guilty party, who then realizes the person is putting two and two together."

"Politics?"

"Or money. Often the two go hand in hand."

She sighed. "Ned, you've been so good to come here, but go on home. I'll sit with him a bit more then head to my place."

"I'll wait a little longer."

"Thank you."

34

"Sounds like an old movie. You know, someone sitting in a newspaper building listening to the telegraph. Going out the front door and giving news of *Titanic* survivors." Harry marveled at the sound.

Miranda smiled. "It doesn't sound like an old movie to me. We used this in my younger years. I remember all of it, and so does Tally. Okay, here's 'How are you?' " She tapped the key.

"I'll never get this stuff." Harry heard the dots and dashes, but didn't know how she'd figure it all out.

"Listen." Miranda tapped out the three words again. "Listen for the longer sounds, the shorter sounds, the times in between. The in-between tells you that the word is finished. Anyway, I thought you'd like to hear it."

"Thanks for setting up your sounder for me, and the key. I can only imagine what this was like during the war, or even in an office. Didn't telegraph operators receive news as to who had died?

The government sent telegraphs of condolence, and someone had to deliver them."

"Yes. Mothers had stars in their window for how many of their sons were in the war. That included nurses. Lots of women served as nurses, drivers. You'd be surprised. I think that war was the biggest force for women's advancement into the working world."

Harry, next to her old friend, touched the key. "I can't imagine getting one of those telegrams."

"Many people here got them. My parents always called on whoever lost their son or daughter. We all brought food, and remember, there was rationing, so that took a community effort. But people did it. We were close then."

"My parents said that. Tally says it, too. G-Pop didn't, because he was at sea. Do you think we'll ever be that close again?"

"I pray we will." A deep breath followed. "Yet this closeness only seems to come during war or disaster. Harry, you'd think we'd learn. I'm old. All this seems so familiar to me, but must seem like science fiction to you."

"It feels as though I've missed something important," Harry honestly replied.

"I'm getting nostalgic. Sorry. Okay, now just give this a try." She placed Harry's finger on the key. "You're going to send SOS. The machine isn't hooked up. You aren't going to scare anyone, but I want you to feel what your grandfather felt. Ready?"

"Yes."

Miranda pushed Harry's forefinger. Three dots, three dashes, and three more dots.

"I know SOS. Think everyone does."

"I should hope so. Now you do it without me."

Harry tapped out three short dots, then three dashes, then three more dots. "Am I leaving enough space between the letters, or too much?"

"You're fine. You need to hear it as a word. Do it again."

Harry pressed the key again. "It's a great sound, isn't it?"

"That wasn't so hard."

"No. I can actually hear it as one word, sort of."

"If you knew the code and practiced, including a lot of listening, you would hear words. It's memory. Time. Okay, I'm going to get the girls on."

Miranda twiddled with her radio, Harry watching every move. This, too, was becoming more familiar. She listened, enthralled, as the "old girls" sang together. After they finished and each said goodnight, Miranda touched Harry's hand. "Sing."

Three full notes followed two short notes. The two women sang it again, as did the ladies on their own radios.

"Very good." Miranda beamed.

"You make it easy and fun. This feels so different from my cellphone."

"I suppose you could sing on your cellphone, but you would have a devil of a time organizing choir practice. Now, of course, you could do that on your computer. But the sound might be clear or faint. With our radios, and we've been doing this for years, we have good sound, as we are all within reasonably close range. It certainly saves on gas plus when the light fades, as it now has, it can be a problem. Many of the girls can't drive in the dark anymore." She paused and watched Harry. "See, that was easy."

"The singing is easy. Using the key would take a lot more time."

"It would. Do you feel closer to G-Pop?"

This question startled Harry. "Uh, I do. I forget how much insight you have."

"I've known you since your childhood, so maybe it's familiarity. I knew your grandfather, too. He had his buddies, but I'd see him on his walks with Moosie. Given Moosie's build, those walks were never long."

"He loved that bulldog."

"Everyone loved Moosie, like everyone loves Tucker. I miss her and those two devilish cats. How many times did I catch Mrs. Murphy reaching into a mailbox as someone put their hand in to pull out their mail. She'd pat their hand. Everyone got used to it. Pewter never did that, she just pulled the mail on the floor after we put it in the box."

"We had fun."

"We did. When are you going to take your technician's test for the ham radio?"

"I have to memorize the book. Really, I do. It's not hard. But I have to memorize frequencies, stuff like that. Fortunately I was good at science. But I was thinking, maybe around St. Patrick's Day. In the meantime, I am making an effort to visit Aunt Tally more. She gets lonesome."

"Ah." Miranda smiled. "A function of age. It's not so much that you're lonesome for people, as they do visit, but you are lonesome for little things, like car keys. I don't want a fat tiny computer in my hand. I want to slide a key in the ignition."

"It is a pain, all this stuff. My prize is my 1978 Ford F-150. Don't use it so much in the snow, but I do have the chains on it."

"Good girl. All right, one more time. SOS."

Harry dutifully punched the S's the O. "Piece of cake." She smiled.

"Now give me 88."

"Oh." Harry concentrated, then touched the key for three dashes and two dots, then repeated the sequence. "Not as easy as singing it."

"Yes it is. You've done well. Memorize the information in that old handbook. You need to go on the air and use call letters, proper protocol, but then you're on. Can go anywhere."

"If our radios could easily be broken into during the war, I'm sure they can be now."

"Yes, but so few of us use them. Were I a criminal, I'd be using my ham radio. If I fenced stolen goods. Stuff like that."

"Miranda!"

"What?"

"How you think."

"Harry, just because I'm in the choir, as devout as I can be, doesn't mean I can't think of nefarious deeds. And I mean it about the ham radio. For a smart criminal, this could be a valuable tool."

"If you start driving around a Porsche Cayenne, I'll know."

Miranda threw her head back and laughed. "If I start driving around in a Porsche Cayenne, you'll know I've lost my marbles."

Driving back to the farm Harry couldn't stop giggling over Miranda. All those years they'd worked together. Fifteen. Once Harry was out of Smith, George, Miranda's husband, the postmaster, had recently died, the post office needed help and Harry needed a job, never dreaming she'd be there that long.

A patch of ice up ahead, dense, slowed her down. Where did the time go? She had no idea. Then she thought about the sounds she'd heard. She paid attention to sounds . . . birds; tires scrunching in the drive, in the snow; the dogs barking . . . but her ears were not necessarily educated. She was learning to listen in a new way. That fascinated her. Then she thought about how terrific the cats' and dogs' ears were, as well as how good her horses' ears were. And those creatures could swivel their ears. Humans' had no movement. No wonder they missed so much.

By the time she pulled in front of her house, Fair's truck was parked next to the barn, under the overhang. She burst into the kitchen, where her wonderful husband was making supper.

"Honey, you won't believe what Miranda taught me." She talked about learning it all.

"*She doesn't hear what I'm saying,*" Pewter moaned.

Mrs. Murphy replied, "*One thing at a time. Maybe someday she will.*"

Lucas woke up that morning not knowing what had happened to him. He remembered the black Jeep, but nothing else. He had no recollection of being cut out of his car, of the ride in the ambulance, of blood flowing into his arm from a transfusion. Nothing.

The painkillers didn't befuddle him. He still felt a little pain. He was wise enough to know without the drugs he would be feeling so much more. He had to be helped to the bathroom. Breathing hurt. He felt the broken ribs more, and while he knew his lung had been punctured, he didn't know how to describe it. But he sure felt it.

His mother and father stayed with him all day. They finally left around six, the sky dark. Winter's early darkness always got to him.

Mom tried to be helpful. She wanted to know, did anyone on the rescue team give him trouble about being trans?

He said no. His driver's license said he was male. Amanda was the person to call in an emergency. All was well. Then his mother brought up the scars from his top surgery. Did anyone notice? He said, how would he know? No one had mentioned it.

He loved his parents but they exhausted him. They'd made the trip from Florida in dicey weather. He was grateful they'd come. They might never understand, but they did love him. That was enough. They left for their hotel to outrun the dark.

Amanda sat by him as soon as visiting hours allowed. He wasn't awake. She left a note by the bed, as she had to go to the statehouse.

He now heard the click click click coming down the hall.

He attempted to sit up straight and lean against the pillows. That hurt. He slumped back down, eyes fixated on the door.

"Lucas." She rushed over, kissed him on the cheek. "You look better."

He half smiled. "I'm glad you saw me and I didn't."

She teased him, "You just looked like someone who had been hit by a Mack truck. It could be worse."

"Ugh." He reached for her note. "Your handwriting is still awful."

"I know. I'm sorry. What do you need?"

"A break from Mom and Dad." He puffed out his cheeks. "I sound ungrateful. I'm not, but they do exhaust me."

"Want me to set up a tour of the Capitol for them?"

"No. That would make me feel guilty. They'll leave the day after tomorrow. They want to talk to all of my doctors, including any that I might need in the future. I'm okay."

"I understand. No one can pluck your last nerve like a parent. Oh, before I forget, the governor made it very clear today he wants a budget."

"Did it light any fires?"

"Not really. The Speaker was questioned, party leaders, our state senators. Everyone knew it was coming. Dolorous predictions, Pollyanna predictions, preening for the media. I walked by Aidan's office, hitting the hallway as hard as I could with my heels. He didn't look up. His door was open. Although he did come to my office later to inquire about your condition."

"Oh."

"Ned Tucker sat with me last night. I so wish he wasn't one of them. Though I suppose given who he is married to, he has no choice."

"I guess, but Ned believes much of his party's platform. Like us, I think. You believe the basics and try to ignore what is batshit. Forgive my swearing."

"Since you have become a gentleman, you rarely swear. This wasn't true at the Delta Delta Delta house, although you did it under your breath."

He laughed, then winced. "Don't make me laugh."

"Sorry. Do you need anything from home?"

"I want to go home."

"Maybe in a few days."

"I'll lose my mind here."

"Be patient. Can you get up and walk?"

A silence followed this. "With help, though I do feel even better than this morning. The painkiller helps."

"Does it hurt? If you walk to the bathroom?"

"The nurse has gotten me up and to the door. She leaves me alone now. I can do okay. At least I'm not peeing on myself."

Amanda shook her head. "That is such useful information."

He reddened. "Well, it is. Really, Amanda, help me go home."

"I will, but you have to do what the doctor tells you, and you'll still need help. Luckily no head injuries, but someone will have to unwrap your rib bandages or take you here to be unwrapped. And you can't take a shower."

"We'll see. Oh, on my desk are two sets of papers. The left side, if you're sitting in my seat, are all the proposed bills with my notes written on them. The pile on the right are specific requests from district people. My notes are on them, too."

"Anything interesting?"

"What you'd expect. Quite a few of your residents are angry about snow removal. Given Ned and Aidan's bill, you might want to respond. I also have clipped to that my research on capital improvements regarding such equipment. And I have non-snow potential expenditures. Loose stone, resurfacing asphalt, and the cost of roundabouts, as well as the time it will take to create them. Also in that list are where we need them in our district."

"Good. But don't worry about any of that right now. Just heal."

"I'll heal better if I have something to do."

"Oh, you will, but you need to be better off than you are now." She paused, reached for his hand, which she held. "Do you think what happened to you was an accident?"

"I don't know. All I saw was a car heading right for me. Out of the corner of my eye, I did see the Jeep swing over in the second lane and turn toward me. I felt it hit me. That's all."

"Perhaps the driver lost control or was on drugs or is a mental patient. Anything is possible. No one has been found yet. But the manner of it is unsettling."

He leaned farther back on his plumped-up pillows. "I'm an easy target."

"I hope not."

"I remember my desk, but I don't remember what I was think-ing or half of what I did that day. I helped Ned move a table. Maybe when I get more clear, I'll have some ideas."

"Call me or text me if you do. I'll be by. Are you sure you don't need anything?"

"No, thanks."

"How about grooming? Do you need me to shave you? The beard only covers part of your face."

He rubbed his stubble. "If the nurse doesn't do it, then you can. I don't have my razor or shaving cream."

"I'll bring some tomorrow." She got up, leaned down, and kissed him again.

When she reached the door, Lucas called out, "Amanda, I love you."

She turned, smiling that megawatt smile. "Ditto."

35

"This is tedious." Harry thought to herself, going through Ned's papers.

Susan was also bent over the makeshift desk.

Both could hear Ned talking in the next room.

"So many of the pages have left or been withdrawn. I miss them," they heard him say to another representative.

Susan, voice low, said, "Maybe it will work out. There are a few pages left. And sooner or later the truth about Reid will be found. It may very well be that he did snort what was in that little jar. Awful thought though. A kid ending his life like that, getting slammed on the road."

"Here's a query about a large pothole near the old Downtown Charlottesville Post Office. Such a pretty building." Harry held up the paper.

"That should go to the City Council, but Ned ought to review it and make a suggestion. This is what drives me around the bend.

All these various territories. What is the responsibility of the City Council, of the county commissioners, of your state representative, your state senator, your national representative and senator? By the time a citizen figures out who to contact, they're exhausted and angry."

"Maybe that's the point." Harry lifted her eyebrows.

"I wonder." Susan put that letter to the side.

"Any more news on Lucas? We couldn't have been four blocks away when he was hit. Speaking of drugs, who knows what that driver was on."

Susan scratched through a line on a letter. "Who knows. Here is someone wanting to design a new website for Ned. Lives in the district."

Harry rubbed her jaw, her fingers were cold. The state was apparently saving money on heat. "Don't throw that out, give it to me."

"Why?"

"If Ned's website doesn't need an update, Fair's does. Young people are much more critical about this than we are; you need the right look."

"What's wrong with what we've got?"

"I don't know, but it wouldn't hurt to get a fresh look. Just give it to me."

Susan handed over the letter as she heard a moan from Ned's room, then someone else's voice saying: "Fifteen more days. I guess we've gotta do it."

"I know. The vote's today. Anyone you need me to lean on?"

"No, everyone . . . even the most unrealistic . . . knows we can't get the job done without more time."

"Okay, Bill. But let me know if I need to give someone a push."

Harry rose from her seat to peer out the open door, but stayed hidden. She put her hands around her sides to indicate fat.

Susan, who had recognized the voice, murmured, "He gets bigger every year. If anyone wants to be fat, not my affair, but your heart sure works harder, and he's in his seventies."

"Be hard to diet and keep up this workload."

"That's the truth."

They returned to their tasks. Harry hummed.

"Harry."

"What?"

"What are you humming? Doesn't sound like a song."

"Oh, Miranda is teaching me how to use a ham radio, and some communications are shortcuts using numbers. That started with Morse code. So she taught me to hum the numbers, and yesterday she had her old telegraph set up and I listened as she punched the key. Numbers again."

"Huh. Can you communicate with Aunt Tally yet?"

"I do from Miranda's, but I have to pass my technician's test to do it on my own. I'm not there yet. When I do pass the test, I'll need to buy a modern ham radio. It doesn't need to be big. I visit Aunt Tally more than usual now. I made a promise. I'm trying to keep it, but it will take some time. So I go over, do odd chores, especially since Blair and Little Mim are in Ocala. Then I talk for a bit, or she talks. It's got to be so lonely."

"I guess at both ends of one's life. You think?"

"Sure. A lot of lonely kids out there, as well as older people who others have forgotten. If someone doesn't have an interest, they are left out. Kids need to try all manner of things to find their interests. Maybe you don't need to do that when you're older, but if someone can't get around easily anymore and no one volunteers to drive them, they're left out. Which brings me back to what I asked you. Lucas?"

"Better. He can walk with a cane. No broken hip, but he's sore. His ligaments and muscles badly bruised. His ribs are wrapped up. That will take time but Ned said he'll be discharged tomorrow and that Amanda has found round-the-clock help for him."

"Sure hope he doesn't need twenty-four-hour help for long. Will cost a fortune."

Susan nodded. "Maybe for a couple of days, but Ned says he's stronger, has a good attitude."

"Any ideas about who hit him or why?"

"No." Susan stopped, put down the paper in her hand. "There doesn't seem to be any ideas about either of the disturbing events that have happened."

"Unnerving." Harry folded the website letter and slipped it in her leather envelope. Harry hated carrying a bag. "Any gossip about Thanatos?"

"That firm has been sniffing around all over Virginia. What they think they will do if they buy all this land is anybody's guess. No one is building shopping centers anymore."

"No, but we need senior housing, more hospitals, maybe a business park or two." She returned to humming.

"What are you humming?"

"All right, listen." She hummed one full note, two seconds, then another full note.

"That's it?"

"That's the dashes and dot for 'go ahead' or 'okay.' Simple."

"Hmm."

"It's the letter K. That's all you need. Here, listen to this."

"What was that?"

"The number 73. Means best regards. I can learn numbers before I learn letters. I don't know if I can learn letters in a short time, but I now know shortcuts and I can talk to Aunt Tally. I don't need Morse code. But she gets enlivened . . . yes, enlivened . . . if I throw stuff in there when I'm with Miranda. You wouldn't believe what Miranda knows. I'm really getting a sense of what my grandfather did."

"Yeah." Susan smiled. "I'm getting a sense of what my grandfather knew, too."

They returned to their work. Given the diminishment of young pages, Harry and Susan weren't the only family members and friends helping out. Mostly the helpers were wives who took time off from their jobs for a day or two to assist. Those who didn't have a job put in more time. Everyone scrambled, some better than others, but the work had to be done.

"Honey, I'm sorry to disturb you." Ned stuck his head in the doorway. "Can you take this down to our whip? And then this to Aidan?"

"They're in two different directions. I'll get my exercise." Susan stood up, stretched.

"I need some exercise, too. Ned, let me drop your papers to Aidan and Susan can go to the whip."

"Okay." He handed each woman papers held together with a big blue pincer clip. They walked out the door, Susan heading down the right side of the polished hall, Harry going left.

Reaching Aidan's office door, which was open, Harry knocked on the frame. "Special delivery."

He glanced up. "If we don't get new pages, you could start a business. Come on in."

She entered the office, handing him Ned's paperwork. "Do you ever think you'll go blind?"

"It's a possibility."

Click click click reverberated down the hall.

It sounded like Amanda was just outside Aidan's office. Three long clicks, almost like slides, then two sharp ones. As she passed right by the door, this was repeated.

Harry's face registered disbelief. "Are you all right?" Aidan asked.

"Sorry. I, uh, thought of something. Work overload for everyone. Do you have anything for me to take back to Ned?"

"No. Tell him I'll get to him."

"Okay." She walked out of the office; the well-dressed, alluring figure of Amanda retreated down the hall, those high heels clicking in a regular footfall.

Harry couldn't believe what she heard. It was 88. She had the brains not to blurt anything out to Aidan, and she wasn't going to say anything to Ned and Susan until she considered this from every angle. But what looped through her mind was: "What the hell is going on?"

That question was somewhat answered by Ellis Barfield in custody. No bail had been set, but something needed to be decided soon. He'd killed no one. He may have sold drugs, but he was not considered dangerous. The hesitation was that they didn't want him to leave the area if he made bail.

He'd admitted to selling illegal alcohol under the table. He'd denied selling drugs. He did not deny taking them. He said nothing about sharing. Or his interrogators forgot to ask.

He also admitted to alerting some businesses as to statehouse discussions, some on committee, that could affect the business pro or con. He accepted financial reward for this, as well as being hired to shoot videos for those informed businesses. He was making good money.

36

Dove gray clouds rolled, turning into darker gray. Squinting through the front windshield, Harry mumbled, "Looks like another storm."

"Does." Susan checked her gas. "Know what, I'll stop in Oilville and get gas. If it starts to snow, gas stations will have lines. Talk to me after I fill it up."

But when Susan pulled into the gas station, Harry hopped out, jacket on, and put gas in Susan's station wagon. As the pump cut off, she punched the button for the receipt, pulled it out, peeled off her coat, and climbed back into the car.

"You didn't need to pay for gas. But thank you."

"No problem. It's my turn. You know, I think the temperature is dropping. Has to be already snowing in Albemarle County, maybe even as far east as Zion Crossroads."

Susan looked both ways, pulled out, and got back on I-64, west. "Now tell me what has you so upset."

"I didn't want to say anything in the office building. I don't know who can easily overhear. And I didn't want Ned to worry just yet."

"Well, what is it?"

"I believe Amanda is sending signals with her high heels. Like Morse code."

"Are you nuts?"

"I could be," Harry calmly replied. "When I dropped off Ned's papers to Aidan, she walked by. I heard her coming. You can't miss it. That click click click. Anyway, before I saw her, I heard the number eight, then again. And as she walked right in front of his open door, she made the same sound, three dashes and two dots."

"With high heels?" Susan was incredulous.

"Yes. She can lengthen her stride or shorten it to a pop. Miranda has taught me to listen by singing. Then she pushed the telegraph key for me to hear it that way."

"Harry, I don't know."

"I can understand. But if she knows Morse code, she can do it. Who else knows Morse code might be part of the answer. I bet Aidan knows it."

Susan drove past the next exit. She felt overwhelmed. She knew her best friend couldn't resist a mystery, a question. But she also knew Harry was not given to fancies . . . plus, she was her best friend, her sister, really.

"Are you going to commit me?"

"No. I'm trying to, uh, process this."

"What if we go to Miranda's, or even Aunt Tally's, and you hear them tap the telegraph key?"

"It's not that. I believe the sounds you described. But to think this is an agreed-upon form of communication between two people who loathe each other, that's a far, far stretch."

"Susan, what if they don't loathe each other?"

"Huh?"

"What if they're in cahoots?"

"Like lovers?"

"They're both married. This would be a good way to deflect people's figuring it out. Love or money? Aren't most crimes love or money?"

"Or both?"

Harry nodded, stared through the windshield. "Really getting dark now."

Susan replied, "Glad we filled up." She slowed a bit. "Power seduces people. Perhaps it's more seductive than love, looks, whatever. The idea that you can control people."

"Never ends. Remember our history classes? We had good teachers."

"We did. But Harry, back to Aidan and Amanda. What set you off? What possible clue did you find?"

"Start at square one. A page is killed on the road. He has cocaine and fentanyl in his system. But what if he didn't use drugs with the other young people, as so many believe? His parents swear he didn't. Granted, one can hide these things, especially if enough other people are sniffing and snorting. Everyone covers for one another. But still. There are no real clues. He could have been offered the vial that was found in his pants' cuff and took it. That doesn't mean he was a druggie. Then the videographer runs out of the building and drives off. He was found in Maryland and brought back here. He admits to selling moonshine as well as information. He admits to taking drugs, but swears he doesn't sell."

"Right. But I still don't see what pushed you to your conclusion."

"My conclusion is that Amanda is communicating with Aidan. She may be communicating with other people, too. Had I not promised Aunt Tally I'd learn to operate a ham radio and get my license, I'd still be in the dark. Now I'm in the fog but not the dark. Anyway, this has turned out to be complicated. Miranda does her choir practice over ham radio with the ladies who can't drive at night, and maybe can't easily get around on their own two legs either, so I go and listen. She showed me how you start the radio, the steps one goes through. I bit off more than I can chew, but she encouraged me."

"And so did Aunt Tally."

"They both did, and I am learning things. When the choir signed off using numbers, Morse numbers, I grasped how efficient this could be. The numbers have a shortcut meaning. Like 'hugs and kisses,' 'goodbye,' 'best regards,' stuff like that. And then there's SOS, although most of us know that. Anyway, I memorized the shortcuts. I'll get to all of Morse code later."

"And you think you heard a shortcut."

"Susan, I did. There is not a doubt in my mind."

"What can we do about it?"

"Nothing that I can think of, but if we heard Aidan tap back, that would be something."

"Ned says he disturbs Amanda's work on the budget committee and even on the floor by tapping his fingers." She paused for a bit. "It's possible he's sending messages."

"I wish I could record that and take it to Miranda and Tally, but there's no way to do that, really. Also, it's random. We don't know when it's going to happen, but I swear it has happened and will probably happen again."

"I should tell Ned."

"No. If he gives anything away, they or whoever is in on this will have time to hide. I'm thinking, is there a way to provoke them?"

"Harry, you don't know what's at stake."

"You're right, I don't. If I could find out whether Amanda knows Morse code, that would help. If I could hear her more, I'd know, even though I don't know words. Maybe she'll send out a sentence. The session will be adjourned before I know enough though; I wasn't planning on learning Morse code right this minute."

Susan, eyebrows knitted together, said, "Maybe we don't have to. Knowing the shorthand might be enough."

"The other thing. Lucas being rammed by a car. What does he know?"

"Ned, who keeps up with him, says Lucas is much better. He was lucky. He really was lucky."

"If he was purposefully rammed, maybe he knows what is going on. Maybe he's balking, or maybe he doesn't know but he's getting close and he scared Amanda or whoever."

"He loves Amanda."

"He does. I think she's fond of him, but would she sacrifice her career?"

"Having an affair isn't going to ruin her career."

"I don't know. Men get away with it. I don't know if we're ready for a woman to blithely break her marriage vows."

"Seems unfair, doesn't it?"

Harry's voice rose. "Where in the devil does anyone get the time to sleep around?"

They both laughed.

"Speaking of Lucas, consider bringing him to your house. Use the excuse he needs a few more days in the country. That also gets rid of his nurse minder, just in case. I don't think Lucas knows anything. I just think he may be getting close. He knows Amanda so well. Surely he has an instinct for what she might be doing. And what if the nurse is a kind of spy?"

"I don't believe Lucas is in on anything."

"I don't either. I'm willing to bet on it."

Susan took a deep breath. "We could be betting our lives."

37

"That dog is huge." Lucas, ever amazed at Pirate's size, gingerly lowered himself onto a wing chair.

"The breed is so gentle. Easy dogs once you adjust to the height," Harry told him. "Susan, I'll start the fire."

"Okay," Susan called from the kitchen.

"It's wonderful of you to bring me here. Everyone is working, the Assembly is in session, no one comes by but the nurse. He's now part-time. I was bored."

"What's it like having a male nurse?"

"Not much different than having a female one. They've seen everything, so no point being embarrassed." He settled in. "What a comfortable chair."

Harry, kneeling in front of the fireplace screen, moved to the side, agreed. "Susan is so good with décor, her furniture and gardens are the best. Snow-covered now."

"My camellias are blooming," Susan called from the kitchen. "And don't forget the hollies."

"You heard her." Harry smiled as she crumpled newspaper.

"I really should call Amanda. She's in session, but I don't want her to worry."

"Just text her, like you did the nurse. That way you aren't bogged down with arguments, too many questions. As long as the nurse gets paid, I doubt he will care. As to Amanda, I don't know. She might get motherly."

Susan carried in a wooden tray with sturdy handles, placing it on the coffee table in front of Lucas. "A little something to hold you until lunch. We whisked you away."

"No one can go wrong with croissants." He plucked one off the china dish.

"Cream, sugar? I have brown sugar, too." Susan pulled a chair closer, as she was also hungry.

"I don't see anything for us," Pewter complained.

"You can eat a croissant." Mrs. Murphy sat under Lucas's chair.

"I want meat, tuna. I could manage some cream." The gray cat lifted her head, smelling the cream.

Owen informed Pewter, *"You'd better forget it. Mom is tough about food."*

"She feeds you from the table. I've seen her do it." Pewter wasn't buying it.

"If you don't behave, she'll throw us out of the room." Mrs. Murphy knew Susan almost as well as Owen did.

Pewter pulled a face, came over to Lucas's side, rubbed against the chair.

"Pewter, don't. I don't want to brush off the side of the chair." Harry finished piling the logs in a square, the middle open.

"She never gives up." Susan laughed.

Lucas looked to the side "She is fat. Has a pretty face."

"I am not fat. I have big bones. You shouldn't fat shame me. It's not nice."

None of the other animals said a word.

"Talkative," Lucas mentioned as he bit into his buttered croissant.

"She has a large vocabulary." Harry grinned as she lit the papers, stepped away, replaced the screen. "Those logs will burn a long time. Love the cherry wood."

"Ned buys this stuff. I tell him to cut on your farm. You have everything. But he goes down to the corner market and buys wood. Talks to everyone."

Lucas replied, "He's supporting local business. Plus, people see him. Good thinking."

"Well, I guess it is," Susan agreed. "But it does seem like spending money that could be used for something else." She held up her hand. "Harry, I've been around you too long."

"All your life," Harry fired back, then told Lucas, "I'm not cheap, I'm thrifty. Susan can be impulsive. If she sees something she wants, she buys it."

Lucas winced slightly. "Me too. It's a bad habit."

"Do you hurt?" Susan had noticed the wince.

"If I turn too much, I feel it. I have to get used to limited movement on this side. The other one isn't bad but . . . well, you learn the hard way."

"That's the truth." Harry sat in the other chair and grabbed a croissant for herself.

"I'm glad you pulled yourself together so fast, and don't worry, Amanda will find out after the session is adjourned. Why trouble her at the beginning? We got to you about ten minutes after everyone was seated. I chatted with Ned. But as we discussed in the car, since we don't know who attacked you . . . and it certainly seems to be an attack, not a drunk driver . . . why take a chance? Whoever did this knows where you live. Perhaps they are waiting for time to pass and then they'll return. I don't want to sound like doom and gloom, but you just don't know. Best to be away briefly," Susan said, thinking the croissants were quite good, flaky.

"Thanks to the drugs, I didn't start thinking clearly until last night. It does cross my mind that I'm vulnerable, especially now."

Harry thought this was a good time to ask a few questions. "Do you have doubts about anyone in the Assembly? You know, maybe you stumbled on corruption?"

"No. The media would jump down your throat if you even have a lunch paid for by a corporation, say like Altria. There's no way any delegate or state senator can do business without meeting people, banking presidents, corporate presidents, supermarket companies. So you have a lunch with them and you pay for yourself. I guess it's okay, but it really seems a leap for me to think that if somebody bought you a lunch, you are suddenly in their pocket."

"You think there are other ways for persuasion?" Susan poured more coffee for Lucas, tea for Harry.

"I don't think influence will ever be contained or even modified. People will be offered advancement, hidden money, a future job when they leave the House. Not everyone listens, but it greases the wheels. I'm not saying anything you don't know."

"You're right. But something is wrong down there. Ellis running away. Reid found with drugs in his system. Those things may or may not be connected, and they may have nothing to do with the business of running the state."

"I've thought about that. I keep coming back to drugs. It's a huge business, and if someone is smart, they can cover their usage. As for that poor kid we all liked so much, what could he know that would endanger him? It seems to be an unfortunate accident to which so many young people are prone. No one believes it will happen to them."

"I'm afraid that's true," Susan replied. "But who could have it in for you? You aren't taking drugs, so if there is a hidden group, you aren't part of it. If you were, it would probably have come out in your blood work after the accident. Some of that stuff stays in the bloodstream a long time."

"I'm a trans man working for a conservative Republican. She's not way out there, but Amanda's not really middle of the road either. And she's hit a nerve with calling out how women are still brushed aside even if they are elected officials. I guess I can be seen as part of all that."

"If you were an elected official, it would make more sense than being an elected official's right-hand assistant," Harry posited. "And you aren't creating trans legislation."

"*Politics is so boring. Aren't you glad we just do what we want?*" Pewter puffed out her chest.

"*Our wants are simpler than theirs. Plus, we have speed, good noses, and fangs. They don't,*" Tucker said, wisely considering her abilities versus a human's.

"*If we fight, it's usually one-on-one.*" Mrs. Murphy couldn't imagine cat warfare.

"True," Owen chimed in. "*They're always thinking about the future. Not right now. Even Susan, such a good person, and she loves me, but even my mom can get wrapped around the axle over something scheduled for June. Know what I mean?*"

"*What future?*" Pirate, still maturing, asked.

"*That's the point.*" Tucker could detect a hint of blood on Lucas.

Knowing her canine roommate well, Mrs. Murphy jumped in, "*That really is the point. There is no future. It's a fantasy.*"

"*Strange.*" Pirate drooped his ears slightly.

As the animals mulled over human peculiarities, Harry felt the time was right, as all were in a good mood. "Lucas, do you know Morse code?"

"No. Why?"

"A thought. Does Amanda know Morse code?" Harry pressed on.

"Actually, she does. She learned when we were in college. She wrote a big term paper about Samuel Morse. She memorized Morse code, gave a demonstration to the class as part of her paper. Got an A+, too. She was always a step ahead." He grinned.

"Yes." Susan struggled to think of where to go next with this.

"Have you mentioned it to her recently?" Harry asked.

"You know, I did. I teased her that if she used her Morse code with party delegates, they could probably outflank those who most bitterly opposed them. I was thinking of Aidan."

"Really?" Harry leaned forward, which provoked further comment.

"She can't say what she really thinks—especially not during a debate, right? But if she could send our delegates messages of what's going on, complete with hateful comments—she can really let those rip—maybe they'd shut down some of the debate. At least everyone would have a laugh."

"Any idea how to do that?" Susan asked.

"Not a one." He leaned back, winced again a little bit. "I really feel it where that tip pierced my lung."

"Bet you do," Harry commiserated, mind racing.

Amanda had heard enough about the Chesapeake Bay. She picked up her cellphone, ringer off, to check any messages. Her face registered surprise, concern. The male nurse had sent a message that Lucas was going away for a few days to rest and repair without him. Lucas said he would contact Amanda after the session was adjourned. Her first thought was, "Where is he?" She couldn't get up and leave. Almost everyone was in their seats, the disposition of the Bay being of utmost importance to most Virginians, as well as Marylanders.

She scribbled on a sheet of paper she pulled out from her small desk. Motioning for one of the few pages, she folded the sheet over, giving it to a page. She hated to communicate with Aidan in any fashion publicly, other than to fight with him. She watched the page put the note on his desk. He looked at her quizzically, then opened the note. Which read: . . . —— . . .

His face registered concern, but he slightly nodded in her direction.

38

The next day, Lucas called Amanda, telling her the brief stay in the country had helped him. He would be back at work tomorrow, but only for three hours. He can sit, do paperwork, and make phone calls. He admitted he tired easily, but he knew the work was piling up. Ned would bring him to the Pocahontas Building, and if Amanda could drive him home, let him know. Failing that, he'd leave with Ned.

She agreed with his promise that if he felt weak or his ribs hurt more, he would go home. If she couldn't drive him early—given voting, etc.—someone else would.

He told her Susan was coming in with Ned. He'd be fine. All seemed well.

Unbeknownst to Lucas, Ned was at Lucas's doctor's office, getting a statement that Lucas needed a service dog. Ned didn't have time to get more signatures, so he fudged it, but the paper looked official.

As Lucas practiced walking with his cane, he felt better. Although he believed he didn't actually need the cane, Susan ordered him to keep it. If he tired or needed to lean on something, the cane would be helpful. His legs, while bruised, were fine, but Susan insisted any kind of injury affects the body's alignment. Use the cane.

As he was practicing walking, Harry came by. She walked next to him while he circled the living room.

"Good."

"Thanks. I feel awkward."

"That will pass. I'm on your left. Pirate is on your right. If you need someone or something else to steady you, here we are. With Pirate, all you have to do is put your hand on his head. He'll stop if you stop. He'll walk with you if you walk."

"I'm very strong," the dog added.

"He's a good boy. He knows quite a few words. The basics . . . sit, stay, come here. Hold hard is one I use if we have to stop suddenly. He's young, but he has a good vocabulary. He's smart."

"I'm amazed."

"Dogs are smart. The different breeds have different abilities. A herding dog is bred to listen to humans, to push along cattle or sheep. Or humans, as the case may be. Tucker is a herding dog. Pirate is a sight hound. Both are smart, obedient. If you use your cane with your left hand, get wobbly, rest your right hand on Pirate's head."

"Okay." Lucas sounded tentative.

"Try it."

He reached over, putting his hand on the Irish Wolfhound's head.

"Now take a step or two," Harry ordered.

"You'll be okay. I'm a good boy," the sweet fellow counseled.

"How's that feel?"

"Okay."

"Tell him he's a good boy and give him a pat. If you sit down, he'll sit down beside you."

"Harry, why am I working with your wonderful dog?"

"He'll go to work with you tomorrow for your first day. It'll be a short day, and he'll be next to you. Ned got a doctor's order for a service dog. I'm probably saying this wrong. It's too much paperwork for me, plus another set of rules. Anyway, you can have him with you for a few hours tomorrow, then you'll go home. A little help won't hurt."

Lucas patted Pirate's head once more. "If only I could teach you how to read."

"*I can chew papers,*" the dog helpfully responded.

"He is a lovely animal."

"He is. The breed is so big, they scare people. While they aren't guard dogs, like German shepherds, he will protect you. The other thing is, they love children. But again, they are so big, you can't really have them around toddlers."

"I see." He patted Pirate one more time. "I think I'll sit down." He walked slowly over to the cushy club chair, leaned his cane against the side, put both hands on the arms and lowered himself down. "Ah. My legs are fine. I feel the bruises, but the pain is in the ribs. Hurts to jostle them. What surprises me is how tired I become."

"I can imagine." Harry looked at Pirate, who was studying her face. "Sit."

He sat next to one of the chair's arms.

Lucas, hand resting there, reached over to rub Pirate's face. "You know, I never had a dog. My parents were set against animals in the house. I missed something."

"You did." Harry clucked. "Susan, you can open the door now."

Tucker, in the kitchen with Susan as Harry worked with Lucas, shot out the door.

"*What have I missed?*" the intrepid corgi asked.

"*I'm Lucas's dog for a few hours.*"

"Oh." Tucker glanced up at Harry, now sitting across from Lucas as Susan walked into the room, taking the other chair.

"How did it go?"

"Pretty good," Lucas said.

"I meant to ask you yesterday. Forgot. Tell me more about your nurse. "

Lucas shrugged. "He was okay. He wanted to help me in the shower, get dressed and undressed. Stuff like that. I can get in and out of the shower myself, but I did need him to put my bandages back on. Fresh ones feel good actually. Like I'm held together."

"But he didn't give you a creepy feeling?" Harry pressed.

"No." He wrinkled his brow.

"Do you know if he knows Amanda?"

"Uh . . ." He shook his head.

"Did he ask about the accident?"

"No. He pretty much stuck to my physical needs, which as I mentioned were not much. The rib bandages. That's about it. I can wash in the sink. If the bandages are off, I can take a very quick shower. Get rewrapped. There aren't deep external bloody wounds. Makes it easier. He was good about putting on fresh bandages, as I said."

"Do you mind if we call the home nursing company? We want to make sure you have the best of care, and we'd like an idea of how long you will need someone in the house with you."

"Me too. But that's up to my doctor."

Susan asked, "Did he give you a time frame?"

"He didn't. There are two of them, and both said they would reevaluate each time I came in, which right now is scheduled for once a week. The nurse has their number, too."

"Do you like them?" Harry wondered.

"Well, I hardly know them, but I trust them. The one is a man maybe in his early sixties. The other is a woman, mid-fifties. After the emergency room, they were the ones who took over. Both specialists. Lung stuff."

"I don't mean to give you the third degree," Susan apologized. "We just want to check out everyone. Until the nature of this accident becomes more clear, it doesn't hurt to be watchful. And I think it's easier for us than you."

"Thank you. I don't want to prevail upon you. Amanda has volunteered to do much of this."

A short silence followed this, then Susan, with a soothing voice, said, "She is an old, old friend, but right now her work is on overload. I know Ned's is, as the session is drawing to a close; even if it has been extended fifteen days, it's drawing to a close. She has to get her ducks in a row," Susan said, using the old expression.

"She does. I have a few other friends I can call upon. Doing the work we do certainly reduces one's social life, but I knew that when I signed on. Still I have a few friends in town. And y'all have been wonderful to me." He smiled.

"Ned says the doctors told him it will only be a few days, a week at the most, before you receive a clear prognosis. Let us be a small part of this, Lucas. Given that my husband is a delegate, I have an understanding of what work you need to get done and the pressures you will be under. But after that prognosis, Ned and I, and Pirate," Susan grinned at the dog, "will be both vigilant and helpful."

"*Don't forget about me,*" Tucker said, sitting in the middle of the floor.

"I'm sluggish today," Susan admitted. "I'm going to make more tea. Harry, come help. We'll bring some out."

In the kitchen, Harry whispered to Susan, "We can't tell him our suspicions. And we can't tell the police or each party's leader. I guess we wouldn't tell them anyway. We have nothing to go on by way of proof. But I know she's guilty. And I'm sure Aidan's in on it. But we don't know what exactly. I know I can flush her out tomorrow."

"Harry, your idea is so dangerous."

"You'll be in Ned's office. And don't tell Ned. He'll try to stop me. We have Pirate, and I can smuggle in Tucker. If I get in trouble, you and the dogs will get me out."

"Does this mean I'm going to the dogs?"

Harry punched her lightly on the shoulder. "Ha. We've done crazier things than this."

"I'm not so sure." Susan sighed deeply. "But I think your idea will flush her out. Maybe him, too."

39

"You look so much better than the last time I saw you." Amanda kissed Lucas on the cheek. "I won't hug."

"Thanks." He kissed her back.

"Pirate is here for his three hours. He's trained to assist him. Mostly Lucas can use him for balance, if needs be." Harry smiled. "Ned worked feverishly yesterday to get the service animal paperwork. And don't worry, Pirate's quiet."

Amanda looked at the dog. "He'll be a help. Well, Lucas, your desk is overflowing." She paused. "I can't believe how quickly you've bounced back."

"I was lucky, plus I was in good shape. And no organ damage or broken bones, other than the ribs. Well, let me get to work." He brushed his hand over Pirate's tall back. "Come on, big boy. I'll teach you how to use a computer."

Amanda smiled then said to Harry, "It was good of you and

Susan to give him some time away from the city. Sometimes a change of scene helps. When the nurse texted me, it put the fear of God into me. Then Lucas reached me and I thought it was a good idea. Ned and I are in opposing parties, but when it comes to the important stuff, it doesn't matter."

"I couldn't agree more. Lucas's speech at UVA is what brought us together. He's a good speaker, great with questions."

"Was at William and Mary, too."

"I'd better get to work," Harry said. "An avalanche of work awaits all of us. I don't know how you do it."

"I don't either." Amanda tilted her head. "It's this mania for data. You can have all the data in the world and still make a bad decision. That's what I think when I look at Aidan Harkness."

"I'll pick up Pirate in three hours . . . and Lucas, too. He thought you'd take him home, but when we looked at today's schedule, there's no way to determine when it will be over."

"We'll work it out. Thank you again." Amanda turned toward her desk and Harry noticed those heels again.

Back in the cubbyhole off Ned's office, the two old friends sorted papers, made notes for detailed responses to inquiries. Tucker, snuck in under Pirate's service-animal paper, lay under the desk. The two cats . . . Pewter snuck in under Harry's jacket and Mrs. Murphy under Susan's . . . lounged on a catch-all table.

Checking the clock, Susan said, "Should be back in another hour. Long day, but they'll get a break. They need to have lunch sometime."

"I hope so. Otherwise, my plan will evaporate."

"As long as you don't. Harry, you have no idea how Amanda and Aidan will react."

"No, I don't, but I do know one thing: Neither of them has a gun, because of all the checkpoint charlies. The only people with guns are the guards. Remember when you could go into public buildings and you didn't walk through a device to check for metal? So if you have a hip replacement, you'll be flagged every time you go through, even if the person sitting there knows you. Rules, rules, rules."

"Could be worse."

"Oh?"

Susan folded her hands. "You could be the person sitting there."

"That's a thought." Harry checked the clock again. "Almost time."

"Ned should be here. I'll tell him. In case."

"Like I said, nobody can shoot me. That's a plus." Harry was taking off her flats, putting on a pair of heels she hadn't worn in years. She stood up. "How did I ever walk in these, much less dance? Okay, wish me luck."

"I do."

As Harry left the office, Tucker followed behind at a short distance.

"Tucker," Susan called. "Come here."

"No." Tucker kept walking.

"What's going on?" Pewter jumped down from the table.

"Maybe we should watch from the doorway?" Mrs. Murphy wisely suggested. *"If she needs us, we'll hear."*

Click click click. Harry strode down the polished hall. She hit the flooring a little harder the closer she got to Amanda's office. Click click click. As she came into view, the clicks changed. Now it was two short clicks. Pause. A long click. A short click. A long click. Pause. A long click and a short click. Then three long clicks, finally ending with a short click and two longs.

She spelled out, in Morse code, "I know," having studied the alphabet last night.

Amanda looked up, puzzled. Harry repeated "I know" in Morse code. She held up her hand, wiggling her fingers, a kind of goodbye.

Amanda's face changed, she stood up.

"I know Morse code," Harry lied. "I know what you've been doing." She turned and left as Amanda hurried to put on her own high heels.

Harry's clicks reverberated, soon followed by Amanda's as she tried to catch up. Harry moved a little faster, followed by Tucker. Amanda was so furious, she hardly noticed the dog.

Two women trying to run in high heels was an unusual sight.

Pirate, hearing them, stood up, pressing closer to Lucas.

Harry ran as best she could in the heels. So did Amanda. Finally, Harry reached Aidan's office. His door was wide open. He looked up. She spelled out "I know" in double time. He froze. She spelled it out again, just as Amanda reached her.

"She's nuts," Amanda shouted.

"I know what you two have been doing," Harry threatened.

Aidan stood up, ran around his desk, and tried to grab Harry. "Shut your mouth."

"How much are you stealing?" That was a long shot.

"No," Amanda shouted as she too tried to grab Harry, who eluded her as well. But Harry knew it wouldn't be for long. Two against one.

"Did you send someone to run into Lucas?"

"What have you told her, Amanda?" Aidan's face was beet red.

Aidan finally grabbed Harry, wrestling with her as Tucker bit his calf. He screamed.

Doors opened that had been closed. Those that had been open had delegates standing in the doorway. No one knew what to do.

Susan, Ned with her, ran down the hallway.

Aidan saw them, dropped Harry, and ran.

"Wait," Amanda yelled. "She doesn't know everything. Wait."

"Save yourself," Harry told her, not quite sure why that popped out.

Tucker, having released her grip on Aidan's calf, tore after him, flying past Amanda, who was now hobbling after him, too.

"Tucker, leave them."

"*He grabbed you,*" Tucker barked.

"Come on, baby, it's okay."

By now, the hall was filling up with people . . . and two cats.

"*We missed it.*" Pewter, tail straight up, thread in and out of the people.

"*Watch out, Pewter, people don't see you,*" Pirate warned.

Lucas used Pirate for balance as he tried to hurry in the direction of the commotion.

A door slammed. Aidan had made it outside.

Amanda lagged behind. A Capitol officer hurried into the hall. "What's going on?"

"We don't know," Ned honestly replied. "But Aidan and Amanda are flying out of here."

The officer ran to the door in time to see Aidan get in his car, with Amanda waving. He left her. She stood there dumbfounded, then, still in her high heels, ran to her own car. She tried to open it, but had evidently left her keys behind. She screamed, beating on the car door. The officer approached her. She turned and hit him. With difficulty, he subdued her. Two other officers joined him. She was yelling at the top of her lungs. The delegates watched from the hall, a few with windows on that side dashed into their offices. Amanda flailed away at the officers, her high heels slipping in the packed snow. With difficulty . . . the snow hindered them as well . . . they brought her to a police car and opened the passenger door. Determined, though, and frantic, she fought to break away. In the end, her heels were too much. They brought her down. Members of the House of Delegates watched, fascinated, as one of their own was shoved into the backseat of a squad car.

"Do you know what this is about?" a delegate from the area asked Lucas.

"No," came the swift reply as he leaned on Pirate.

The running effort had hurt his broken ribs. He rubbed his

hand on his chest, turned to go back. Harry turned with him. She walked on his other side.

Susan and Ned turned also, as did Tucker, Mrs. Murphy, and Pewter.

"What are cats and dogs doing in here?" a delegate from the Valley asked.

"Running for office," the delegate from the Fauquier area quipped.

"Does anyone know what's going on?" a female delegate from Richmond asked.

Everyone was bewildered, shocked to see Amanda in an uncontrollable fury.

Harry led Lucas to Ned's office, as it was a bit closer. He dropped down in a chair.

"*He looks peaked,*" Pewter observed.

"*He hurts,*" Mrs. Murphy answered.

Pirate stuck right to him.

Harry kissed her big boy on the head. "You're a good boy."

Pirate lifted his head to her, then turned to Lucas. "*Are you all right?*"

He was, but his broken ribs created a sharp pain.

"I have no idea what got into her." Lucas held his chest.

"Need a pain pill?" Susan asked.

"No. I shouldn't have tried to run. I'll be fine. What happened?"

Ned and Susan stood in front of Lucas.

"You have no idea?" Susan asked not as a challenge, but because of the cleverness of it all.

"No. All I know is I heard Harry clicking. Then Amanda got up and as her heels hit the polished floor, I heard Harry say, 'I know' and Amanda took off."

"I clicked out a message in Morse code."

"What?" His eyes grew big.

"I clicked out 'I know,' and she went off her rocker. She and Aidan are or were up to no good. I'm not sure what they've done but whatever it is, both ran out of here. He left her. We can hope she tells the police everything. Ellis is still in jail. If you count him, you might be their third harmed person. I believe this is all connected."

"Oh my God," he said quietly. "What would be worth this?" He glanced up at Harry hovering over him. "Morse code?"

"Yes. I knew once you said she wrote a paper on Samuel Morse, and she'd learned Morse code, that she and Aidan had sent each other messages using the code. Ned said that Aidan would tap his fingers on the table. Everyone thought it was to irritate her. That was the game they played. But he was tapping out information they wanted no one else to know. I expect some of it was about money."

"Oh my God," Lucas said again.

"Your accident was probably not an accident." Harry felt this was wretched information, as Lucas loved Amanda.

"But I didn't know anything." His voice shook.

"You had to have been getting close." Ned put his hand on Lucas's shoulder. "This will all come out. If Aidan gets away, my bet is Amanda will sing to save herself."

"*Tucker, you should have bitten Aidan harder,*" Pewter mentioned.

"*I did bite him. Hard. I let go when he started to run. He was too big to hold.*"

"*No claws. That's the problem with dogs. If you could have sunk your fangs and claws at the same time, his leg would have been shredded. A permanent limp,*" Pewter said with relish.

"*I'll remember that next time,*" Tucker said sarcastically.

"Lucas, stay here. I'll get your coat. Anything else?" Harry asked.

"No. Here are the keys. Lock the office. Oh, and turn off the computers."

"I will."

Ned took his own coat out of the small closet, as well as Susan's and Harry's. "Lucas, come home with us again. You shouldn't be alone. This is devastating. Just devastating."

"Do you think they were lovers?" The blond fellow kept shaking his head in disbelief.

Susan held her hands palm upward. "It may have started that way, but there has to be more. Her bracelet fell out of his car in Crozet when he parked at the school. Remember?"

"Right. She made a big deal of him stealing it." Lucas began to put a few scattered pieces together. "She must have been in his car."

Harry came back. "All done. Let's go. I asked the officer in charge if we could leave, and he said we can be questioned tomorrow. Come on. Lucas, let me get on your left side."

The four of them, along with Pirate, Tucker, and the two cats, walked across the cold ground, a frigid wind touching their cheeks.

Ned drove, Susan sat in the front passenger seat. Harry and Lucas sat in the backseat, while Pirate and Tucker were in the folded-down third row, lying on blankets. The cats sat with Lucas and Harry.

Lucas, stunned, whispered, "Do you really think they thought I would harm them?"

"Maybe they just wanted to put you temporarily out of commission," Harry replied with a touch of hope.

"She was my best friend." His eyes clouded up.

Ned suggested, "Try to keep an open mind. We'll know more soon, I hope."

"It can't be good." Harry felt terrible for Lucas.

40

Windowpanes rattled as the wind howled. Night's dark made the group stay close to the large fireplace. Susan and Ned kept the warmth steady, constantly placing heavy oak logs into the flames. The fireplace, not as big as a walk-in fireplace, was nonetheless impressive. Harry and Fair, along with the two cats and dogs, joined Susan and Ned. Lucas sat deep in a comfortable chair. This was his fifth night staying with Susan and Ned. His injuries hurt, plus he was shattered by the drama. Susan, wise about people's unexpressed needs, had told him he was coming home with them. A small cottage of six hundred square feet was attached to the back of the house by a covered walkway. In summer, thick wisteria draped over the thirty-yard walk. In the winter, the open sides were closed with paneling, so one could go to and fro without shoveling or being knocked sideways by whirling winds. Given Lucas's injuries, staying there was a sensible solution. He'd have privacy but be close.

"Think you'll be called for more questioning?" Harry asked Lucas.

"I told them everything I know over the phone. They have the keys to her office after you returned with them as you know." He propped his legs on a hassock. "I provided as much as I could, going back to William and Mary days. I'll do what is asked of me."

"For now, you stay here. You've suffered two devastating shocks." Susan pulled a light throw over her legs. "Anyone else want a throw?"

All shook their heads.

"I'll take one." Tucker hopped into the bed, a replica of a banana, with snuggle room.

"She offered it to me first." Pewter's whiskers swept forward.

"You sat on your fat butt." The corgi grinned, digging deeper down into the cute yellow bed.

Mrs. Murphy joined Tucker. "We can both fit."

"Because we're not fat." Tucker turned on her side.

"How rude." Pewter walked to the sofa, jumped in Harry's lap.

"Pewter, get off the furniture," Harry commanded.

"I'm not on the furniture. I'm on your lap." She looked up with her most adorable look.

"Don't worry," Susan advised. "No one is shedding all that much right now."

"I could gag," Tucker grumbled.

Pewter, at the purr volume, said, "I'm on the cashmere throw Harry pulled down from the back of the sofa. It's divine. Absolutely divine."

Pirate, head on his paws, remained silent, ear tuned to the crackle and pop of the fire, as well as the wind. He was beside Lucas.

"Did they ask you anything that surprised you?" Ned wondered.

"They asked did I have a gun," Lucas replied. "I said I did not."

Ned, Susan, and Harry were glad the police had questioned Lucas over the phone. They agreed to take him to the station for

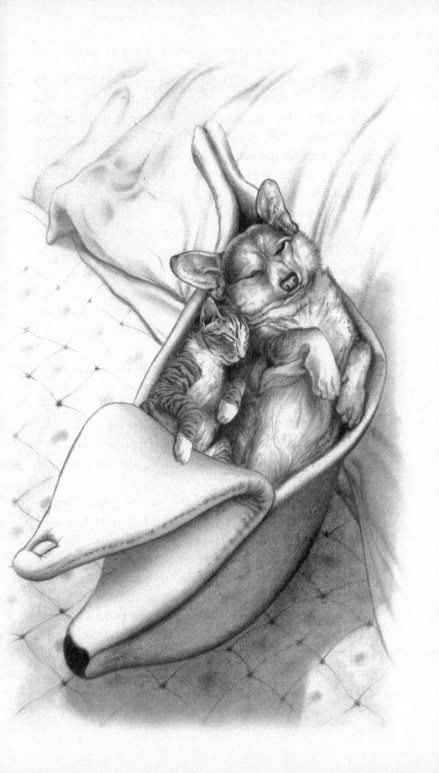

in-person questioning when the police scheduled it. They had their hands full. Yesterday, the girls . . . as Harry and Susan were known when they were together . . . had gone to Lucas's and packed some clothes, a good pair of shoes and heavy boots, sweaters, his computer and notebooks.

Meekly, Lucas agreed to stay for a bit longer in Crozet. He couldn't think too clearly, being so stunned, and he found Susan and Ned's cottage charming and private.

Two days had passed since he'd learned about Amanda and Aidan. He was in better shape.

"Amanda blames Aidan for everything." Ned had been in touch with the party whip.

The officers of both parties were informed by the police. Partly they wanted to make sure no one else was involved in this, that it was only Amanda and Aidan.

"I should have known. I was blind. She paid too much attention to him. He's handsome and he's younger. She has a quiet terror about growing old." Lucas kicked himself.

"There was no way to know," Ned soothed him. "They were too clever. Think of it, Morse code. That's damnably clever."

"When you all were at William and Mary, was she ever wildly in love? Just out of her mind?"

"Oh, every two weeks." He smiled. "She settled down, and the only man I saw her be serious about until she met Ron was a medical student at New York University medical school. They met at the Outer Banks two summers after graduation. They seemed crazy about each other, but eventually she ended it because she said she could never live in New York. If she did, she'd always be in his jetstream. When she met Ron about a year later, they clicked, and he supported her ambitions. Her career took off. We stayed in touch, would go out to lunch when I'd come down from graduate school at American University."

"Do you want to talk to her? She's out of jail, but in a place for safekeeping. She threatens to harm herself," Harry asked, perhaps a bit too directly.

He paused, dropped his hand to feel Pirate's head, then said, "No."

"This has to be so painful. They had to be losing it." Susan reached over to pet Mrs. Murphy.

"Oh, I don't know, honey." Ned considered the situation. "Surely they were having a torrential affair. But there was money at stake. Had to be. Payoffs for land sale or business trips. Dipping into campaign funds. There's always a way."

"I showed them everything." Lucas grimaced. "I pointed out where she had withdrawn fifty thousand dollars, yet to be replaced. She took more, as we now know. She was terrifically clever hiding the money. The books looked clean to me; but then, I'm not an accountant. Now I realize why she didn't want me to hire a part-time bookkeeper. She paid me extra for doing the books, but that wore me down. She insisted she didn't want people she didn't trust in her business."

"Did you ever see Aidan and Amanda together?" Harry asked.

"Once he popped his head in the office. Two minutes. If there was major electricity, I didn't feel it."

"Maybe all those times she was lasering in on state budget, she was also doing hers," Ned opined.

"She was very, very good with numbers. One of those people for whom math is like breathing." Lucas thought a moment. "I don't understand why she would risk a potentially big political career for wild sex, or whatever it was. As to the money, I think she would have repaid it. For all I know, she used it to create more money."

"Actually, if you think about it, it makes sense. If they could be public enemies, it would be great theater. They'd be in control. No matter who would win politically, both would profit. Their separate followers would stick with them. More money would roll in.

The higher one rises, the more money. Gifts don't have to be money. There are so many ways to reward someone who votes your way, or as the expression goes, 'is in the tank.'" Ned was beginning to see the beauty of their plan.

"And both keep their perfect marriages public. No reason for the wife or husband to know."

"Whoever succeeded would drag the other one along as an antagonist. Think about it. Should she have become our first woman governor down the road, he could slam her relentlessly, which would be red meat to his followers and vice versa. As each would know what the other would ask or do, they could be prepared. It would be like a prize fight that was fixed to go ten rounds. Lots of blood and close calls." Ned filled this out more.

"Theater." Harry's voice dripped with disdain.

"Harry, a lot of politics is just that. This happens to be theater on a whole new level." Ned half smiled. "But you still have to deliver something for your constituents. We are all in that vise. Well, it's not a vise, it's why you're there, but if you continually underdeliver, you won't be there for long.

"A challenger from the opposite party running for your seat can bash you as woke or a spendthrift or being close to being a Proud Boy. Whatever would cause the most damage in the district, but if you delivered services, maybe even attracted a big business to the area, you'd be damn hard to dislodge."

"Do you want to go back to the statehouse?" Harry asked Lucas.

"I can't think about that," Lucas honestly answered. "I'd like to think I was good at what I did, but now I don't know. I missed so much."

"Don't feel bad about it. Nobody else caught it either. We all fell for the drama. Amanda, by the way, declares that Ellis Barfield was selling drugs. She was considering him for video work but noticed his pupils were often enlarged when they shouldn't be. She also swore Aidan took a cut of the business. He himself never used drugs."

"Ellis denies all of that, except for selling information and hooch," Susan added, having kept up with the developments.

"Bull." Lucas wanted to sit up straight but it would hurt, so he stayed leaning back in the cushy chair. "Ellis made money on the side filming videos for corporations around Richmond. She would ask me if I thought those corporations were approachable on issues, issues that aligned with her own, like business invest-ment, land investment, business parks, stuff like that. I expect she and Aidan both fed Ellis information that could help a business, so he could use it to make money . . . probably for all of them. I know it's a big business." Lucas rubbed his temples. "If Aidan wanted to put me out of commission or kill me, why didn't Amanda stop him? She had to be in on it. Maybe she thought because of our long relationship I would get too close, or I had by pushing her to replace the fifty thousand."

"I expect she'll deny everything. Who is to say he didn't keep some things from her? He had no trouble leaving her in the snow. What we do know is, she's suicidal, depressed, and under care. That excuses nothing, but perhaps she knows how destructive this is." Harry then added, "I don't mean to be hurtful. But she had to have known more about Ellis. Maybe he was blackmailing them. Or her. But if he was shooting footage, being a go-between, he could have proven difficult, especially if he was taking drugs himself."

"I don't know if he was," Lucas stated. "We only have her as-sertion."

"Do you think she was?" Ned asked.

"At this point, I could believe anything." Lucas's voice had dropped.

"We all feel the same way. Shocked. Confused. Without Aidan, who is to say?" Susan, unhappy though she was with the events, enjoyed the warmth from the fire. "Honey, will you put another log on?"

"Certainly." Ned rose from his chair and brought back a three-foot hardwood, moved the screen and laid it on, carefully. "Maybe another." He put on another one, then returned to his comfortable chair.

"What do you think about Reid?" Harry wondered.

Ned answered, "Amanda knew a bit about the drug trade, but kept out of it. She'd seen so much while working on TV. She said Ellis gave Reid cash to run errands, deliver things both in and out of the House. She said Reid didn't know what was in the packages. Ellis could have given Reid the vial as a gift. That would be tempting. Poor kid. Takes a toot and it helps to kill him."

"I don't know." Fair shook his head.

Ned was firm. "There had to be more. And I just don't believe that bright kid would be so stupid."

Susan carefully thought this out. "We may never know how or why, but we do know he had drugs in his system. It's a different generation, honey. They are exposed to so much more than we were. Their music heroes sing about drugs. It's part of their life."

"Amanda swears she had nothing to do with any of this." Ned paused. "But how can anyone believe anything she says? And Aidan is still on the loose. I check in each day to see if anyone knows more."

Lucas shivered despite the fire. "I believed she was my best friend. If she were, she would have stopped Aidan."

"He turned on her in the end. Left her in the cold, literally, drove away." Ned wondered, "Maybe Amanda was only guilty of blind lust or love. Anything is possible. The longer she is in care, perhaps the more we will know. She may confess, or provide real evidence against Aidan. Until he's found, we just don't have enough. All we know is that she took money from her own funds, ran after him when Harry tapped out a message that said, 'I know.' "

"What if he's never found?" Harry petted Mrs. Murphy.

"Sooner or later he will be. You know what I think of, the last scene in *Five Fingers*, when James Mason is looking out the window, having gotten away with everything, and there's a knock on the door." Ned loved old movies, especially political ones.

"Whatever, Lucas, you need time to repair. Don't blame yourself. There's no way you could have known," Susan again reassured him.

"I thought we were so close. I should have known. I loved her. I truly did. She was my best friend." He took a breath, tears coming to his eyes. "I was her maid of honor at her wedding. We stuck together through the years."

"Maybe she changed. Power seduces people. She was famous. People knew her as a newscaster, but that's not the same as the power she was gaining. As a great-looking woman, now middle-aged, she obviously had an Achilles' heel. She made a mistake many women make, fighting age, believing a younger man loved her. Only hers was on a bigger, grander scale," Harry calmly said. "Some younger men do love older women. Perhaps not Aidan."

"I'll say," Susan rejoined.

"*Love or money,*" Mrs. Murphy mentioned to her friends. "*That's what Harry often says when there's a crime.*"

"This will be drawn out. There will be a trial. She'll have the best lawyer. There is enough that's questionable. Who is to say, she may not be convicted." Lucas felt the fire's warmth, a help to his pains. "She can be so convincing. Even if Aidan is caught, he would deny her innocence, and him being the main perpetrator. She could still not be convicted. A woman wronged."

"She is likable," Harry conceded. "All of that is a ways off. Right now you need to heal and recover from a terrible shock."

"You all have been kind to me." Lucas's eyes moistened again.

"That's easy to do." Ned smiled. "Even if you are a Republican."

This made Lucas smile. "Actually, I'm an Independent. Amanda told me to keep it to myself, which I did. I can't muster much enthusiasm for either party, but we need to get things done."

Ned smiled. "We do. We will."

Once Harry and Fair were home, the wind nearly blowing them off the road, she gave the cats and dogs treats. They had put up the horses before they left for Susan and Ned's. Once safely in the house, the wind banging on the old, solid structure, they sat for a moment in front of their own fireplace, Fair having started a fire.

"Well, honey, what do you think? Are we correct in our identification of guilt?"

"I believe so, but unfortunately I expect others will be tarred and feathered simply by association. Mostly, I feel sorry for Lucas," Fair replied.

"I do, too. But part of me thinks she must have loved him. She stood by him when he went through the sex change, all that stuff."

He half smiled. "The older I get, the less I know about people. You'd think it would be the other way around. I'd like to believe she loved him."

Harry squeezed his hand. "You aren't missing things, people's behavior. This has been a once-in-a-lifetime crime. At least I think it is. Is money filched every day? Yes. Do people cheat on their husbands and wives daily? Yes. But this was on another level." She squeezed his hand again. "Who would think my trying to make Aunt Tally less lonesome would lead to me figuring out not what they were doing but how they were doing it? Miranda was a big help. I made a promise. I bit off more than I could chew." She jumped a bit as a branch scratched a window in the wind. "They would still be getting away with what they were doing if I hadn't started learning about ham radio and a tiny bit of Morse code."

"Serendipity."

"I wonder what will happen to her shoes?"

"Harry." He laughed.

"Well, I do. Think of it if they go to Goodwill? Thousand dollar shoes."

"Do you want me to buy you red-soled shoes?"

"No." She grinned. "Maybe a new tractor?"

He kissed her cheek. "You know if you wanted red-soled heels,

I would buy them for you. As to a tractor, we'll have to count our pennies, but I bet there is a John Deere, new, in our future."

He left to take a shower. She sat in front of the fire, the cats on the sofa, Pirate and Tucker snuggled together near the fire. She rose, picked up her grandfather's picture from the bookcase.

"G-Pop, you led me in the right direction." Moosie's collar hung over the photo. Harry lifted the collar and rubbed it on her face, inhaling the old leather scent.

Tears rolled down her cheeks. She didn't know why.

ACKNOWLEDGMENTS

My friends, as always, carried me along. No one had any idea about this book. Often a friend, an expert in some area or who runs a business, is a great help.

I kept this story line all to myself in the hopes that I would fool them.

Ever and always,

Rita Mae

PS. I even fooled the cats and dogs.

AUTHOR NOTE

Dear Reader,

Bet I fooled you. I had great fun writing this book. Maybe you enjoyed reading it.

My publisher informed me that many of you have complained about the eighteenth-century story line that has been included in many prior novels. They tell me the timeline is confusing.

I regret that as I had been moving that story along these many years to get right to what I would have included in this novel, which is the grotesque excesses of the French Revolution. Our new nation was divided between those who thought the uproar good and those who did not. Passion ran high but most people backed off when the death toll accelerated. We still don't know how many died. The rough estimate is 40,000, with another 200,000 fleeing the country. Given the population of France at the time, about 28 million, that is a great loss of life, people.

I was eager to show how this affected us, especially Bettina and DoRe, whom some of you will remember. They leave Cloverfield's, being granted their freedom, to start a business at Wayland's Crossing, which is now Crozet.

I am fascinated by our history. It's like a parrot riding on our shoulders. Perhaps in the future I will be able to write a novel

about that time with the characters some of you have learned to love.

We are all looking at the future through the shadow of the guillotine.

May you be well.

Ever and Always,

ABOUT THE AUTHORS

RITA MAE BROWN has written many bestsellers and received two Emmy nominations. In addition to the Mrs. Murphy series, she has authored a dog series comprised of *A Nose for Justice* and *Murder Unleashed*, and the Sister Jane foxhunting series, among many other acclaimed books. She and Sneaky Pie live with several other rescued animals.

SNEAKY PIE BROWN, a tiger cat rescue, has written many mysteries—witness the list at the front of the novel. Having to share credit with the above-named human is a small irritant, but she manages it. Anything is better than typing, which is what "Big Brown" does for the series. Sneaky calls her human that name behind her back, after the wonderful Thoroughbred racehorse. As her human is rather small, it brings giggles among the other animals. Sneaky's main character—Mrs. Murphy, a tiger cat—is a bit sweeter than Miss Pie, who can be caustic.

To inquire about booking Rita Mae Brown for a speaking engagement, please contact the Penguin Random House Speakers Bureau at speakers@penguinrandomhouse.com.

ABOUT THE TYPE

This book was set in Joanna, a typeface designed in 1930 by Eric Gill (1882–1940). Named for his daughter, this face is based on designs originally cut by the sixteenth-century typefounder Robert Granjon (1513–89). With small, straight serifs and its simple elegance, this face is notably distinguished and versatile.